PRAISE FOR RACHEL VAN DYKEN

"*The Consequence of Loving Colton* is a must-read friends-to-lovers story that's as passionate and sexy as it is hilarious!"
—Melissa Foster, *New York Times* bestselling author

"Just when you think Van Dyken can't possibly get any better, she goes and delivers *The Consequence of Loving Colton*. Full of longing and breathless moments, this is what romance is about."
—Lauren Layne, *USA Today* bestselling author

"The tension between Milo and Colton made this story impossible to put down. Quick, sexy, witty—easily one of my favorite books from Rachel Van Dyken."
—R. S. Grey, *USA Today* bestselling author on
The Consequence of Loving Colton

"Hot, funny, and will leave you wishing you could get marked by one of the immortals!"
—Molly McAdams, *New York Times* bestselling author on
The Dark Ones

"Laugh-out-loud fun! Rachel Van Dyken is on my auto-buy list."
—Jill Shalvis, *New York Times* bestselling author on
The Wager

"*The Dare* is a laugh-out-loud read that I could not put down. Brilliant. Just brilliant."
—Cathryn Fox, *New York Times* bestselling author

THE MATCHMAKER'S PLAYBOOK

A WINGMEN INC. NOVEL

STAND-ALONES

Hurt: A Collection (with Kristin Vayden and Elyse Faber)

RIP

Compromising Kessen

Every Girl Does It

The Parting Gift (with Leah Sanders)

Divine Uprising

THE MATCHMAKER'S PLAYBOOK

A WINGMEN INC. NOVEL

RACHEL VAN DYKEN

SKYSCAPE

Published by Skyscape, New York

www.apub.com

Amazon, the Amazon logo, and Skyscape are trademarks of Amazon.com, Inc., or its affiliates.

ISBN-13: 9781503934481
ISBN-10: 1503934489

Cover design by Shasti O'Leary Soudant

Printed in the United States of America

To Jilly. Thank you for pushing me with this book and listening to me freak out over all the scenes that I knew I had to make hotter. You make me smile.

CHAPTER ONE

The tea? Cinnamon.

The coffee shop? Secluded. Dark. Inviting.

The girl? Late.

And not just fashionably late, but the type of late that had me thinking she was going to be a no-show, which was common for a first meeting. At least 15 percent of our clients were no-shows. It was nerves. And fear that our system wouldn't work for them and they'd be in worse shape than before.

The wood chair creaked as I leaned back and examined the small shop. A year ago people would have asked for my autograph. Then again, a year ago I had just been drafted by the Seattle Seahawks.

I rubbed my knee self-consciously as the aching pain returned, causing a raw edge of irritation to burn through my chest.

I checked my watch again, biting my cheek in annoyance.

Twenty-three minutes late.

With a sigh, I reached for my tea one last time, drawing out the sip as I peered over the cup. Two more minutes and I was leaving.

The glass door shot open, the bell nearly clanging to the floor as it slammed against a nearby chair. A small mousy girl with plain brown hair stumbled through; her pale skin turned crimson as she touched her cheeks and nervously glanced around the room.

Most would give her a passing glance.

But I wasn't most.

I stared.

Hard.

When her fidgety eyes finally settled on me, she blushed even deeper. It wasn't unattractive, just very telling.

I pushed my chair back and stood.

I had a feeling she wanted to run.

They were always nervous. Which was expected. Besides, I knew what I looked like. I wasn't being vain, just drawing a logical mathematical conclusion after adding how many times I'd gotten laid to how many times I'd been asked if I was an underwear model.

Chiseled? Check.

Caramel-blond hair that somehow managed to look wavy and thick all the damn time? Check.

One dimple on the right side of my cheek? Check.

Sexy crooked smile? Check.

Rugged badass-looking scar near my chin? Check.

Smoldering hazel eyes? Check.

And don't even get me started on penis size. Really, it just gets better the farther south your eyes go—trust me.

She took a faulty step backward, colliding with the magazine rack. Several copies of the *Seattle Weekly* went flying across the floor.

With a flutter of busyness, she bent down.

Her jeans ripped at the knees.

Yeah, I was going to have to rescue her. She was already a danger to herself.

With a patient sigh, I slowly walked from my seat and approached her. Lowering to her level, I peered over at the newspapers, calmly collected every last one, and stood.

She was frozen.

It happened. Often. And unfortunately, it was a huge time-waster. Because my business? It was flourishing, and time was my currency.

She was late.

Meaning she was wasting not just my time, but my money. Typically, I met my clients elsewhere, but I was short on time and wanted to see her in action. I was having some serious second thoughts as she grabbed one of the paper napkins and proceeded to blow her nose before stuffing the napkin in her front pocket.

"Stand," I instructed, trying to keep the scowl from my face.

She gaped up at me, her mouth ajar, her eyes widening as her skin went from pink to white, all within a few seconds.

"Or," I whispered, pinning her like a bug with my stare, "you can sit. But I highly doubt that's the way to get on the good side of that barista you've been trying not to check out ever since you walked in that door."

"But I haven't—"

"You have." I nodded, giving her an encouraging look. "And if you don't stand right now, you'll lose your chance with him. Most experts believe that jealousy is the most crucial emotion men feel before falling in love." I held out my hand.

She stared at it.

"I won't bite." I smirked, then leaned down and whispered in her ear, "Yet."

She gasped.

"Take it." I gave a curt nod. "That's what I'm here for, remember?"

With reluctance, she placed her hand in mine and stood on wobbly legs. I eyed the barista with mock annoyance as I helped my new client to her seat.

"What's this?" She pointed at the red cup in front of her chair.

"Tea." I yawned. "But yours is probably cold."

"I hate tea."

"No." I shook my head and leaned forward, my hands placed directly in front of her cup as I scooted it closer to her. "You love tea."

She frowned.

"Smile."

"What?"

"Just do it."

She forced a smile, which actually transformed her face quite nicely. A bit too much tooth and faux enthusiasm, but I could work with enthusiasm. Apathy, despondency, despair . . . not as easy.

"Hey . . . you, uh . . . guys need anything?" Jealous Barista asked as he wandered over to our table. Any jackass with half a brain knew that if we wanted something, we'd just go to the counter and ask.

"Nope." I didn't give him a second glance.

"Oh." He didn't leave. Idiot. "I just—"

"I'll send my girlfriend over if I need something, how's that?" This time I did meet his gaze. Sometimes it was just too easy. Really. His eyes burned through me, nostrils flared, fists clenched. Dude may as well have been wearing a sign that said "Mine" with an arrow pointed at Mousy Hair.

"Thanks, though," my client squeaked, tucking that flat hair behind her ear in a seminervous gesture that asshat probably found cute.

We were going to have to work on that squeak. It was endearing . . . like a fat puppy that couldn't walk.

But in order to gain the barista's attention? She needed to move on from fat puppy to something more like a greyhound—sleek, beautiful, unique.

Jealous Barista walked off.

"He hates me." She slouched.

I let out an irritated sigh as I reached for her hand and gripped it. Clammy fingers. *A personal favorite,* said no man ever.

"Stop fidgeting and sit up straight." I squeezed her hand.

Her chest rose and fell like she was running a marathon. Shit, if I had another fainter, I was going to walk.

"Sorry," she huffed as she leaned in. "It's just that he's actually talked to me only a few times, and only ever to ask if I wanted sugar in my coffee."

"He hates coffee," I whispered. "Every time someone orders coffee, he actually sneers. It's hard to tell if you don't look for it. But his nose lifts, his eyes narrow, and the bastard *sneers*, as if coffee is the equivalent of getting high behind the Dumpsters."

"But . . ." She bit down on her bottom lip. It was plump. Juicy. Finally! Something I could work with. "He works at a coffee shop."

Impatience pounded through me. "And you run five point six miles every day at three in the afternoon, yet you hate running. We all do what we gotta do to get what we want. You want a nice body? You work for it. He wants to pay for parts for his motorcycle? He works for it." Damn it, I really needed to stop taking clients when I was running on no sleep.

"Should I be taking notes?" she asked softly.

"You love tea. You hate coffee." I reached out and brushed my thumb across her bottom lip. "He despises public displays of affection, probably because he wishes he was the one involved with a girl who can't keep her hands off her man."

Her head swayed toward me, eyes heavy, cheek pressed into my hand. Bingo!

"Touch me," I instructed.

"But—"

"Do it now."

Gulping, she reached across the table and placed her hand on my shoulder.

On. My. Shoulder.

"Lower."

"But . . ." Her eyes darted to the counter.

"Stop staring or we're done."

She moved her hand lower and ran her hand over my chest, her forefinger grazing my nipple. Probably by accident, but the barista's reaction would be the same.

"Now laugh."

"Laugh?" She giggled nervously.

"That works too." I grinned smugly. This was always my favorite part, the part that solidified me as a certified genius. A rich one too. The moment when the guy suddenly realizes there's something brewing between him and the girl who's been vying for his attention for weeks, years, whatever.

Jealous Barista waltzed back over. "Shell, if you need anything besides tea, let me know." His chest puffed out as he crossed his arms. I fought the urge to roll my eyes and give the douche the finger.

"No." Shell met my gaze with a reluctance that slowly turned into triumph. "I think I'm good with my tea."

"You hate tea," he pointed out.

"No," I said. "She *loves* tea."

"Asshole," he grumbled under his breath before walking away.

"He knows my name." She gave a rapturous sigh of longing.

Again, the urge to roll my eyes was so strong my cheeks twitched. I shrugged and leaned back.

"Who are you?" she said.

"Ian Hunter." I nodded. "Master wingman and your only chance in hell of getting"—my eyebrows lifted as a sigh escaped between my lips—"that."

Jealous Barista stared at us with his lips pressed into a firm line.

"When do we start?" Her words rushed out so fast they nearly ran into one another.

I smirked. "Three minutes ago."

CHAPTER TWO

Shell was reciting a monologue. Lucky for her, I was used to my clients rambling nervously, their words toppling over one another until I felt my head start to ache. So while my hot tea turned to ice, I let her talk, let her get every damn thing off her chest.

"And then my cat started getting sick, and we couldn't figure out what was wrong."

Gentle nod.

"I'm so upset with my mom! She never told me I was pretty!"

Pat on the hand.

"Do you think I'm pretty?"

Aw-shucks look followed by a wink.

"It just makes me so angry. The way guys ignore me like I'm some sort of nerd. If I knew how to wear lipstick, I'd freaking wear lipstick! I just, for once, want the hot guy to notice *me*."

"I completely understand." I needed to pick up my dry cleaning in about ten minutes, and she was going longer than I'd originally projected.

"I know." Shell sighed helplessly, her posture making my entire body itch to strap her upright to the chair and put a book on her head. "I just wish . . ."

You know what I wish? That we could go back in time and I could reschedule her as a client for my wingman, Lex. Damn, she's a talker.

"Stupid, huh?"

Shit. I dropped the ball. What did she wish? "I don't think anything you say is stupid." Blanket statement.

She grinned.

Nailed it.

"Th-thanks." She grinned again. "You know, you're a pretty good listener."

They always forget they pay me to listen. Always.

Shell's eyes zeroed in on my mouth. Oh, here we go. Had to admit, she was moving through my playbook stages a lot faster than I'd anticipated.

"You're really . . . hot."

"I know," I said in a bored tone. "But remember, you're my client. I'm helping you so you can help yourself."

Shell frowned. "So you don't ever date your clients?"

No, because all of my clients were in love with someone else, and I didn't have time to play the hero. I almost always created a catastrophe that their crush had to save them from, solidifying that relationship and breaking them away from whatever hero worship they had of me. It made sense, if you really thought about it. The women I dealt with were so starved for male attention that they had a hard time telling the difference between my acting and actual feelings. It's why I always made my rules very clear.

"Never," I said, keeping my voice crisp. "Shell, sweetheart. I'm going to e-mail you the schedule for the next week. Let me know if you have any issues, but no phone calls, do you understand?"

She nodded slowly.

"Only texts and e-mails. We don't talk on the phone. And if you see me around campus, you don't know me. Outside of our business arrangement, we're strangers. And if anyone asks about Wingmen Inc. . . ."

She sighed. "I know, I know. Give them the red card with the Superman logo on the front and the giant *W* on back."

I winked. Our cards were genius. They just looked like stupid Superman cards, when, really, the message was on the back. The message was always in the details people rarely paid attention to. "Great." Standing, I held out my hand. "Seven days is all I need."

She glanced over at the barista, who was still blatantly shooting daggers in our direction. "I hope you're right."

With an eye roll, I pulled her in for a quick kiss on the lips and whispered, "I'm never wrong."

"You smell spicy."

Aw, how cute, a compliment. Maybe I'll only need six days. After all, one of the days was completely dedicated to learning how to stroke a man's ego. Look how fast my little grasshopper was learning!

"Thanks." I placed my hand on the small of her back and guided her out of the coffee shop.

"Bye, Ian." She walked toward a red Honda and hopped in. Damn, I'd had her pegged as a green Jetta type of girl. Well, can't win 'em all.

The minute I jumped into my Range Rover, my phone rang.

"How was she?" Lex yawned on the other end of the phone. I imagined he was probably shit-deep in e-mails, since it was two weeks after New Year's, meaning everyone with a pulse had just created New Year's resolutions to change their lives. "Because your waiting list is hella long, and if she's not a good fit, I have another girl that offered to pay me in sexual favors to move her to the top."

"Cross her off," I barked. "If she knows how to give favors, she knows how to get her own damn man."

"Noted." Lex chuckled darkly.

I made a mental note to make sure he actually checked her off the list rather than making fake promises just so he could get his rocks off.

"Oh," Lex said, "and Gabi says if you don't make it tonight for dinner, she's going to glue your hand to your penis. Though she was much more graphic."

"Always is." I grinned. "Text her and let her know I'm on my way."

"Done." He hung up.

I didn't pick this life. It's not like I woke up one morning and went, *Wow, wouldn't it be so badass to help dowdy women get the guy?* And before you stomp off in a huff, look at the facts. Almost 60 percent of women marry down, meaning most women go for a man with the dad bod. The guy who is more than likely going to make less than them; never work out; eat hot dogs for breakfast, lunch, and dinner; and, let's face it, need Viagra by age forty.

All it takes is a simple Internet search to get the facts.

Women are, by nature, insecure creatures, and if by the tender age of thirty-five they haven't settled down, they'll most likely marry the guy with the unfortunate bald spot and a heart of gold.

And there is absolutely nothing wrong with that.

It's kind of like when you go to the pound and pick the dog with the lazy eye because you feel sorry for it, and you know without a doubt that bastard will never stray.

So what's the difference between settling and settling?

The first type of settling is cute. The dog with the lazy eye, or in this case, the man, really is what's best for the girl. A match made in heaven. They're the couples you see holding hands while you wonder if the girl's legally blind. It's the hot tall mom and the short dad. The sorority girl and the guy with the beer gut. The cheerleader and the science nerd.

For some reason, the universe accepts this. I accept this.

What I don't accept? The insecure type of settling, desperate in nature. Granted, that's rarer.

But getting more and more common.

It's when a girl never reaches her own potential, thus settling for less than what she's worth. It's the quiet girl who was never taught how to wear makeup. The chubby girl who eats her feelings but has a hilarious personality, who should by all means be paired with the quarterback.

It's the matches who never find one another.

It's my sister.

Quiet, shy, a bit desperate, but gorgeous. She used to crush hard on a guy from my team. And when I say hard, I mean, she ran her car into a mailbox once when I had him over for the Fourth of July.

The crazy part? He was totally into her, but because of her insecurity and awkwardness, she never pursued him. She was too scared to take that next step and meet him halfway.

I was too selfish to care, and she made me swear not to intervene.

A year went by. He got tired of waiting; she got tired of "rejection." And she settled for her lab partner, Jerry.

Now she's married to some loser who thinks video games are an Olympic sport, and that when the beer is gone, a magic beer fairy restocks the fridge while he sleeps at night. Idiot probably thinks buffalo are extinct as well.

My friend, on the other hand? He just got drafted by the Steelers and was recently in a Nike commercial.

I was sitting on my sister's couch, at her birthday party nine months ago, when my life clicked. My knee hurt like hell, but it was nothing compared to seeing the look of complete devastation on her face as she watched my friend on national television while Jerry yelled for her to pick up the baby so he could keep on playing Xbox.

My sister deserved better. *Deserves* better. And as I iced my knee, thanks to an unfortunate incident I didn't want to dwell on, I had an epiphany.

If only she had been more secure, known how to read the signs, known how to get the guy she really deserved, she would be happier. An ounce of confidence would have changed her life, and knowing how to read guys, to read a situation? Hell, just learning *one* rule in my playbook would have changed her life.

She wouldn't be stuck in Yakima, Washington, the place that's known as the Palm Springs of Washington but really, if you ask me, is drug and gang central, worse than LA.

She's a Seattle girl surrounded by cows, drugs, tractors, and a weekly date night at Applebee's.

To make matters worse, it's not like she can move back to Seattle, not with her husband taking over the family tractor business and with his entire clan having lived there for over forty years. There was nothing I could do. Nothing she could do except the occasional call or text.

So basically she was stuck in hell until something shifted in their situation. But by the looks of it? World peace would be accomplished before that ever happened.

She's completely lost to me.

The only family I have left.

Besides Gabi, but I don't count her, since she's not a blood relation and would probably stake me with the closest sharp object if I referred to her as my sister. Something about not wanting all the available men to run away when they find out our connection. One time. I threatened a guy in high school one time, and now she refuses to tell me any sort of information about her sex life or lack thereof.

I shuddered. Whenever she wears a short skirt, the only feeling I can conjure up is that of fierce protectiveness and the sudden need to pick up sewing so that I can add fabric to the length.

So, yeah, that's my story.

It's how Wingmen Inc. got started.

Think about dating like you would a football game. Coaches have their playbooks, ones that a player will memorize for days, weeks, years on end even, and they work. It's not enough that you know how to play the game; you have to know how to read the plays, read your opponent.

That's what Wingmen Inc. is about. What if you could study a play-book for dating? We have rules for every type of relationship scenario, and our process works. Basically, we created a dating version of *Minority Report*. We see the "dating disaster" before it happens and make amendments accordingly.

Nothing angsty about it. I'm not a sad, lonely bastard in need of therapy because my parents ignored me when I was young—though they did, and probably still would have if they hadn't died in a freak plane crash when I was seven.

My heart wasn't broken by the girl next door who finally noticed me and then left me for my best friend. Please. Have you seen me?

And, no, I'm not trying to make up for things in small packages. I think it's already been established that all's well in the mechanics department.

I'm rich.

I'm brilliant—ask my professors.

I get more ass than even a man with my appetite can keep up with.

And I'm basically the modern-day Superman, saving women from themselves while my best friend, Lex, plays sidekick.

Before you ask—yes. It sucks. I'm pissed I can't play in the NFL. But when one can't play . . . one teaches.

And I was more than just a football player.

I was *the* player.

Of sports.

And . . . of women.

The best of them all.

So who better to teach women how not to get played than an actual player?

Exactly.

It's not like I've turned over a new leaf; I've just learned to use both sides. Brilliant? Absolutely.

"Shit." I nearly ran into the small Corolla in front of me as Gabi's ringtone blared over my speakers.

"Yes?" I answered. "To what do I owe this pleasure?"

"I'm not your client, Ian," Gabi shouted. "Cut with the smooth-talking love coach voice. You promised!"

"I did." What the hell did I promise? Movie night? That's what I thought I promised. The light turned green. My thoughts were still blank. A horn blared behind me, and I took off.

"You forgot, didn't you?"

"About our date tonight?" I laughed. "Of course not."

"Sometimes I wonder why we're friends."

"Because you like to stare at me when I sleep?"

"One time, Ian!" She growled out a loud curse. "You're lucky I'm forgiving. I'm having a welcome party for my two new roommates, and you were supposed to bring the chips and dip. And the party started a half hour ago."

So much for my dry cleaning.

"Was this party on my calendar?"

"You and your freaking calendar!" she shouted. "Sorry that I don't have time to log into Gmail and plug it in so that you can make time for me."

"It would be a lot easier on Lex if you did."

"You know Lex is more your bitch than your friend these days?"

"Harsh," I coughed. "You better hope I don't tell him that."

She fell silent. Because that was what she did when we talked about Lex. She pretended she wasn't planning on setting his bed on fire with him in it, and I pretended not to notice that even when they were fighting, it seemed like she was still clamoring for his attention, no matter how negative.

But we both knew the elephant was standing in the room with his face plastered all the hell over it.

I sighed. "Sorry, Gabs. I'll be there in about fifteen minutes, alright?"

"You better," she grumbled. Then the line went dead.

My music started up again as I quickly pulled into the closest grocery store parking lot and ran like hell to grab the snacks I'd promised. The busier I got, the worse my memory became, which was why I had a calendar and an online schedule that even my professors knew how to access just in case I wasn't in class, since I was a TA. I was an A student; I'd trained them to keep up with my schedule well, and it was an added bonus when I could teach their classes while they did more important things.

I grabbed all the chips and dip I could find that promised lots of empty calories, then groaned when I noticed only one checker was open and the guy in front of me had ten coupons.

I was ready to pay for his groceries if the dude would just let me go first.

"I can help you over here, sir," a perky voice said to my right.

A slow smile spread across my face as I turned. "Oh wow, thank you."

The girl blushed and flicked on the little light at her check stand.

"Hmm, going to a party?" The scanner beeped as she ran each item through.

"For my sister. Well, she's basically my sister. And I'm the tool that forgot to bring snacks."

"You don't seem like a tool to me." Her voice was throaty as she arched her eyebrows.

"Well, maybe you should tell her that, which would save me from having to grovel . . ."

Her eyes lit up. "I get off in ten minutes."

"Aw, it would only take me five. Tops."

"What?"

"Your top." I pointed to her plain white shirt. "Looks gorgeous with your skin tone."

Her eyes dilated right before me.

Sometimes, it was just too easy.

CHAPTER THREE

"Finally," Gabi shouted as she opened the door and jerked the groceries out of my hand in one fell swoop. "I thought you said you fifteen minutes."

"Did I say fifteen? Could have sworn I said twenty." And there was that one checker who needed my help, so . . .

Gabi's eyes narrowed. "You smell like cheap perfume."

"Gross, right? Who wears Vanilla Fields anymore? I think your grandma still buys that shit, but she's eighty. She's allowed to be a creature of habit."

"You did it again, didn't you?"

"Did what?" I played innocent while I unpacked the shopping bags. Gabi lived a few blocks away from the University of Washington campus, and I, in turn, lived a few miles away from her. It was convenient for both of us.

I made sure no idiots plagued her with their existence.

And she cooked for me.

Sometimes she even packed me little-kid lunches with smiley faces.

I'd probably starve without her. A point she liked to make on a daily basis.

Gabi rolled her green eyes and quickly pulled her long auburn hair into a low messy bun. "Sometimes I want to kill you." She exhaled. "Wow, I feel so much better getting that off my chest."

"That's what I'm here for." I winked. "Your own personal therapy."

She scrunched up her nose. "Seriously. You smell bad, dude."

I held up my shirt and winced. "How the hell did five minutes with Shopgirl lead to me being a walking perfume commercial?"

Gabi sighed, then pointed upstairs. "Go. Shower. I'll put out the food. Your extra clothes are still in my room. Just"—she sneezed and wrinkled her nose—"get rid of the skank."

"She has a name," I teased. Not that I actually remembered it. But in my defense, while her lips were wrapped around me, her head was blocking the view of her name tag. See? Not my fault.

"One day." Gabi shook her head. "You're going to get smited." She frowned. "Or is it smote?"

"Oooo." I shivered and leaned in, pressing a kiss to her cheek. "Sounds dirty. Can't wait."

With a hard shove, she pushed me off of her and slapped me on the ass. "Upstairs. Go, before you start attracting more."

"Attention?"

"Girls with no future." Gabi nodded seriously. "You know, the type you like to give quick—"

"Lex!" I interrupted her on purpose when my best friend sauntered into the kitchen. He was six foot five inches of pure muscled man-slut. Worse than I was.

Which meant he probably deserved some sort of medal.

Or badge.

Or at least a patch with the letter *W* for "whore." His own dirty scarlet letter.

Next to me, Gabi tensed.

"I'll just go take that shower," I said, leaving them alone. I knew full well that it was best to stay out of the way where they were concerned.

I hated breaking up fights. Last time I earned a black eye and a kick to the balls trying to keep the peace.

And with all the clients I had piled up for the rest of the semester, the last thing I needed was to show up to a meeting with both my eyes swollen shut.

I took the stairs two at a time, made sure to knock on the bathroom door before I let myself in, then quickly stripped out of my clothes and jumped into the shower.

All of my essentials were where I'd left them, in the little caddy I kept in the corner.

And before you go getting all suspicious on my ass, remember, Gabi is like a sister to me—as in, the only time I even thought about kissing her was during eighth-grade skate night, and I'm pretty sure that's because someone had spiked my Mountain Dew.

Regardless, we kissed, and it was awful. She actually puked. But we're 99 percent sure it was the stomach flu and not my bad kissing skills that caused it.

We shook hands a few days after that.

Swore each other to secrecy.

And haven't had any issue since.

So, no, I'm not jealous of her fascination with Lex, though if he ever pursued her, I'd probably hang him from a telephone pole and light his nuts on fire. It was cute, her obsession, and I knew it would never go anywhere. Because she was a virgin.

He wasn't.

And guys like Lex know what girls like Gabi are worth—gold. He couldn't afford her, not even if he sold his soiled soul.

The familiar scent of my Molton Brown body wash floated into the air, burning my nostrils but relaxing me at the same time.

I only kept Molton at Gabi's.

Jean Paul Gaultier was for my place.

And if I was staying overnight and had to meet a client the next day, then I brought along Old Spice. It was another numbers thing. At least 30 percent of guys in college used Old Spice, meaning the girl would start to associate my scent with that of other men, pushing her boundaries, making her comfortable. Because as any dating expert knows, scent is the easiest way to establish memory as well as comfort.

You can't make this shit up.

Which is another reason Lex is invaluable to the company: he loves his charts, data, and fun facts.

A loud knock shook the door. "I swear to the shower gods if you don't hurry your ass up, I'm going to break the door down and flush the toilet."

"Five minutes, Gabs."

"You and your fake time limits!"

I quickly turned off the shower, wrapped a towel around my waist, and made my way down the hall into her room.

With a sigh, I shut the door behind me, dropped the towel, and flipped on the light.

Did she get a new dresser?

Hers was brown.

This was black.

And the perfume on top was new.

Frowning, I picked up the Prada bottle and sniffed, just as the door to the room opened.

"Holy Garfield and lasagna!" a tall brunette with an exorbitant amount of long wavy hair said. She covered her face with her hands and stumbled backward. The door had already halfway shut behind her, so the doorknob gave her butt a nice high five. With a wince, she stumbled forward, reaching for the hamper next to where I was standing.

It was plastic.

Not steel.

So naturally, the minute she put weight on it, it broke. Laundry scattered all over the floor, and she fell to her knees, her ugly black basketball shorts hiking up to reveal muscular thighs.

Grinning, I leaned down, still naked, and pointed to a pink thong. "Kinda had you pegged for a boy-shorts girl."

The girl's brown hair was covering her face like Cousin Itt from *The Addams Family*. Slowly, she pushed her hair out of her eyes.

"What are you doing in my room?" Her voice was accusatory low, and kind of sexy—if I closed my eyes and thought of it belonging to a different body.

"You mean Gabi's room?"

"No." Her nostrils flared. "*My* room."

"And you are?" I held out my hand, because I was a gentleman first, a certifiable man-whore second, and because my grandma used to swat my ass every time I introduced myself without a firm handshake.

Her eyes widened as she stared at my naked body.

"Fine," I said with a half shrug. "But I literally only have three minutes before Gabi hands me my ass. You want the bed or the floor, since you're already there?"

And Gabi said I wasn't charitable enough? Damn, look at me, just ready to hand out orgasms for free.

"What?" New girl's wide roaming eyes finally lifted to meet mine. Hell, some people charge for that kind of staring. "What are you talking about?"

"Okay, now we're down to about two and a half minutes. I'm not gonna say it won't be difficult, but I could probably do something that would at least conjure up a little panting. Maybe a scream or two."

"Scream?" she said, her eyebrows drawing together. "What are you talking about? And why are you naked?"

"I was looking for clothes before you barged in on me."

"In *my* room."

"Look." I glanced at my watch. "Now we're really getting into dangerous territory. I've been nicknamed Superman in bed, but I'm not actually sure I can do a repeat of 2014, though I'd love to add another instance to the record books. So if we're going to do this, you need to hurry up and take at least your shirt off."

"Are you"—her cheeks reddened—"a stripper for the party?"

Hmm. The idea had merit. I could do a free show, which would make me a saint, considering what I typically charge each client.

"No." I held out my hand. When she didn't take it, I took it upon myself to lift her from the floor and onto her feet.

She kicked. She even tried to bite me.

"There we go. A little enthusiasm!"

"Put me down!" She jerked away from me.

I set her away from me and crossed my arms. "Sorry, time's up. You have ten seconds left, and even I can't perform a miracle of this"—I pointed at her baggy shirt, baggy shorts, and, holy shit, was she wearing tube socks?—"caliber." I swallowed. "Just a guess, but were you homeschooled?"

Her face reddened with either embarrassment or anger. "No! And I live here. This is my room!"

"But it's Gabi's room."

"We switched this morning!" She stomped her foot. The girl was wearing old-school Adidas flip-flops.

They still made those? Huh. It was like seeing a real live T. rex.

"Why are you staring at my feet?"

"They have to be worth a mint by now." I tapped my chin and continued staring at the ugly rubber flip-flops. "Impressive. Really impressive."

"Are you even listening to me?" she shrieked. "Put some clothes on and get out of my room. Or don't put clothes on and just get out of my room. Whichever."

"Exactly." I nodded seriously. "I was just about to do that when you tumbled in. Now," I said slowly, "you say you switched rooms?"

She nodded.

"Which makes Gabi's room . . . ?"

She pointed down the hall. I had a brief moment of recollection in which Gabi had mentioned something about switching to the smaller room because the two new roommates were going to share.

"Ah, you must be Serena."

"Blake," she growled. "Serena's blonde."

I'd have bet she was hot too. Serena was a hot-girl name. Blake? It was what you named a girl that you thought was going to be a boy and therefore projected all your boyhood dreams onto her. Ten bucks that her dad had made her play every sport in the book and she was either the product of divorce or single parenting.

"Why are you still standing here . . . naked?" This time she looked away, covering her face with her hands.

"What's wrong with being naked? You do know you were born that way, right?"

"Just"—she didn't look again, but pointed at the door—"go."

"Your loss." I laughed. "Could have rocked your world."

"My world doesn't need rocking."

I paused midway through the door and turned back, moving in close, making sure my breath would blow across her neck as I whispered, "Now that's where you're wrong, Blake. Every girl needs to allow her world to be rocked, at least once. Or if said rocking is coming from me? Twice."

Her stance was rigid, and the only clue I had to her emotions was the fact that her breathing picked up along with her pulse. I leaned forward and licked a spot on her neck that was taunting me. Then I stepped back. "Nice meeting you."

The door slammed behind me, nearly slapping my ass in farewell.

Can't win them all. Not that I would want to win anything with Adidas Girl. I had too much on my plate already. The last thing I needed was some sexually repressed tomboy who wore sweats because they were comfortable.

CHAPTER FOUR

I was still shaking my head after I got dressed and made my way back down the stairs and into the small living room. I mean, Adidas flip-flops?

Lex was busy chatting up the chick I guessed to be Serena, who had blonde hair, big doe eyes, and a cute little body that would probably be under his lazy ass in a few hours. Or better yet, she'd be on top doing all the work while the bastard placed his arms behind his head, yawned, and said, *A little to the right.*

He was bossy in bed and out of bed; he probably handed his girls manuals they had to memorize before getting the honor of doing him.

Blake wasn't downstairs yet.

And *Game of Thrones* was playing on the TV. Season three, just where Gabi and I had left off. I wasn't above faking an illness during the next episode so that everyone would go to bed and I could watch it without interruption. I'm a giver like that.

"Ian," Gabi growled. "It's been ten minutes. Tell me you didn't."

"Didn't." I winked at Lex and grabbed a beer from the counter, then started piling my plate high with chips.

Gabi pinched me in the side and twisted.

"Shit!" The chips nearly fell off my plate. "What was that for? I showered, I no longer smell like baby prostitute, you're welcome!"

Gabi released my skin and shoved me in the chest. "Where's Blake?"

"Is she on the basketball team?"

"No." Gabi rolled her eyes, then gave me a familiar and suspicious look. "Where is she?"

"Soccer?"

"No."

"Tennis?"

"Ian, if you touched her, I swear I'll rip your golden locks from your brain one by one."

I crunched down on a Cool Ranch Dorito. "Golf?"

"Volleyball," Blake supplied, coming up beside us. "Actually."

I snapped my fingers. "That explains the clothes."

Gabi looked back and forth between us. "The clothes?"

"What's wrong with my clothes?" Blake looked down.

I laughed.

They didn't.

Clearing my throat, I crunched on another chip, flashed a smile, and said, "Absolutely nothing."

"He belong to you?" Blake was pointing at me like I wasn't part of the conversation.

"Unfortunately." Gabi sighed. "You know how your parents always tell you not to feed the strays?" Her eyes met mine. "He was so cute at first, like all puppies. Then he started biting all my friends."

"Love you too, boo." I kissed her on the forehead and slapped her ass. "And they're love-bites."

Blake watched the exchange with wide eyes.

"Ian," Lex shouted. "Are we going to do this or what? I have a test in the morning."

That was his angle.

And he was so damn good at it that even I had to bow down and give him a pat on the ass.

He was a computer genius.

A hot science nerd.

I imagined he was what would happen if Bill Gates were reborn a Greek god. One day Lex was going to take over the world. That was, if he stopped banging the wrong chicks, i.e., his professors' favorite students.

Girls adored him because he had a brain. Too bad he used his powers for evil. In a way, he was the villain to my hero.

I saved the girls from settling for tools, losers, and frat boys; that is, I saved them from guys like Lex. And Lex made sure, via his illegal computer programs and research, that our clients were legit.

He took the evil ones.

I helped the good ones.

I think we fed off each other's powers. The perfect balance between good and evil.

Serena giggled at something Lex said. Hell, she'd probably giggle if he spelled "astronaut" correctly.

I fought the urge to roll my eyes. Don't get me wrong, I did girls like that on a biweekly basis to blow off steam, but that's all they were good for; the one contribution they had to society was that they didn't care about anything beyond the fact that guys like Lex and me had six-packs and we let them touch each muscle while giggling.

"Yup." I tossed my muscular body onto the couch and stretched out. "Final episode. Feel free to watch, girls, but if anyone talks, I'm taping their mouth shut."

"Not yet!" Gabi ran and stood in front of the TV. "It's a welcome party for my roomies. We have to socialize first."

"Oh." I nodded. "Right."

The room was silent.

"Well, if this isn't like a forced blind date," I said to myself. Sort of.

Hey, it was a small living room.

"You would know." Gabi's eyes narrowed. And I froze. Because if there was anything we agreed upon, it was that we never talked about Wingmen Inc. It was like Fight Club, only better, because it revolved around keeping sad girls from having sex with douchebags.

Stop shaking your head. What I did in my spare time, off the clock, was totally different. I didn't bang sad girls; I banged stupid girls. Note the difference.

"Come on, Gabs." Lex pushed Serena away from him. "Get off it. We met the roomies, Ian brought food, and you're still single." He sneered in her direction, running his hand over his dark buzzed hair. "All is right in the world."

Gabi lunged for him.

I jumped in between them and quickly pulled her body back against mine as we sank into the deep leather couch. Gabi might have been small, but she was scrappy.

"Shh," I whispered in her ear. "You know he's just being a prick because he hasn't gotten laid this week."

Lex cursed and rejoined Serena on the couch. He was a pretty easy-going guy, unless he was in the same room as Gabi. Then he lost his shit and resembled Crazy Eyes from *Orange Is the New Black*.

"Let's just watch the last episode," I suggested. "Then we'll have dessert."

I eyed Serena when saying "dessert."

So did Lex.

Gabi elbowed me dangerously close to the groin.

"He already peed on her," I whispered in her ear. "Don't worry."

"You disgust me." She pressed "Play" and leaned back against me. With a smirk, I whispered back in her ear. "You love me, little sis."

"Sometimes I wonder why."

"I bring up the group average by at least two points, admit it."

"Only because you have nice hair," she grumbled.

"That's my girl."

Smiling, I comfortably set her next to me, but felt like I was being watched. I turned just in time to see Blake cover her face with that giant mop of hair again and look down at her ugly flip-flops.

Huh. I wondered what her story was, but only until I heard the familiar music of *GoT* and was sucked back into a fantasy world that made mine look like child's play.

Ten minutes in, I felt the staring again.

I adjusted myself on the couch and turned.

Blake wasn't staring, but she was texting.

During *GoT*.

Which was the equivalent of falling asleep during a Marvel movie.

I cleared my throat.

And when she still didn't look up, I moved away from my spot on the couch, sauntered over to her little barstool, and picked her up out of it.

She shrieked as I dumped her onto the couch and wiped my hands on my jeans. "There, now we're all snug and together. Phones on the table." I eyed the one in her hands. "Now."

Narrowing her eyes at me in a sinister glare, she tossed her phone onto the table with the rest of ours and crossed her arms.

"Shouldn't have fed him that first treat," she whispered to Gabi.

Gabi patted her hand and whispered back. "Haunts me day and night, Blake, day and night."

CHAPTER FIVE

Mornings. I relished mornings. Starbucks in hand, I sat in my usual spot near Drumheller Fountain, more famously known as Frosh Pond. I'd dunked many a freshman in my day, though as a senior, my maturity level had clearly grown leaps and bounds.

The morning mist was chilly—it was always chilly—but I refused to pick another spot.

I was like Sheldon from *The Big Bang Theory*.

The pond was my leather couch. The space right in front of Bagley Hall, my own personal couch cushion.

"Damn." Lex yawned loudly as he walked up to me, his own coffee clearly not doing the trick. "It's early."

"It's seven." I took another sip of my drip Pike Place Roast. "It's only early if you stayed up all night with . . . ?"

Lex grinned. "Serena. Wildcat in bed. Forgot my name twice. Asked if I believed in unicorns. Has attended Comic-Con three times, every time as a different character from *X-Men*. Her strength is her ability to say the ABC's backward, and when I asked for her number, she cried."

"Shit." I let out a low whistle. "Must have had your A game going for you last night."

Lex rolled his eyes. "I'm never off my game."

"Right," I said patronizingly. "So that one time you hit on Gabi was a fluke?"

"I was drunk," he said defensively. "Can we not talk about Gabi this early in the morning? It ruins my entire day."

"Sure, whore. Now let me see the schedule."

We moved over to one of the benches and sat. That was the thing about Wingmen Inc. We never did business meetings in the house, never brought clients to the house. It was an unwritten rule. No mixing business with pleasure. We figured we needed some pretty strict ground rules, especially since the last thing we wanted was for everyone to actually know who was behind the company.

We did all of our work strictly on campus.

Granted, the girls knew once they met one of us.

But they were sworn to secrecy. Basically they signed a contract that said if they uttered one word about Wingmen Inc., we'd sue their asses.

I'm sure you're wondering how other people on campus haven't caught on.

It's easy.

Remember how I said we don't mix business with pleasure? I'll repeat it. We don't mix business with pleasure. So from the outside looking in, it's all pleasure.

We were players before; we're players now.

People just assume we date every color of the rainbow; every size, every shape—we don't discriminate. It's why we're also so approachable to every female on campus. One day I'd date a model; the next I'd be helping a blind chick learn how to ride a bike for the first time.

You get the point.

In our world? Every woman is beautiful. Every woman has a purpose. Every woman has one guy she's been after, one unobtainable piece of man art.

Just think of the two of us as the brokers.

You're welcome, world.

"So . . ." Lex pulled out his phone and held it near mine. Immediately, an Excel spreadsheet popped up on my screen. "You have Shell for the rest of the week and then an opening before you're booked for the next two months straight. Two girls a week, starting in three weeks. Can you handle that, or do you want me to take one?"

I scrolled through the names after Shell. "What's the story on her?"

"Avery Adams." Lex let out a dark chuckle. "Oh, she's a fun one."

"Fun as in, I'll actually *have* fun, or I may want to end my life after spending a week with her?"

"The second, I think." Lex nodded, furiously tapping on his phone, then pulled up a full profile with her age, height, major, favorite foods, hobbies, dreams, dress size, and coffee drinks she liked. Let's just say our intake form was extensive. It typically took each client a few hours to fill out. "She's in love with her study partner."

"Aren't they all?"

"He's a chem major, a year younger than her."

My eyebrows shot up in interest. It was usually the opposite—the guy was older. Younger was a fun change.

"And he's more interested in ring strain in cyclopropane and cyclobutane, which is exactly what he's helping her with right now. She keeps pretending not to understand."

"Well, I'd have to pretend *to* understand. What the hell is a ring strain?"

"Business majors," Lex huffed.

"Science nerds," I countered.

"So she's failed three times, he's starting to think she's stupid, which she isn't, and it's clearly affecting her chances at settling down with him."

"Settling down." I let the two words roll around in my head a bit. "So this isn't a quick trip to Bangtown. She wants—"

"Babies." Lex shivered while I made a face of disgust.

"Great." For her. "Does anything in his background give us an idea of how open he'd be to commitment?"

"Parents have been married for twenty-five years. Basically, from what I've seen, he's just shy and awkward. And the girl's kinda cute if you take off her glasses. My guess: he's intimidated. I put both of their info into my program, and it's a perfect match." He scrolled to the bottom of the page. "If they can successfully get past the first date, my data says they have a ninety-eight percent chance of staying together and"—he grunted the next word—"committed."

"She does know how to kiss?" I took a slow sip of coffee, and it burned down my throat. Not much worse in life than teaching a girl how to kiss. Awkward, time-consuming, and—I shuddered—most of the time they did this weird tongue thing that made my mouth feel like it was being held hostage by an alien.

"Passed that test with flying colors, though she seems to be confused on what her tongue's supposed to do once the kiss deepens. I gave her an A for effort, C-plus for execution."

I supposed I could work with that. "Body?"

"All women's bodies are beautiful."

And people called us jackasses.

At least we knew that all women had something to offer, regardless of how oddly shaped the package might be. There was always something. Always.

"And?" I prodded further.

"She's a bit on the short side. So is Romeo."

"Sexual experience?"

"She's had two partners and marked both down as bad."

"That may be a problem if he doesn't know what he's doing."

"We can always make sure to give him a few pointers or conveniently have a conversation while he's grabbing his daily coffee about how to please a woman. If he doesn't know what he's doing, he'll stay and listen. If he does, he'll walk off smirking."

We both nodded.

I squinted as the sun started pushing through the clouds. "She'll be easy then."

"Yeah." Lex scrolled through the next client. "This one actually just popped up on the site this morning, but since your schedule is kinda full, I wasn't sure if you wanted me to let her apply."

"Do it." I didn't even look at the screen. "I have some time."

"But—"

"I need to go." I stood, stretching my arms and my coffee above my head. "Shell has an early class with Douchepants, and I'm supposed to walk her to it while carrying her books, then kiss her on the forehead."

"Tale as old as time, my friend." Lex let out a halfhearted laugh. "It's not the tongue kissing that gets the guy to notice."

"Nope." I fist-bumped him and started walking off. "It's the gentle kiss."

"It's always the gentle kiss," Lex yelled after me.

I had a sneaking suspicion that once we graduated and this shit went viral, Facebook was going to try and buy us out for a billion dollars.

CHAPTER SIX

The UW campus was buzzing with excitement. Students shuffled past one another as the wet morning mist hung in the air. Just another reason I loved Seattle—the weather was crisp, full of promises.

Shell gripped one of my hands as we stopped in front of one of the business buildings. I used my free hand to wave at Gabi as we passed by. Her eyes locked on mine. It was times like these that I was convinced I could read women's thoughts just by staring at them—and I was the only lucky bastard who could do it.

See? Superhero.

Her look said that.

Asshat, another one? Already? Didn't you just get done helping out that chick last week with the sob story about how she really wanted world peace but nobody ever took her seriously because she has a nervous laugh?

Stella had been an easy one. She took four days. Dude didn't even know what hit him. One minute they were just friends. The next, I saw his car parked outside her apartment all . . . night . . . long.

"Gross," Gabi had said. "You were doing recon during their sexcapades?"

"I'd like to call it research," I said.

"Didn't she laugh at his dad's funeral?"

"Right. It's a nervous laugh, and it's a real thing."

Another eye roll. "Lunch later?"

"Sure thing."

"Have fun saving the world, one girl at a time."

"Don't I always?"

Okay, so maybe she didn't say "Have fun saving the world." I may have exaggerated that part for my own benefit.

"I'm nervous," Shell said, squeezing my hand. "What if he doesn't notice me again? Or worse, what if this doesn't work, and—?"

"You read our stats. When has it ever not worked?" I took a deep breath. "That's why we give you our success rates along with the FAQ sheets, so you know without a doubt that what we do works. But you have to follow the rules, understand?"

Shell bobbed her head. Her new haircut did wonders for her face, and her bangs brought out a cute trendy side of her that Mr. Barista would totally dig, if he recognized her in the first place. I made sure to give her pointers on what to wear, but I always—and I do mean always—told the girls one thing: A girl should never change herself for a guy. Ever. And if she did? Then they weren't meant to be. We helped improve what they already had, but we never changed them.

Though thanks to Lex, we usually knew if it was going to be a bad match before it happened, and we very strategically steered those girls toward more successful matches.

All in a day's work.

Jealous Barista rounded the corner and was just about to look our way.

"There he is." I stopped and pulled Shell against me. "Smile."

"I'm trying."

"You look nervous."

"I *am* nervous." Her lower lip trembled slightly.

"Hey, hey." I cupped her face. Flirting was always more realistic when they were nervous, because nerves could also appear to be tenderness, trust, love. "You'll do just fine."

She already was doing fine. Her body leaned into mine, her eyes wide with fear, but from this angle, my guess was Mr. Barista was ready to punch me in the jaw at her obvious adoration.

I kissed her cheek, gently rubbing mine against hers before whispering in her ear, "If he looks over here, avert your gaze like you're guilty."

"But—"

"Do it, Shell. I have a class too." And unlike her building, Paccar Hall was a good twenty-minute walk across campus, meaning I had to haul ass.

She tilted her head.

"Now, grip my back with your fingertips like your hands are almost digging into my skin. Make it look desperate."

She did.

"Ouch."

"Sorry," she whimpered.

"Good." I pulled back and kissed her forehead, my gaze meeting Mr. Barista's as he swore and jerked his head away from the show.

"Did he notice?" Her voice rose in excitement.

"Oh, he noticed." I grinned, then tapped her chin with my finger. "Now, during class he'll most likely sit next to you. Let him, but try not to talk to him. If he engages, be polite, but not overly excited. He'll think I told you not to talk to him, which will make him try harder. He'll drive himself crazy, because you look sad and nervous, and he'll think something's wrong with our relationship and basically bother you the rest of the day until you tell him all the gory details. Give him your phone number, but don't answer the first text. Answer the third. Always the third."

I'd just blazed through rules one, two, three, and four.

Rule one: Make them curious, slightly jealous.

Rule two: Don't appear too interested. Always be polite.

Rule three: Give them a method of contact, but keep the ball in your court.

Rule four: Never answer the first text, call, e-mail, etc. For some reason, the brain picks up on the number three as being the final try before you look desperate.

"What if he doesn't—?"

"He will." I winked. "Now, off you go."

"Third text, evasive, polite," she mumbled to herself as she took purposeful steps toward the building.

"Kind of like watching little ducklings hatch and finally make it into the water," a deep voice said beside me.

I grinned. "Lex, what brings you to my side of campus?"

"Have you checked your schedule?" His grin was way too big for nine in the morning.

"What did you do?"

"Not me." He held up his hands. "I'm sure I'll be hearing from you later."

I was just about to open my schedule when I noticed the time. "Shit." I ran like hell toward the Paccar building, hoping I wouldn't be late again. Pretty sure my whole "my aunt was sick and needed someone to talk to" excuse wasn't going to go over well for the third time, and this particular professor hated me because Lex had screwed his daughter.

We may be best friends, but at least I looked before I laid, you know? Lex didn't care who his appetite affected; if he wanted something, he took it. Odd, considering he put so much damn time and energy into Wingmen Inc. It was his baby, his love child. Then again, even though we were best friends, Lex was private. He shared things with his computer, and sometimes, if it was a good day, he shared personal shit with me, but it was rare.

There were two things Lex trusted in this world: technology and sex. Neither had ever let him down. Hell, thirty years from now Lex will be sitting on the front porch of his mansion sipping lemonade with his computer/automated robot, whispering sweet nothings into its ear.

I nearly collided with a bench as I continued my sprint.

Shit. Shit. Shit.

With one minute remaining, I jerked open the door to the classroom and ran right into a short boy.

"Sorry, bro." I leaned down to help him pick up his books.

Pink nail polish? Well, to each his own, I guess.

"You," a very female voice said.

A hood was covering the she-man's head. I peered closer and really wished I hadn't.

Blake.

And she was pissed. Then again, my girl parts would probably be pissed off too if I strapped on a tight sports bra, tank top, and long basketball shorts. And, damn, those flip-flops just wouldn't quit.

"Why are you always . . . everywhere?" she spat, wearing a look of outright distaste.

Class still hadn't started, but I was a very self-aware individual. Meaning I knew that every damn eye in that room was trained on me and probably wondering why the hell I wasn't charming the chick in dude clothes.

Can't charm the asexual, folks.

I handed Blake her books. She jerked them out of my fingertips and huffed out a breath, pulling the hood from her hair.

That I could work with.

Her hair was a pretty golden-brown, thick, glossy, the first thing you noticed about her—other than the flip-flops, mind you.

"Business major?" I pointed to her books.

"Gen ed. Why else would I be here if I didn't have to take the class?"

"Stalking." I winked. "Wouldn't be the first time I've been followed. Probably won't be the last."

"You clearly have too high an opinion of yourself."

"Some may say not high enough." I let out a low chuckle as a few girls in the front row started whispering loud enough for anyone with two ears to hear:

"So hot."

"Three times! She said it was the best night of her life."

Blake clenched her teeth and shot poison darts with her eyes. "Fans of yours?"

"The club has an opening."

Blake shoved past me to make her way up the stairs to the last few empty seats. I followed her, mainly out of curiosity but also from the need to distance myself from the girls in front, who would have most likely tried to fondle me the entire class.

Last time that happened, I couldn't even finish!

And by "finish," I mean finish my finance class.

"They made posters last year," I said with a sigh, plopping into the seat right next to her.

Jaw slack, she pointed at the other seats on either side of us, seats that would at least put a few empty desks in between us.

"Desks. Chairs. It's a classroom, so that's to be expected. Anything else I can help you with?"

"Sit in any chair but that one."

"This one right here?" I patted my seat right between my legs and grinned shamelessly while her cheeks burned bright red. "Something on your mind, buttercup?"

"Just . . ." She dropped her book loudly onto the desk and put her bag on the floor. "Don't talk to me."

"Okay."

She blinked at me, the shape of her mouth forming a small *O*, giving me the best possible daydream of her on her knees in front of me. I sucked my lower lip, allowing my thoughts to trail into dangerous territory. Then again, she was blushing now, blushed often, and was probably too uptight to take direction on any sort of oral activities. Pity.

Smiling, I kicked back in my seat. I did my best studying in silence . . . I didn't need to talk to her to get to know her. Most of the important things about people were learned by simply observing.

Besides, class was starting.

The professor droned on and on about business organization and different organizational roles within a corporation.

I tuned him out, because I had my own corporation. I knew how roles worked. It was like going back to first grade after graduating with honors. But I stayed glued to my seat and studied Blake out of the corner of my eye.

Her face wasn't bad. She had a smattering of freckles around her nose and cheeks, like someone had just dropped a few for effect right on her face when she was born. She would be cute if her hair wasn't constantly falling over her eyes, making it impossible for me to really see what shape her face was or what color her eyes were.

With a huff, she pulled back her hair into a low ponytail.

I let out a small gasp.

Purely by accident.

"Are you going to make it?" she whispered harshly.

I leaned over, my hand grazing the back of her chair, fingertips dancing along her neck. "Are you?"

"I'm not . . . interested."

"In men?"

"In you," she said pointedly. "Now, stop whatever it is you're thinking about and pay attention. I just transferred here from Boise State this semester, and I already feel like I'm behind."

"Ohhh." I snapped my fingers.

"What? What 'ohhh'?"

The world suddenly made sense. "You're from Idaho? Hit me with the town you were born in, because it sure as hell wasn't Boise."

She shifted in her seat, moving farther away from me as she gave me a quick sidelong glance. "Riggins."

"Dear God, save me from small towns with only one grocery store."

"Stop," she hissed, "talking."

"Okay." I shot her a calculated half smile—just enough to make her wonder. "I got all I needed anyway."

I could tell she wanted to ask me what the hell I was talking about, but she had impressive self-control. I'd give her that.

She was from a small town in Idaho. Transferred here . . . for what purpose? My guess was her dad. I was still banking on the single-parent thing. He got a job transfer. I racked my brain. Boeing? Possibly Microsoft? Maybe even Amazon. Hell, Seattle boasted so many different corporate headquarters, it was a toss-up.

I glanced back down at her flip-flops.

I was going to go with Microsoft. Computer-nerd dad with no fashion sense who used to work from home via satellite. Bingo!

I tried to pay attention to the lecture but kept getting distracted by the way she tapped her pen.

And the fact that she had on perfume and pink nail polish. What girl who dressed like she did wore pink nail polish and Prada perfume? Did she have that pink thong on under those basketball shorts? Now those I could definitely work with when the time came. They would look so good dangling from one ankle with her legs in the air. Parts of me twitched with interest just considering the possibilities of exploring all of her diverse . . . nuances.

A mystery.

I hadn't had one of those in a long time.

Or a challenge. Hah, too bad she wasn't a client. I could do a lot with those legs. Granted, they wouldn't be wrapped around me, unfortunately, since I never got involved with clients. Not for lack of trying on their part.

The lecture ended an hour later.

We both stood. I let her walk by me and whispered, "Blue."

She froze but didn't turn around. "What?"

"Your eyes." I squeezed by her and whispered in her ear, "They're a really pretty ice blue."

"Like my soul." Her eyes narrowed. "Now, will you please leave me alone?"

"Why would you want that?" I fell into step beside her as she lengthened her stride. "Besides, any friend of Gabi's is a friend of mine."

"That's really unfortunate for me."

"So you saw me naked," I said loud enough for people walking by to hear. "Big deal."

Wide-eyed, she slapped a hand over my mouth and backed me up against the wall. I grinned against her palm.

She leaned in. "I wasn't impressed," she whispered amidst a cloud of minty-fresh breath.

I pushed her hand away and laughed. "You're a shit liar. Then again, that may have been your first time seeing a naked man, and therefore, you're waiting to compare me to the sad, unfortunate soul-sucking individual you're going to end up with. I bet he'll have glasses."

She frowned. "What's wrong with glasses?"

"And a bald spot." I nodded thoughtfully, then pointed to her temple. "Right here."

Rolling her eyes, she stepped back and escaped.

For the record, I let her.

She was out the door maybe five feet before she turned around one last time.

They always did.

They always would.

I waved.

She flipped me off.

She might as well have kissed me.

Chapter Seven

Sunlight broke through the clouds, a rarity in January, when it was usually rainy and gray. The calming sound of the fountain was broken the minute my Superman ringtone went off. Duty called.

"It worked!" Shell screamed into the phone. I barely managed to save my eardrum by pulling the phone away while she continued to shriek.

"Of course it did," I said with a bored tone. If I didn't know what I was doing, I'd suck at my job. A few girls walked by my bench and waved. The wind picked up, causing some of the water from the fountain to sprinkle across the girl closest to me. Her revealing white shirt was most definitely getting wet. And I didn't miss the fact that she leaned into the water, turned to make sure I was looking, then stuck her finger in her mouth and sucked. Hard.

What a shame that she had to ruin her shirt in order to gain my attention. I almost pitied her, and then, she turned toward me.

Or not. Not a shame. God bless America.

She blew me a kiss.

I winked in response.

Her friends giggled at our exchange.

At this point I expected either the solitary giggle or the hateful stare. I usually only received the second if I'd already been with the girl and forgotten her name, or the fact that we'd slept together in the first place. That's why I had Lex! And my damn calendar. So I didn't forget important information.

"Shell, remember what I said about phone calls." She needed to calm the hell down. Unless his penis was made of gold and he could single-handedly take down every Avenger, the screaming wasn't necessary. Not one bit. Again, the man liked *tea*. Enough said. "I need you to listen very carefully."

She sighed into the phone. "I know, I know. I was just excited. It won't happen again, Ian. You're the best!"

I know. "He's going to try to get you alone. Say no."

"But—"

"Rule number five: Tell him you're busy. From here on out, you are *always* busy, until *I* tell you that you aren't. Got it?"

"But, Ian, it's working. I mean, he asked me out twice today."

"Twice is nothing, and we aren't through the rules yet." I reached for my old-school planner and wrote down the number two next to day two. He was moving through the stages fast for a tea-drinking hippie. Guys usually hit the first stage of jealousy and hang out there for a while, rarely making a move or stomping on another man's territory until day three or four. "The minute he's done asking, he'll move on to telling. That's when you have him. Not when he asks you out, but when he demands your time and waits outside your dorm until he gets it."

"Wow," Shell breathed. "That's . . . romantic."

"I know guys." I checked my watch. "Gotta run. New client."

"Thanks, Ian. Bye. And—"

I hung up.

I didn't have time to form relationships with my clients, especially not the ones who'd cry once I told them to cut off all communication at the end of our contract. Better that I keep all conversations short and to the point rather than let our little transaction turn into a romantic entanglement that could potentially destroy my business.

With a relaxed sigh, I leaned back against the bench. My dark D&G sunglasses hid my eyes so I could study people as they passed. It was usually easy picking out new clients. They almost always approached the bench I was sitting on looking like they were going to puke. Several had turned around and started walking the other way while others had marched right up to me and burst into tears.

Frowning, I glanced at the calendar app on my phone. Lex had written in "noon." It was five after. I could be eating Thai with Gabi instead of sitting in the chilly wet weather waiting for some chick to grow a pair and approach me.

Granted, they never knew it was me behind the business until they saw who was sitting on the bench. That was part of the beauty of the cards.

Lex and I decided to keep things simple. If the girls never knew our identities until after we took them on as a client, then we didn't have to worry about the aftermath if we rejected them.

And we rejected plenty of applications, but that was all before the meeting ever took place.

Irritated, I swiped my thumb across my phone to call Lex and tell him to drop the client, when someone stumbled into the spot next to me.

Curious, I glanced up.

"Blake?" I almost laughed out loud. No way in hell.

Face pale, she glanced away and mumbled, "You really are everywhere."

"Like God, only less powerful."

"Surprised you can say his name without getting struck by lightning."

"Well, don't sit too close, just in case."

With an exaggerated eye roll, she scooted to the farthest part of the bench, crossed her arms, and tapped her foot.

"Waiting for someone?" Oh, this was too good.

Blake pretended not to hear me. Her hair was still pulled back into a tight bun, her baggy Nike shirt had paint on it, and her pink Nike shorts would be cute if they were actually the right size. Had she been overweight once and then just never went shopping for new clothes?

"Look." Blake uncrossed her arms and turned toward me. "I'll pay you to leave right now."

"In what?"

"Huh?" She started chewing on her thumbnail. That nervous habit would have to go. I should probably start compiling a list.

I leaned closer. "What will you pay me in?"

"Rupees." She glared. "Cash, you idiot."

"No can do." I scooted over so that our thighs were touching and pretended to be staring at my phone. Curiosity always won. I just had to wait it out.

"Fine, how do I get rid of you?"

Bingo! "Easy." I was still staring at the locked screen on my phone that had a Superman emblem with a *W* in the middle. "You pay me in whatever currency I designate."

"You have your own money or something?"

"Or something." I pulled off my sunglasses and shoved them in the front pocket of my leather jacket. "Either you pay me with ten minutes of your time, or you pay me with a kiss. Since it appears you'd rather eat shit than spend another second with me, I'd go for the kiss. It'll be over quicker and will most likely increase your popularity. You may even get lucky and find your picture on my Twitter feed."

"No." She burst out laughing. "Not happening."

"Fine." I put my sunglasses back on.

"Look." Her voice became desperate. "I'm kind of meeting someone, and it's important, and I don't want you here. In fact, I was specifically told that if I didn't come by myself, the contract would be . . ." She glanced down at her hands. "Just . . . go. Now."

"One kiss," I whispered under my breath. "Am I that ugly? That you can't even kiss me?"

Gritting her teeth, she muttered a curse, then grabbed my face and planted one of the quickest kisses of my lifetime—on my cheek.

On. My. Cheek.

"What was that?" I touched the spot where she kissed. "Seriously? What the hell?"

"A kiss!" She threw her hands into the air. "Now go!"

With a laugh, I swiped the screen on my phone and opened up the file with her information. I always waited until after the first meeting to learn the client's name and read their file, since I felt it would be unfair of me to judge someone based on reputation alone. Lex knew the names, but I never did until they sat on the bench.

It was part of my process.

She was from Idaho, which I already knew, but she didn't move with a parent. Good ol' dad was still back in Riggins. *Points for the single-parent guess, though.* Nope, she'd moved a few states over . . . for a guy. "Interesting."

"What?" She chewed harder on her thumb. "Never mind. I'm leaving. This was a stupid idea."

I let her walk three steps before speaking. "You think David would approve of that attitude? Says here he values optimism above all things." I paused for half a beat as though considering. "Shit, what's he studying? Spiritualism?"

Blake froze. Then she turned slowly, her face white as a sheet. "How do you know that?"

"I hacked your e-mails."

Ouch. Didn't realize it was possible for her to pale more.

"Wow, you look a little green." I stood, then grabbed her arm and started walking with her. "And I was kidding." Once we were under the nearest tree, I pushed her against it and pulled off my sunglasses again, this time allowing my eyes to fully inspect her face. Strong chin, blue eyes, the freckles again, pouty lips. "Very pretty."

"What is this?"

"Wingmen Inc.," I said in a cocky tone. "But since we're already on a first-name basis . . ."

"No." Blake shook her head. "There has to be some mistake."

"Sorry." I pulled back enough so she could have some breathing room. "No mistake. Lex and I are the masterminds behind the fastest-growing relationship service in the Pacific Northwest."

Blake exhaled slowly. "But . . . you're a . . ."

"Whore?"

She nodded.

"I enjoy women." I shrugged. "And I help women, all types of women, find their perfect match. Is that so wrong?"

"But—"

"We have a lot of work to do." I tilted my head. "Do you know what Victoria's Secret is?"

"You're an ass."

"Duh, I'm a guy. But, I'm also your new love coach. I don't charge two hundred bucks a day to be your friend." I nodded, and my body buzzed with excitement over the challenge—she'd be one, that was for sure. "I'll do it. That is, if you're still interested in this David."

She looked hesitant. Her body language was closed-off completely, so I knew she'd be a tough one to crack. Especially since I could tell she wasn't my biggest fan. Then again, she didn't need to be. Maybe I needed to remind her of that.

"Look." I licked my lips and held out my hand. She took it, thankfully. "We have a ninety-nine percent success rate. Follow the rules, follow my advice and guidance, and you'll be popping out little Davids in no time."

"Kids?" she choked.

47

"Or whatever it is you want. I'll get it for you. The only time our process doesn't work is if you refuse to play by my rules." I arched my eyebrows at the sound of her teeth clenching. "Or when the match isn't your ideal match. But if you're here, that means it's already been settled, and if you listen to me, you'll have your guy. But if for some reason this David isn't a soul-saving Mother Teresa saint who shits rainbows, or if you change your mind about him, then we'll find you someone else who's a better match. It's the perfect program. Believe me—Lex designed it, and he's a genius."

This was always the part I hated. The thinking part, when I waited for the client to say yes or no. Women overanalyzed *every*thing, and again, I didn't have time for it. Patience made me shaky.

"Anonymity is key. In public, people speculate that we're dating or maybe even together. In private, I coach you, help you find whatever dormant sexuality you've kept hiding under all that hair and those flip-flops. And after a few days, or"—I winced at her clothing—"maybe in your case a few weeks"—she glared—"we part ways with a handshake, or a high five, if that's your preference, and you skip off into the sunset with your one and only true love."

"Can I think about it?"

"Sure." I nodded. "You have two minutes. Also, did you miss the part where I said sunset? True love?"

"Two minutes?" She started breathing heavy.

"My time is precious. Next to kissing, it's another one of my currencies, the most valuable thing I have. Don't waste it."

"It was an impulse! A girl on my team gave me your card after I was complaining about being invisible to David, and—"

"Megan," I said, snapping my fingers. "Nice girl. Helped her pick out her wedding colors before the poor bastard even knew she liked him."

Blake's mouth dropped open. "You mean you were the one that said to go with orange blossom and white?"

"They complement each other so well. Besides, he's a football player and legally color-blind in both eyes. Guy can't see worth shit, and she needed help."

"So not only do you know everyone at this school, but you know every athlete too?"

"I possess a lot of school spirit. Wanna hear the fight song?"

Blake stared down at the ground.

"Thirty seconds."

Her head jerked up.

"Twenty."

Panic was starting to set in as her eyes darted back and forth between me and a route of escape.

"Ten."

"Fine," she yelled. "Fine." With a jerk she pulled her hair from her ponytail holder, then retwisted it. "What?"

I frowned. "Is all that real?"

"What?"

"Your hair."

"Yes."

Without asking permission, I tugged her hair out of the rubber band and ran it through my fingers, savoring the silky feel. "It's perfect. Men are suckers for long hair. I think it goes back to the early days when cavemen would grab women by the hair and tug them back to their sad little hay beds and make sweet love to them."

"That's"—Blake shook her head—"probably one of the most offensive things I've ever heard."

I shrugged. "Get used to it. As of right now, you'll hear a lot of shit. That's because I don't believe in candy-coating anything. Honesty is key, and, baby, I've gotta be real honest here." I let out a loud sigh. "If you want to turn the head of the captain of the basketball team, we've got a lot of work to do."

Her shoulders slumped.

"But I'm the best." I wrapped my arm around her waist and tugged her against me. "We start tonight."

"Tonight?"

"I'll e-mail you the questionnaire for the second stage, and the schedule once I talk to Lex." I stepped away from her. "Oh, and if David seeks you out at all during this process, talk to me first. If he texts you today, ignore him. If he calls you, tell him you're busy with your new study partner."

"Is that you?"

"I'm not just your study partner, Blake. From here on out? I'm your everything."

"Great," she grumbled.

"Oh, it is." I winked. "Believe me."

CHAPTER EIGHT

"You're going to want to see this," Lex yelled the minute I walked into our shared house a few miles off campus. We had a sick view of Puget Sound, thanks to the house that my wealthy parents had left me when they died. Rather than paying Lex for his services, I let him live with me for free. Not that he really needed it. He already worked for Apple and was basically able to name his price for all hacking activities done on the side.

Selfishly, I kept wishing Microsoft would come knocking so he'd stay local. We'd been inseparable since we were kids, and the last thing I wanted was to retrain a best friend.

But in his words, "Working for Bill Gates would be like working for the enemy," and he viewed using Windows as the equivalent of spitting on Steve Jobs's grave.

Our two-story house was a relic from the fifties, but it had been completely gutted and remodeled before we moved in last semester, so while the outside still had old-home character, complete with a front porch and white-framed windows, the inside was an HGTV dream home.

Each bedroom was its own master suite, complete with a fireplace and balcony. We had an extra two thousand square feet of outdoor living area that had a kick-ass barbecue, a fire pit, and a bar that over-looked Lake Union.

Another reason we didn't mix business with pleasure: we were pretty sure that if we let any girl see our man cave, they'd never leave. And then we'd find sparkly toothbrushes, tampons, and homemade cookies in all the wrong places. I shuddered at the thought as I tossed my keys onto the granite countertop and made my way to the living room, where Lex was working.

"In all my time with Wingmen Inc."—Lex didn't take his gaze away from the screen—"I've never seen one of the clients answer questions like this."

"Which one?"

He snorted. "Which do you think?"

"Our little athlete who wears Adidas flip-flops like it's still 1992. I bet she named her first pet Slim Shady."

Lex burst out laughing. "Close. Eminem."

"Damn it."

"I know you pride yourself in taking less than a week for a client to gain true love's kiss, but damn, man, she's . . . a piece of work."

"She can't be worse than Tara."

We both shuddered.

Tara had been one of our very first clients. Never kissed a guy, sported a unibrow, and when Lex tried to tutor her, she started crying midkiss because she was afraid he was going to bite her.

When he asked her why she would think that, she said it was because her daddy told her all boys bite.

I'm assuming what was meant to be a warning against teen preg-nancy ended up making it so that Lex got punched in the face and I had to finish the kissing lesson.

It was horrible.

When she finally managed to figure out that kissing could be special, personal, and romantic, she latched on to me and Lex emotionally, making it nearly impossible for us to get her to follow any rule.

Hell, she was the reason we had rules and why we never made exceptions. The last thing we needed was another Tara.

Lex chuckled. "On that note, I've rearranged your schedule and taken on two of your clients to free up some time for"—he motioned to the screen—"this."

"It can't be that bad."

"No," Lex said. "Actually, it's worse."

"You mean she's a little virgin who's never kissed a man, can't spell the word "orgasm," blushes when people talk about sex, and believes in love at first sight?"

Lex remained silent.

"Shit," I muttered. "Did you print off the questionnaire?"

He thrust a stack of papers in my face. "Check out number fifteen."

My eyes roamed across the questions until I found fifteen through twenty, which pertained to relationships: *What would you wear on a first date?* Her answer: *Something comfortable. I tend to sweat when I'm nervous, so maybe a baggy sweatshirt? Or a hat. Hats are good because they look mysterious.* I had a sudden vision of Blake in a giant pink hoodie and a Yankees hat that flattened her ears.

"Number sixteen's my favorite." Lex smirked, putting his hands behind his head as he watched me read.

My first kiss was . . . Her answer: *Hopefully it will be great!* She had typed in a smiley face with a heart emoji. This did not bode well for my workload. I barely managed to keep myself from groaning out loud.

I sighed. "No wonder she kissed my cheek."

"She what?" Lex nearly fell out of his chair. "She kissed you . . . where?"

I pointed to my left cheek.

Lex stared hard, like he was still having a hard time believing it. "No shit?"

"She grew up in some faraway town named Riggins."

"Dude, need I remind you that my grandparents had a ranch in Montana with about fifty thousand head of cattle. There are no excuses for that."

"I'm meeting with her tonight." I sat on the couch next to Lex, my eyes furiously reading over her answers. "Did you want to do the rest of the testing with her, or—?"

"Oh, no." Laughing, Lex threw his hands into the air. "That's all you, bro. I just took two of your clients, meaning my schedule's about to get just as shitty as yours. I won't have time to do the dirty work anymore."

The dirty work always included a quick kissing test followed by a few very personal questions involving sex.

Lex had never minded it before.

And I sure as hell didn't want to sit in front of Blake with a freaking diagram of the human body and ask her to point to erogenous zones.

"Hey." Lex slapped me on the back. "Look at the positive side."

"Which is?"

"Marissa called." He stood. "She wants a little TLC, and according to your schedule, you've got around two hours to kill before you're balls-deep in Sex Ed 101."

"Remind me who Marissa is?"

"Red tank top. Last week at Dante's, she tried to grope you. I intervened. She was too drunk and sloppy. Gave her your phone number."

I shook my head. I seriously didn't remember her.

Lex sighed. "Big boobs?"

I frowned.

"Her jeans were painted onto her body, and she was wearing brown cowboy boots."

"Ohhh." I nodded slowly. "Damn. I remember the boots, because they made her ass look huge, in a very inviting please-spend-some-quality-time-with-me way."

Lex laughed and slapped a piece of paper in my hand. "Cell number, e-mail, and the usual background check. She's clean, but be careful. According to her Facebook profile, her only goal in life is to save the wolves."

"Well." I grinned shamelessly. "We do need saving."

"That we do." He joined me in laughter while I quickly dialed her number.

"Hello?" She picked up on the first ring. Rookie mistake. Did no girl understand? Third ring. *Always* wait until the third ring. If you answered on the first, it meant you were desperate. The second basically said the same thing and gave the guy the idea that you were sitting around stalking his Instagram just waiting for him to call.

"Marissa," I rasped out. "It's Ian."

"Hi!" I pulled the phone from my ear. I'd already had enough shrieking for the day. "How are you?"

"Free. You?"

She let out a throaty laugh. "As free as you want me to be."

"Where do you live?"

"Why can't we go to your place?"

"Sorry." I winced. "It's getting remodeled. Crazy, but a wolf actually got loose from the zoo and somehow made its way into my home. I saved it from getting shot, using my own tranq gun, but the damage to the floor was already done. They have such sharp claws, you know?"

I could almost feel her nodding her head in agreement while I snatched my keys from the counter and walked out into the rainy weather.

"I just love wolves."

"Aren't they the greatest?" I said as I rolled my eyes. "Now, what did you say your address was, sweetheart?" Shit, I'd already forgotten her name. Melissa? Manila?

She fired off an address a good twenty-minute drive away, so by the time I got to her house I'd only have an hour before I needed to make the trek back to campus to meet up with Blake. Shit. I still had to check in with Shell too.

"Ian? You there?"

"No, but you will be soon," I joked, then hung up the phone.

The minute I got to her house on Queen Anne Hill, I smiled. If her house didn't just scream sorority girl . . .

I knocked.

She answered the door before I could knock again.

Did no woman understand the power of three?

I hid a wince. Too eager. But for this visit? It didn't matter.

Remember, I slept with stupid girls, not sad ones. And by the look of her? She was too brainless to feel such an emotion—you know, unless someone shot a wolf. Then I'm sure she'd be crying all over the place.

"That was fast." Her chest heaved as she opened the door for me to walk in.

I sniffed. "Did you bake cookies?"

She nodded, tucking her hair behind her ear. "I thought you might be hungry."

"Oh, I am," I said never taking my eyes off her mouth. "And if it's okay with you, I'd like to take a bite."

"Sure!" She started moving away, I assumed in the direction of the kitchen. I tugged her back against my already needy body.

"I wasn't talking about the cookies."

Her body softened against mine. "You weren't?"

I nibbled the side of her neck. "Hell no. I think I've found something sweeter."

She moaned, rubbing her body against me.

"Bedroom?" I panted, already pulling her shirt off.

"Last room on the"—I flicked her bra off—"left."

"Good." I tossed my shirt onto the floor, then moved her backward, in the direction of her room. "Because I only have one hour, and I really, really want to make it worth our while."

"I'm sure you will."

"Believe me." I pulled back and gazed into her brown eyes. "I always do."

She yelped as my mouth met hers in a frenzied kiss. "Mmm," I hummed against her lips. Then I whispered, "Were those cookies chocolate-chip?"

"Yes." More breathless moaning as I quickly tugged at her leggings and discarded them, along with the rest of my clothes.

"You don't waste time." Her lips were puffy from my hard kisses. Her cropped blonde hair was pushed away from her heavily made-up face.

"Time . . . is everything." I leaned down and kissed her harder, then lifted her by the hips and wrapped her legs around me.

"Oh." She bucked beneath me. "Oh wow."

I licked and tasted down her neck as I let my fingers do most of the work—the work I didn't have time or the energy for. She fell apart in my arms five minutes later.

Ten minutes after that, she was screaming my name while her headboard nearly took out the wall.

And fifteen minutes after that, my sweaty body collapsed onto hers while I whispered, "Did I mention I really love wolves?"

~

"Shell." My voice was calm, but my head was pounding. I was starving, and the last thing I wanted to do was argue with a client about why I was right and she was wrong. "I don't give a damn if he's outside your room serenading you with Drake. Don't let him in."

"But"—her voice was whiny; hell, why were they always whiny?— "he's being so sweet!"

"Guys are always sweet when they want a piece of ass," I grumbled, then sniffed the air. Damn, what kind of perfume did Wolf Girl wear? I smelled like I'd just walked into a confused saleslady in the cosmetic department, who'd squirted me with five different brands of "I'm easy." You pay me to help you succeed. You won't succeed with him if you keep trying to break the rules. The rules were established in order to benefit you, not hurt you."

"I know." Shell's voice shook. "I just . . . it's hard."

"It will be worth it"—I pulled into the closest parking spot on campus I could find, which basically meant I was still going to have to jog three miles in order to meet Blake on time—"I promise."

She was silent, then whispered a thanks before ending the call.

I'd broken the rule of phone calls with Shell only because her text gave me the assumption that she was about two seconds away from tossing her body out the window into Jealous Barista's waiting arms.

Clients always argued when things were going right. When things went bad? When they realized that Prince Charming was a jackass? They cried. Loads of tears. During those times I gave them numbers to a few counselors on campus and made sure they understood that, although I was sorry, I wasn't their girlfriend. I refused to be the sounding board when they started lamenting about why all men were the spawn of Satan.

I turned off the car and raced across campus. I was meeting Blake at the Husky Union Building. I was starved, so I was going to officially break one of my own rules—I was going to share a meal with her.

Maybe I should have taken some of the cookies from—what the hell was her name again? I closed my eyes as my mind did a quick rewind of a few hours ago when I'd pounded her against the wall, she screamed my name, and I yelled . . . "Marissa."

I nodded. Damn hard name to remember. She'd offered me cookies again upon my exit, but girls only did that as a way to lure you back in. Offering a guy a cookie after sex is like telling a kid to pee before you put them in the car for a long road trip. Suddenly they're all *Yeah, I really do need to go to the bathroom.* You plant the thought.

Ergo, had I taken Marissa's cookie, it would have planted the thought that I wanted more of her cookies. And the last thing I needed was to allow her, or any girl for that matter, to think I was committing just because I had a sweet tooth.

Just the thought of it had my body buzzing with warning.

But eating with Blake was different. It wasn't a booty call.

And it sure as hell wasn't a date.

I never ate with clients. I shared a coffee, had a beer, but never food. Food meant something else was going on, something deeper. It was like the minute food was brought to the table, a girl's entire demeanor changed, as if the fact that I bought her steak meant I could keep it in my pants and wanted to get into hers for more than one night.

That rule I'd learned the hard way.

Lex, sorry bastard, was still traumatized over his last date over a year ago. He still refused to even do so much as a happy hour with a client. It was coffee or water. Shocking that he and I almost always got the same results when we took on clients. My methods were gentler, as opposed to Lex's. Let's just say he had a hell of a bedside manner.

Sweat pooled at the back of my neck as I pulled off my leather jacket, throwing it over my arm, and opened the door to the HUB. This was Blake, I reminded myself. There was absolutely no worry of her having higher expectations based on meal-sharing. She could hardly tolerate being in the same room with me. Safe to say my Indian did not like her Pilgrim.

I let out a sigh, and there she was, checking her phone, her shoulders hunched, flip-flops visible—only this time the girl was actually sporting a pink scrunchie.

Did they still sell those things? Or was she seriously just buying shit off eBay to mess with my head?

"Blake?" I called her over, crooking my finger in her direction. I wanted to see how she walked toward me, how she approached men. With a shrug, she shoved her phone into the deep, baggy pockets of her basketball shorts and stiffly made her way over. Walking like she had a stick up her ass.

Her hair was pulled tight into a low ponytail, making her face look like it would hurt to smile.

Without acknowledging that she was in front of me, I swore and tugged her hair free.

"Hey!" Her head jerked back with the force of my tug. "Ouch!"

"No." I held the scrunchie in between us. "Just . . . no."

"But—"

"Never," I said slowly as I launched it off my finger, rubber-band style, in the general direction of the trash can. It missed by a few inches. Meaning some poor soul was possibly going to discover that sad, ugly little treasure and put it to good use. Let's hope not, for everyone's sake—for the sake of eyes everywhere. "May it rest in peace."

Blake hunched her shoulders as a crowd of guys stomped all over it. "It's the only thing that keeps my hair back."

"We'll find you something else that doesn't make you look like you starred in *Napoleon Dynamite*, okay?"

Her eyes narrowed.

I staggered back a few steps. "Whoa." Gripping her shoulders, I leaned in. "Did you change eye color overnight?"

"No." Her eyes widened. "Why?" She pressed her hands to her face. "I didn't get much sleep last night. My eyes are probably bloodshot."

Actually, just the opposite. They were gorgeous, clearer than they'd been in class. She had a bit of green that outlined the irises. It was . . . mesmerizing.

"Ian?" Blake whispered. "What's wrong?"

"Nothing." I jerked back and forced a laugh. "Just . . . let's go. I could eat a herd of cows right now." I clicked open a text from Lex and scanned the busy eating areas.

```
Lex: Every night after practice he eats
     at Asian Fusion. Gross. You'll find
     General Tso at his usual spot.
```

"How's Asian sound?" I didn't wait for Blake to answer, just steered her toward the line and fired off an order for fried rice and something that looked like chicken but had a gray tint to it. "What do you want?"

"Nothing," Blake said quickly.

I frowned. "You mean you want no food? None at all?"

"I, uh"—she blushed—"didn't bring my purse with me."

My mouth dropped open. "Holy shit . . . you own a purse?"

"Very funny."

"Is it Guess?" I grinned.

She punched me in the arm while I kept guessing. "Tommy Hilfiger? Calvin Klein? Oh damn. Please, please tell me it's actually a Caboodles case masquerading as a purse. That would make my entire week."

At Blake's blush, I knew I was close.

"Coach." I sighed. "We'll get you a Coach purse."

"But that doesn't match my clothes."

I eyed her up and down and forced my lips shut so I wouldn't say something else offensive. To be honest, I was damn curious about what would match her clothes and equally horrified with the possibility that she'd have an answer.

"What?" She put her hands on her hips.

"Food or no food?" The guy at the register looked like he was ready to quit.

"I already said I don't have my purse."

"We know," the dude said in a bitter tone. "But I'm sure Daddy Warbucks can spot you a five."

I rolled my eyes. "Are you hungry?"

She nodded.

I waved my hand over the register like magic. "So you eat. I'd order," I whispered out of the corner of my mouth, "before he spits in your food."

"Egg rolls." She nodded again. "Four."

"Finally," he muttered, keying it into his register and taking my twenty. The minute money exchanged hands, I felt the tingle again.

It wasn't a good tingle, like the kind you feel postorgasm.

It was a bad tingle, like the kind you get when a girl reaches for your balls in an unfriendly manner.

With a heavy swallow, I moved down the line, frowning. Was it possible? Was that meal the first one I'd purchased for a woman since high school?

I stared at my receipt like it was a death sentence, then quickly shoved it into my pocket. Out of sight, out of mind. It wasn't a date. I wasn't feeding Blake because I liked her. I was feeding her simply because I was hungry, and I felt guilty eating in front of her.

"Are you okay?" Blake touched my shoulder.

"Of course." Keeping my cool, I waited for the food, then carried our tray toward the back table. As we made our way through the scattered crowd, whispering commenced. I never tired of it.

Of the way girls stared at my body.

The vibe they gave off when I walked a little too close, letting them get a good whiff of my cologne, or gave them the "accidental touch" as I rubbed my body against theirs in order to get to my spot.

"You're disgusting," Blake announced once we sat.

Steam billowed off the food. "Is that how you repay your pimp during your hungry time of need?"

"Not my pimp." She scowled. "And how can you do that? Lead girls on like that? Every single one of them is still staring, whispering, staring more. One of them took a picture."

"Two, actually," I said with a shrug.

"Why?" Blake shoved my plate off the tray. "It's not like you're famous or something."

My hands froze.

Actually, my entire body seized. It wasn't necessarily in regret. But she touched on a sore subject, one she apparently didn't know existed. The damn phantom pain returned. Clearing my throat, I reached for my bottled water while Blake continued to stare me down like I was a puzzle that needed solving.

"Are you?" she finally asked.

"Was." Where the hell was the soy sauce? I was searching beneath the napkins for the tiny packet when Blake handed me one. "Thanks."

"Are you going to just leave it like that? Or are you going to explain?"

"Not much to explain." Shit, it felt like a date. I started sweating immediately. Again, this was why I didn't share meals with clients! It made them think we had something real, something personal. Damn it! "My sophomore year, I got an exemption to enter the NFL draft. I played for the Seahawks but I was"—the sound of metal crunching together jolted me out of my waking nightmare—"injured . . . So here I am."

She gawked. "You actually came back to school? After that?"

"Chew with your mouth closed, please. It aids in digestion. And why not?" I tossed the empty soy packet back onto the tray and started digging into my rice. "I wanted to complete my degree."

"But—"

"We could talk about me, but you pay me to talk about you. So?"

Her posture went rigid.

It was a jackass thing to do, basically reminding her I was the wing-man for hire, not her friend. I'd paid for her egg rolls, end of story. She paid me for my services, not my life story. Maybe I needed the reminder just as much. I didn't share personal shit, the end.

Blake suddenly paled and slumped, folding into herself like she was trying to become invisible, only she lacked the superpower to pull it off.

"Whoa, what happened just now?"

"He's here." She spoke through her teeth.

"I know." I didn't turn around. He'd just walked in with DJ, a senior guard, and a few more guys from the team. "We're doing a little recon . . . You've known him, according to your profile, since you were four, and you used to take baths together. Why are you suddenly shy around the guy? He's seen the goods, sister."

"I had no goods then!"

"You may have no goods now." I shrugged. "No way to tell, considering how loose those damn shirts are. Are you even wearing a bra?"

"Yes!" Blake's pale cheeks went crimson. "It's a sports bra!"

"No," I said in fake disbelief. "Tell me something I don't know. I bet it's white. I'm guessing Adidas."

More blushing. "We need to go before he sees us."

"And that would be bad because?"

"Every time I'm with him I act like one of the guys. I don't want him to see me like that anymore. It's bad enough that sometimes he still calls me 'buddy.' It's time for more. I want more." She slumped onto the table, leaning her head on her hands. "I want him to know I have boobs."

"Need I remind you the jury's still out on that one?"

"I do!"

"Show me."

"No!"

"Do it."

"We're in public."

"Fine." I moved to her side of the table, scooting my chair loudly across the floor until I was thigh to thigh with her. I wrapped an arm around her shoulder and tugged her against me. "I guess I'll just have to cop a feel."

"I will seriously cut off your fingers if you cop anything."

"No, you won't," I whispered in her ear. "Just imagine it's David."

She tensed even more.

"Relax," I whispered. Her hair smelled like Hawaii. Fresh flowers and suntan lotion invaded my senses. It was . . . refreshing. Slightly dizzying, in a good way. I lifted some to my nose and inhaled.

"Are you sniffing my hair?"

"Is David watching?"

"No, he's eating."

"Bastard must be clueless then, because no doubt he's seen you. There's only fifteen people in here. Okay, turn away from him, toward me."

"I'm uncomfortable."

I kissed her just below the ear.

A whoosh of air left her lips.

"Good. Relax toward me." My right arm clenched around her while my left hand inched up her thigh toward her shirt.

Eyes wide, she watched my hand move until it slid under her shirt. Then her gaze met mine, like it was a scary movie and she was afraid to look.

It was exhilarating, watching her watch me. Most girls looked away, most girls just closed their eyes and screamed my name.

She stared right through me.

Eyes trained on mine. Eyes that trusted way too easily.

"Breathe," I instructed. "In and out."

Blake's eyes closed for a few brief seconds before she opened them again and exhaled slowly.

My fingers danced along her ribs. I fought the urge to frown. Why the hell was she hiding her body? She was fit, really fit. Then again, she was an athlete. Her skin was soft, velvety. My hand reached the edge of her sports bra. I didn't go underneath; that wasn't my job. Actually, feeling her up wasn't part of my job either, but I had a dual purpose.

The minute my hand came into contact with her bra, she sucked in a deep breath, her chest heaved, and her body tensed.

Holy shit. I kept my response on lockdown. Her breasts were perfect, and clearly they existed. The itch to feel more than a few seconds was enough to make my body throb. Instead, I slowly pulled my hand away just as David approached our table.

"Blake?" David was around six two, the current point guard for the Huskies. He had dark curly hair and dimples that I guess girls might find attractive. He was a bit on the lean side, but from what I'd heard, he was a nice guy. Really into his game, though, didn't date, rarely partied, and liked to go home on long weekends. Yawn. "I didn't see you." His gaze fell to me. "Who's your . . . friend?"

I stood, knowing full well that my height matched his perfectly, but out of the two of us, I could easily kick his ass. I had a football player's body, and I'd worked hard to keep it that way even after my injury.

David's eyes narrowed as I held out my hand. "Name's Ian."

"Ian!" DJ held up his fist. I bumped it. His fiancée was another happy client, one of Lex's, not that he knew. "How's it going, man?"

"Oh, hey, do you guys know each other?" DJ asked. "David, you should have seen this guy play."

"Oh?" David crossed his arms. A hundred bucks said that the last thing he wanted to hear was my glory-day stories.

"Nah, let's not bore him." I chuckled. "Nice to meet you, David. Are you a friend of my girl's then?"

"Your *girl*?" He repeated, his eyebrows nearly getting lost in his hairline. "*Your* girl?"

And this—this reaction was what I lived for, what I waited for. I'd just touched Blake, intimately. She was still feeling the effects of the buzz, riding the chemicals that were released when any sort of intimate action was explored. Men, for some reason, picked up on that kind of hormonal release, meaning that for the first time in his entire life, David was finally seeing Blake as a woman.

Her blush helped.

And the fact that her hair was down.

Back ramrod-straight, she puffed out her chest a bit. My fingers itched to cover up the treasure I'd just discovered. Instead, I winked. "Yeah, my girl."

"Didn't know you were dating," David muttered as his gaze drifted toward her chest, then flashed away.

I burst out laughing. "What are you? Her dad?" When he didn't say anything, I pushed further. "Aw, how cute. Have you always been like a father figure to my Blake?"

Blake made a whimpering noise beside me as I held out my hand to her and helped her stand.

"What? Hell no!" He let out a nervous laugh. "We've been buds since we could walk."

"Cute story." I nodded like I was faking being impressed. "Well, it was nice meeting Blake's dad." I laughed. "Kidding. It was nice meeting you, man." I shook his hand, then draped my arm over Blake's shoulder, waving good-bye to DJ as I dropped our tray off and left the eating area.

Blake was deathly silent until we reached the parking lot.

This was usually the part where the girl freaked out and jumped up in down in triumph, or tried kneeing me in the balls.

Granted, I'd never actually groped any of my other clients, but desperate times and all . . .

Kissing them? Yeah, that's typically how I got the first reaction out of the clients, but Blake had never been kissed, and I was still a gentleman. It wouldn't be my right to take that kiss from her, not when she'd clearly been saving it for him.

A voice in my mind screamed that I'd done a hell of a lot more by touching her boobs, but the ass in me shrugged off the voice.

Hormones released. Reaction given. It worked. Bingo!

"You okay?" I let go of her.

"That was"—she pressed her hands to her temples—"really stressful."

I let out a laugh as adrenaline surged through me. "It usually is."

Her bright eyes met mine. "Thank you. I think that was the first time he's actually looked at me—"

"Like you had boobs."

Blake laughed harder. It was deep, and a bit addictive to listen to. She nodded in excitement. "Exactly."

"So now will you go to Victoria's Secret?"

Sheer delight made her eyes sparkle. "Only if you go with me."

Shit.

Typically, I didn't need to do this much work. Typically, my clients knew what lipstick was.

I eyed her up and down. Yeah, she wasn't typical. Not at all. She was special, but for the life of me I couldn't figure out why.

"Fine," I grumbled. "But you better treat me to froyo after."

I waved good-bye as she jogged off toward her dorm while I slowly made my way back to my car.

My phone buzzed with a text.

I knew it was probably Shell, but I didn't want to think about my other clients. I wanted to think about Blake. And in all my time being a wingman, I'd never done that.

I'd never given a girl a second thought. I never took business home with me.

But I was still thinking about Blake long after she left.

And it wasn't in a sense of *Gee, how can I help her?* It was mostly about why the hell she was chasing after some guy who clearly hadn't seen that he'd had a good thing in front of him for over ten years.

I was reading too much into it. Guys were blind, end of story.

Damn egg rolls.

Yeah, let's blame those.

CHAPTER NINE

"I'm going to count to five." I banged on the dressing room door one last time. "And then I'm coming in."

"No!" Blake's voice was muffled. "I'm . . . It's . . . I'm . . ."

Cursing, I pressed my forehead against the pink wood door. "Blake . . . I'm starving!"

"You're always starving! Why don't you eat before our meetings?"

"I'm busy! I hate protein bars. I forget. And Gabi didn't pack me a lunch!"

She was quiet. And then, "Gabi packs you lunches?"

Groaning, I made another feeble attempt at grabbing the doorknob and twisting. Still locked. "Gabi sucks. She was supposed to come."

"Gabi had a test."

"Wanna know how many tests I've flunked because of her?"

Absolutely zero, because she'd never needed me during a test, but I would have gone to her. Maybe. If she was dying, or if the only way for her to pass her class was for me to have sex with her professor.

"Seriously?"

"No. But best friends make sacrifices!"

Blake let out another pitiful groan. "I don't think it fits."

"They measured you. It fits. Just tell me if it looks okay so we can go." I checked my watch. "Gabi said dinner was at six, and it's already a quarter till."

"This is too much pressure." Her voice was frantic. "I can't do this. I mean, how do I know if it looks good? They're boobs."

I groaned. "Boobs always look good. Believe me."

"Boobs are gross!"

Said no man ever. Even the gay ones.

One of the salesladies eyed me up and down. "Are you two okay?"

"Great," I chirped. "Just having a very heated discussion about the beauty of breasts." I dipped my chin to the sales lady's chest. "What are you? A double D?"

Scowling, she marched off.

Thank God.

"Blake," I hissed.

No answer.

I'd never had such a difficult client. If anything, they jumped when I told them to, asked how high, and then kept jumping until I was satisfied. Blake fought me at every turn.

"Open the door before I crawl underneath it. I'll pick the bras— you can close your eyes if you want so you don't have to watch me look at you, alright? My stomach literally just ate my liver. I need protein. Open. The. Door."

The door slowly creaked open. Taking advantage of the small crack of air, I pushed it farther, then clicked it shut behind me and turned around.

Blake was facing me, hands on hips, face beet-red, body . . . freaking perfect. My tongue almost lolled out, like a dog.

Most girls starve themselves to have abs like that, which was disgusting. But her abs? They had muscle, actual muscle, but still appeared feminine.

She also had a nice tan, just enough to show that she spent time outside, or maybe she just had naturally darker skin.

My throat went completely dry as I continued to stare.

"Well?" Her voice was weak. "How awful do I look? On a scale of one to ten?"

I'd convinced her to buy some new workout clothes to replace her old ones. I knew I'd never get her to actually completely change her style. She liked workout clothes? Fine, at least buy the kind that fit and actually point to the correct gender. I tried to steer her away from the boyfriend sweats and sweatshirts, but she eventually wore me down, so I told her if she bought at least five new pink outfits that had spandex in them, I'd let her get one pair of ugly slouchy sweats. You'd think I'd just given her a million dollars, from her reaction.

Currently, she was sporting a short pair of bright-blue yoga shorts.

And a black push-up sports bra that did wonders for her boobs.

And the world just in general.

Holy shit.

I gulped as I became more and more irritated with the fact that my body was reacting as if it had never seen a girl without her shirt on before. "Blake, it's great."

"You sound bored!"

I had to, damn it! What did she want me to do? Sound interested? Turned-on? Intrigued? Curious? I was all those things. I just tried to ignore the insanity bouncing around in my head and blurted, "Your boobs look really good. Perky, happy, just . . . awesome."

Did I just call her boobs "happy"?

"You think?" She stared down at her breasts, then grabbed them.

Holy shit, was she seriously feeling herself up? I braced my hand against the door and sucked in a breath.

"They still feel comfortable," she said.

"Do they?" I managed to choke out while she continued bouncing them a bit in her hands. Dear Lord, did she know what she was doing?

Waving a flag in front of a bull. My jeans suddenly tight in all the wrong areas, I tried to envision Lex naked, anything to get my dick to clue in to the word "client," meaning I was in a no-play zone.

Another first.

It was because I was hungry.

And Marissa? Melissa? Hadn't satisfied me. I'd gotten off, and made sure she did too, but the entire experience left me feeling empty, bored, and—if I was being completely honest?—a bit depressed. Besides, her tits paled in comparison. I had to wonder what the hell I'd been doing all my life if this was the first time I was having such a strong reaction to boobs.

Something about Blake had me wondering if I'd been satisfied at all up until this point. And I had no idea what the hell was so confusing about her, and about the situation. I was unable to put my finger on it, and the more I thought about it the more my head hurt.

Hunger does weird things to guys.

"Yeah." More bouncing, then turning and staring in the mirror. I wasn't sure what was worse. Her staring at her own boobs or touching them. "I'm just no good at this stuff. I didn't grow up with a mom, and I hit puberty really early. The girls made fun of me, and the boys pointed." Her shoulders slumped inward again.

Could we please go back to the bouncing? I was a fan of that Blake. The one that rolled up like an awkward armadillo? Not so much.

Which was a good reminder of why I was helping her. Sprinkle a little confidence fairy dust all over her tight little body, throw her in some hot workout gear, and steer her in the general direction of the gym for round two. Piece of cake.

"A woman should be proud of her body." I met her gaze in the mirror. "If you feel good about the outside"—my hands twitched to cup her breasts, to outline the silhouette they gave off, to point out the all the angles and curves that drove a man insane, that made a man want—"then it directly reflects in the way you carry yourself." I pulled back as we locked eyes in the mirror, and then took a step closer, this time placing my hands on her hips and lightly running my fingertips up her sides. "Guys are turned-on by sight, girls by touch. By wearing something that fits, you're guaranteeing that he won't still see you as a buddy, but as a partner. And that's what you want . . . right?"

She licked her lips and nodded. "Right."

My heart sank.

I had no idea why.

I quickly released her and laughed out a simple "You look fantastic. David's going to be a very lucky man. He'll be eating out of your hand in no time."

The moment was lost.

If that's what you could call it.

Food. Low blood sugar. Aliens invading my body. I needed to leave that small room before I did something stupid, something undoable.

"That confident in your abilities?" she said. Her eyebrows arched.

Staring at her in the mirror, I could already visualize him falling for her. Underneath all that hair, she had a really pretty face, a gorgeous body, and a full C cup that would make any guy with two eyes weep with thankfulness.

"No," I said honestly. "But I'm pretty confident in yours."

The saleslady knocked. "Everything okay in there?"

"Yup," I answered for Blake.

"Sir, you need to get out of the dressing room. We don't allow customers to . . . er . . . play in the product before they purchase."

"Play?" I said dumbly.

"Hanky-panky."

"Oh," I said loudly, winking at Blake in the mirror. "Do you mean sex?"

She knocked louder. "Sir! Get out this instant."

Blake's horrified expression made it all worth it. I smirked. She needed to step outside her comfort zone if she was going to make it to that first kiss with David.

Her cheeks reddened.

Virgins.

"Almost . . ." I started panting, then hit the wall with my hand. "But it's so good."

"Sir!"

"Wait for it."

"*Sir*, right now! I'm going to call security!"

Blake opened her mouth, but I covered it with my hand. "Oh yeah!"

She bit me.

"Ouch!" I jerked away, shaking my hand. "Did you draw blood?"

"What's wrong with you?" She smacked me on the chest and jerked open the door. Three salesladies and at least a dozen customers waited on the other side, mouths open. "He was kidding."

I poked my head out. "Not kidding. Have you seen her? Oh, and we'll take it all." I pulled out my platinum Visa and winked.

Nobody moved at first, then the saleslady closest to us grabbed the card while Blake handed her the clothes. "Anything else?"

"Yeah." I gave her a wicked grin. "Do you have security cameras for each dressing room, or is that illegal? Because whatever just went down in there really should have been on tape, you know?"

Blake ducked and covered her face with her hands while a few of the salesladies gave me sultry nods of approval.

"He's kidding." Blake smacked me again. "He's been drinking all day. All week, actually."

"Stone-cold sober."

"He's a pathological liar too." Blake pushed me toward the sales counter while we made our purchases.

"This feels wrong." She watched as the woman went to the counter and started ringing things up, then swiped my card.

"What does?"

"You paying for my lingerie."

"I always pay for my clients' clothes, makeup, yoga, whatever's necessary, then I bill you at the end. It's easier on my taxes."

"Yoga?" Blake asked once we walked out onto the street.

"Yeah, once. I had a client who really needed to learn some new moves. Missionary was her one and only trick, and even then her guy still had trouble taking her to O-Town." I threw on my sunglasses and laughed. "To this day, she still thanks me for the suggestion."

"O-Town?" Blake frowned. "Like the boy band?"

I froze, then very slowly shook my head. "Riggins, Idaho, you say? Do you even have Internet there? McDonald's? Tell me you at least have Taco Bell."

Blake still looked genuinely confused. "What kind of moves did she need? You know, besides"—she gulped—"the other."

I gave her a soft pat on the shoulder. "Baby steps. You just bought your first real bra. You can barely crawl. Those types of moves are for sprinters."

"I can sprint."

I winced. "No, you can't."

"Yes, I can!"

"You do realize I'm talking about the *Kama Sutra*, right?"

More confusion. "Is that a type of food?"

A guy next to me grunted, and his face fell as if saying, *Poor bastard has to go home with her?*

"No." I shook my head as we pushed our way through the crowds at the University Village shopping center. "And the fact that you actually asked that—out loud—greatly disappoints me."

"I was a tomboy," Blake said defensively.

"Tomboys should still know the terminology, Blake." I opened the door for her, ignoring the fact that she'd said "was," as in past tense. Someone really needed to buy her a mirror, then burn all the boy clothes in her room.

"One more thing," I said. Speaking of rooms. And beds in general.

"What?"

"It's day two."

She chewed her lower lip. At this angle, I could imagine myself tasting her, meeting her mouth, teaching her the art of kissing. "Okay?"

"Typically"—my eyes trained in on the pink color of her tongue as it slid over her top lip, wetting it—"by day two I know what skill level you're at."

"Because of my questionnaire?"

I nodded. "And a few other . . . tests."

"I thought you were hungry. Spit it out already."

My stomach growled on command. "You know what? We'll talk about it tonight after dinner." My attitude perked up. "Dessert?"

"Sure." She grinned. "Okay."

Yeah. We had two very different meanings for that word. And she was about to find out very soon. She may have just gone through one stage of my training, but she was about to start the boot-camp phase, and I was very thorough when it came to making sure my clients knew just how to handle the guy they were trying to land.

CHAPTER TEN

Weekly dinners with Gabi were starting to get more and more intense. Not because she was busy, but because Lex and I were a package deal, and ever since freshman year when he mistook her for someone other than my best friend from childhood, things went from bad to worse.

Now? Every time they were in the same room together, I half expected one of them to end up in the hospital.

The minute we got to the house, Blake ran upstairs with her bags. I focused really hard on her flip-flops out of necessity. The rest of her looked tight, toned, tan. I angled my head as she made her way to the top of the stairs and turned. Her breasts were really starting to be the highlight of my day.

Something smacked me on the back of the head.

"Hey!" I turned around and faced Gabi. She had her angry face on. No smile, eyes narrowed. "What was that for?"

"If you hurt her, I'm going to break off your favorite appendage."

"Silly Gabi." I grinned. "Is that an invitation to touch?"

"Guarantee if I ever do touch you, it will only end badly."

"Tease." I winked.

"Stop that." She flicked me on the nose. "Your sexual prowess is dead to me. Dead!"

Rolling my eyes, I wrapped an arm around her and steered us both into the kitchen, where the smell of French bread and spaghetti filled the air. "Have I told you how much I miss our weekly dinners? Think we should do it daily? You know, so I don't starve?"

Gabi shrugged out of my embrace. "Learn how to cook."

I jutted out my lower lip. "It's not for lack of knowledge." I broke off a piece of warm bread, then poured myself a large glass of wine. "It's because yours always tastes better."

Gabi groaned loudly. "Damn, do the girls really fall for that? Still?"

"Eh." I shrugged and made a so-so motion with my hand. "Nine out of ten."

"You disgust me."

"You say that every day."

"Because it's true every day."

"When's dinner ready?" Serena bounced into the room, literally, her head bobbing from left to right. Maybe that's how girls like her built up more brain cells. They shook the air, and the pressure between their ears exploded, making tiny little brain-cell babies.

Gabi poked her head into the fridge. "When Lex gets here."

"So it's ready now?" she asked.

Never mind. No brain-cell babies. I fought the urge to point to the steaming spaghetti and bread sitting on the breakfast bar. Didn't it look ready, kiddo?

"Technically," I answered for Gabi. "But we aren't *eating*"—I stressed the word "eating" even though I'd just taken some bread—"until my sidekick gets here."

"Sidekick, huh?" Serena crossed her arms, forcing her boobs to kiss one another and nearly hit her in the chin.

"Oh, I thought you knew." I gave her a sad face. "I'm the hero in this scenario . . . Even own my own cape. He's basically the Robin to my Batman."

"Batman's hot."

"So is Robin," Gabi said defensively.

Whoa. Did she just defend Lex? I felt her forehead. She pushed my hand away and handed me some Parmesan cheese.

The door flew open, and Lex stepped through, holding up two bottles of Cab. "Sorry, traffic was shit."

"Language," Gabi called.

Lex and I shared a look before Lex stomped over to the swear jar and tossed in a dollar bill.

Gabi and her freaking double standards. She swore frequently. But she didn't allow swearing in the kitchen. She was half Italian, and kitchens in her family represented peace and love and some other shit I always forget. So swearing during dinnertime? Off-limits.

Which, knowing Lex, was like asking him to turn into a chick and give me an openmouthed kiss. He said when he was in Gabi's kitchen, he cursed on the inside and drank to keep himself from slitting his wrists.

On that note, Lex muttered something under his breath, stole the wineglass from my hands, and chugged it.

"We doing this?" he asked, wiping his mouth with the back of his hand.

Serena hadn't taken her lustful eyes off Lex yet. Highly doubted he'd actually called her, but he was the king about making things seem easy and less awkward when it came to shitting where he slept and vice versa. I wondered if Gabi knew.

She wasn't hitting him.

Therefore, she was probably in the dark.

"Where's the other roomie?" Lex asked, pouring himself more wine and then tipping it back.

"Here!" Blake walked into the room.

Lex spit out his wine. All over the floor. Then he started coughing and choking.

Gabi patted his back furiously, probably knocking a few ribs out of place. "Are you okay?"

"Shit!" Lex yelled, voice hoarse after his choking spell.

Gabi held out the swear jar while Lex grumbled and stuffed in another dollar.

"What's wrong?" Blake asked, crossing her arms, making her body appear just . . . hotter, if that was at all possible.

The flip-flops were present.

But everything else from the ankles up was . . . damn, it was good.

Tight-muscled legs poured into short blue yoga shorts, an off-the-shoulder white tank top hung loosely on her body, and a leopard sports bra pushed the girls up exactly where they were supposed to be.

And her hair was down.

Makeup-free, she was three times the girl Serena was. And Serena looked like she'd just robbed a Sephora and tried on the entire stash.

"I'm—" Lex coughed into his hand. "Sorry, I just . . . Low blood sugar."

"Good one," I whispered under my breath.

He sent me an irritated glare but said nothing. Silence began a slow stretch to awkward proportions.

"Shall we sit?" I rubbed my hands together and moved to the small table directly next to the kitchen, around which sat a mismatched group of green and blue chairs as well as two gray folding chairs. The table was something Gabi had grabbed from a yard sale, and the plates had been passed down to her from her grandma. They had little flowers on the sides and always made me ponder what life would be like with an actual family where kids sat down with their parents and ate food, and they all participated in family conversations.

Not where nannies made the food and the parents called once a week.

And then stopped calling.

And then died.

"So, Blake . . ." Lex spooned a liberal amount of sauce over a pile of steaming spaghetti and handed the first plate to Gabi, since she'd cooked. In Gabi's kitchen, cooks always ate first. "I like the new look."

"Thanks." A bright blush flamed across her cheeks. "Ian was a huge help."

"Oh, I bet." Lex grinned.

I kicked his foot under the table while he continued serving everyone. Serena was staring at Blake. Hard.

I knew that look.

Dinner was about to get real.

"I guess it's okay." Serena gave a slight shrug. "I mean, if you're into working out."

"Which clearly she is," I pointed out. "Look at her."

Serena's lips twisted into something that looked a lot like a snarl. "It's not like she's wearing a dress. She's wearing spandex. Didn't that go out of style a few years ago?"

"Says the non–gym rat?" I shrugged. "I don't know. Didn't hair extensions go out a few years ago too?" I was pretty confident if I tugged on her hair I could come away with a piece.

Serena's face heated to a dull red color before she jerked her plate away from Lex and not-so-accidently dropped it onto Blake's lap. "Oh my gosh. I'm so sorry. It slipped."

Gabi jumped to her feet, grabbing napkins, while Blake just stared at her lap. Then, in a move I wouldn't have ever seen coming, she started piling the spaghetti onto her own plate before licking each finger.

I gripped the chair with both hands. Holy shit, that was hot. Spaghetti sauce—who knew?

"It's alright." Blake laughed. "I can always toss them in the wash. They're workout clothes, after all. I'm sure a few weeks from now they'll be in worse shape than this after practice."

That shut Serena up.

Dinner was blessedly quiet, except for the chink of flatware against china. I knew it wouldn't last. After all, Gabi and Lex were sitting next to each other.

It was against the laws of nature for them not to fight.

"Wow." Blake patted her flat stomach. "That was really good, Gabi. Thank you so much."

"Thank Ian. He begged for spaghetti night."

"I beg every night," I said. "And not just for spaghetti. Last week I wanted ravioli."

"You sure you aren't Italian?" Gabi laughed and started collecting everyone's plates.

"Nope." I stood. "You cooked. Lex and I will do cleanup."

Lex's eyebrows shot up. "We will?"

I stared.

Slowly, he scooted out his chair, stood, and helped me take everything into the kitchen. Once the girls were out of earshot, he whistled and said, "Dude, nice work. I didn't even recognize her."

I smiled proudly. "She looks cute, right?"

Lex burst out laughing. "Are you high? She looks more than cute." He stepped backward and peered around the corner, then made his way back into the kitchen. "She looks hot."

"Hot?" I let the word roll around in my head a bit, then abruptly snuffed it out. "I guess."

"You guess?"

Dishes. I needed to wash dishes, because if I focused too much on Blake's small transformation, I was going to be in a world of hurt, and not the emotional kind. Hell no, it would be all physical. Already my body was responding as if my hands weren't in soapy water but sliding all over her body.

I inwardly groaned. I had no time to stop by some random girl's house and alleviate the hurt.

"Have you kissed her yet?" Lex asked as I held out a plate for him to take. It dropped out of my hand, but luckily he caught it before it smashed into the floor. "I'll take that as a no."

"She's never kissed a guy. It would be . . . wrong." I held out another plate. Lex didn't take it. Instead he stared openmouthed at me.

"Are you . . . *falling* for her?"

"What?" I burst out laughing. "Hell no. Have you seen her flip-flops?"

"Not like she'd be wearing them in bed, amigo."

"What's our number one rule?" I scrubbed the next plate vigorously as visions of her perky breasts invaded every logical corner of my brain.

"Don't fall for the clients."

"Don't. Fall." I scrubbed harder. "For." My hand was starting to cramp. "The clients."

"I think it's clean, bro." Lex jerked the plate out of my hands and gave me a pat on the back. "And you're the one who made the rules. Not me."

"We have a legitimate company, one that both of us are hoping will eventually take over as the number one dating app in the world. Why screw that up because you fall for a sad girl who wants the guy who's never looked twice at her?"

Lex smirked, his toothy grin making me want to inflict violence on his person. Or another damn dish. "Why, indeed?"

"You're seriously shitting up the wrong tree, and you're pissing me off. Go argue with Gabi or something."

"So no kissing?"

I sighed and braced myself against the porcelain sink. "No. Not unless it's absolutely necessary."

"Hmm."

The girls' chatter got louder as they made their way into the kitchen.

"No dessert?" Blake piped up.

I froze.

Lex and I were both still facing the kitchen window, and I could see his smug expression in the reflection. Just like he could see me flipping him off right above the dishwater.

"Dessert? I didn't get any," Gabi said, "but—"

"Actually." I turned around quickly. "About that . . . Blake, can I talk to you upstairs for a minute?"

"Sure." But she hesitated.

"Great." I grabbed her hand and tugged her toward the stairs, praying that Gabi and Lex would get into it so I'd have an excuse to call the police and get the hell out of that house before I embarked on more rule-breaking.

Once we were in her room, I shut the door behind me and stalked toward her. She moved backward until her legs collided with the bed.

"You look upset," she said.

Frowning, I grabbed her spaghetti-stained shirt and tugged it over her head.

Blake let out a little squeak as I dipped my thumbs into the span-dex shorts and tugged them all the way to her ankles. Thankfully, she stepped out of her flip-flops as well as the shorts.

I stood to my full height.

And blinked.

Was I hallucinating?

"You're—" I coughed into my hand. "You're"—I glanced away, seeking to restore the balance of power—"in a thong." It was one thing to hear about her wearing one, but actually seeing the proof? Damn near intoxicating.

"They're comfortable," Blake said with a shrug. "And it's not like I planned on getting a spaghetti bath or having my love coach strip me down to nothing."

"Love coach." I still wasn't looking at her. "I love the way you say it."

"Does this stripping have a purpose?"

I jerked my head in her direction. "Stripping should always have a purpose."

Her eyebrows rose.

My eyes were fighting a battle with my head. My eyes wanted to stare at her nearly bare ass, while my head told me that there was no part of the screening process that involved me groping her smooth skin or asking her to turn around, bend over, and arch her back. Unfortunately.

Blake's hair lay tousled around her shoulders, giving her this wild sex-kitten look that I was about 200 percent sure David wouldn't know what to do with.

Damn David.

"Ian?"

"We need to wash your clothes," I said dumbly.

"And I needed your help getting them off, or what?"

"Next lesson." I seriously needed to get my mojo back before I lost my shit. "Kissing."

Blake slumped onto the bed and let out a little whimper. "You read my answer. I've never been kissed."

"I'm not going to kiss you."

Her head jerked up, blue eyes burning a hole through my chest, making it itch, or tighten, or—what the hell was wrong with me? "No."

"Is that normal? Do you usually kiss your clients or just teach them?"

"Each client is different," I said smoothly. "But right now, I'm going to focus on teaching you how to get him to kiss you, as well as how to get him to see you in a sexual way. Think you can handle that?"

She nodded.

Her boobs bobbed slightly. I ruffled my hair and then stalked over to her small closet. "You got any giant hoodies in here or muumuus or something?"

Blake came up behind me. Her body heat blasted me. A few more inches and her breasts would be pressed up against my back, and in that position I could almost lean forward, then in one move twist her around so that she was in my arms, straddling me.

Too easy.

"Right"—her arm brushed mine—"here."

"Honest moment." I frowned at the ratty blue hoodie. "Why the hell do you wear clothes like this?"

Blake tossed it over her head and huffed out. "We all have our things, right?"

"Guess so."

Funny, a day ago I wouldn't have looked twice at her in that sweatshirt, but now that I was actually getting to know her? And knew what was underneath? It looked sexy as hell as it hung past her hips to midthigh. It teased me.

And I didn't do well with teasing.

I was an instant-gratification type of guy.

She sat on the bed and crossed those gorgeous legs. My mind went wild with different possibilities, angles, positions.

"Ian?"

I rubbed my hands together. "Right. So tomorrow we're going to work out together. I took another look at David's schedule, and he works out from five a.m. until seven. We need to be at the gym before he gets there so we catch him by surprise. Your schedule said you typically work out as he's leaving the gym. Is there a reason for that?"

Blake chewed on her thumbnail. I tugged her hand down and held it firm, my eyebrows arched as I waited for her answer. "I figure it's the easiest way to get him to talk to me. If I show up at the end of his workout, he's tired, and his walls aren't up. Is that stupid?"

"No." I was thoughtful. "Not stupid, just misinformed. The last thing a guy wants to do after he works out is flirt with a girl. Now, beforehand? Even during? No problem. Adrenaline pumps during workouts, and if a hot chick's watching, you better believe the entire hour's going to be eye-screwing."

"You said hot chick." Blake shrugged. "Not cute."

"You're hot," I grumbled. "Believe me. Just wear one of the outfits we picked out, alright?"

She nodded, her chest puffing up slightly. I itched to unzip the hoodie. Five seconds, that's all I needed, maybe six, then I'd walk out of the room and leave her to it.

"Right." I removed my hands from hers. "So when he sees us together, we need to flirt. The issue is that you flinch most of the time when I touch you."

"I do not!"

I cupped her face. She flinched, and then her eye twitched. "I'm touching your face, not spitting on your eye there, sweet cheeks."

Her teeth clenched.

"Good." I nodded. "That look right there, the very pissed-off one you're giving me? It's often confused with lust. So maybe I'll just piss you off the entire workout. Shouldn't be hard, just imagine me heckling you the entire time. In fact, imagine me staring at your ass and tits the entire time. Because I guarantee you, that will be happening. Ninety minutes in heaven. Can you believe I get paid for this shit?" I was goading her on purpose, even though I probably *would* be staring at her. Who wouldn't?

Her chest heaved as she pushed against me. I used the weight of the push to pull her back on top of me. "Now"—I looked at our bodies as they pressed together—"say this happens tomorrow. What do you do?"

"Get off." Blake tried to wiggle away. I locked my legs behind her.

"Oh, I'm sorry. That's incorrect." I tugged my ankles against her ass, forcing her against my chest. "Next question. If we're this close, do you fight, or give in?"

She was strong. I'd give her that. Blake tried to buck away from me, her hands dangerously close to my face.

"Fight." Her lips nearly brushed mine. It was painful when she didn't break the rest of the distance. The lust I was feeling for her was so unnatural I didn't know what to do with it, so I tucked it away.

"Wrong." I grinned, flipping her onto her back and pinning her arms above her head. "Body language is everything. You don't want to appear too pissed at me, but you don't want to be meek either. Right now you're doing a good job balancing both of them. If things start going south, I may need to kiss you, and I need to know that if I do you aren't going to knee me in the balls or scratch my eyes out."

"I may." Her teeth clenched as her eyes lowered toward the goods. A smug smile crossed her features. "Guess you'll have to find out."

"Don't play a player," I instructed smugly. "It never works, sweet cheeks."

"Why are you calling me 'sweet cheeks'?"

I released her wrist and moved my hand down her side to her bare thigh, then very slowly inched my fingers around until I came into contact with one butt cheek. "Sweet cheeks."

Rage crossed her features as she let out a little bellow and tried getting from underneath me.

"Lesson's not over." I pressed my body harder against hers. "If I kiss you, you don't have to kiss me back, but don't push me away. Just let it happen."

"Why does it matter?"

"Because." My position was starting to make my body ache in more ways than one. "If he sees us as too happy, he won't think he has a chance. If we're fighting, he'll think you're a bad lay, or worse yet, he'll think you're dramatic. We need the perfect medium. Just let it happen, and try not to lose your shit when you feel my tongue."

"Is that necessary?" she asked, voice desperate.

"Not at all." I grinned.

"I think lesson time's over." Blake glared.

"Great." I jumped off of her and dusted my hands into the air. "I'll pick you up at four thirty."

"So early," she grumbled. "This better work."

"It's never *not* worked." I reached for the door. "Unless"—I turned to face her—"you're having second thoughts?"

"No!" Blake stumbled toward me, getting her foot caught on the comforter.

I caught her before her face collided with the floor, but the impact of her body slammed me against the door.

Our mouths touched.

Accidently.

But in my current state, it was enough. Like lighting a fuse, pouring gasoline on top of a roaring fire.

I leaned in.

"You sick *son of a bitch*," I heard Gabi yell. "Ian, get your ass down here *now!*"

"Aw, hell," I grumbled as I released Blake, tore open the door, and ran down the stairs.

Gabi was currently beating her fists into Lex's back as he carried her around the kitchen, his eyes frantic, like he was searching for a switch to swat her with.

"Everything okay down here?" I chuckled, folding my arms across my chest as I leaned against the doorframe.

"Oh, just great," Gabi yelled, lifting her head briefly to make eye contact before slapping his ass again.

"A little to the left." Lex bounced her up and down. "Or if you're feeling really frisky, I can dig a squeeze."

"I'm killing you in your sleep!" Gabi shouted.

"What happened?" I asked Lex while Gabi started cursing.

"That's five bucks, slut," Lex laughed. "We're in the kitchen!" With his free hand, he scooted the jar to the end of the counter and then heaved Gabi toward it.

"You sick bastard!"

"I take it she found out about Serena?"

"Stop"—Gabi pounded his ass again—"sticking"—another smack—"your diseased"—two hits, and Lex burst out laughing—"dick"—I winced as Lex heaved her higher over his chest, and her face suddenly smacked his ass—"in my roommates!"

Lex smirked as he locked eyes on her. "It was an accident."

"Accident." Gabi's eyes were wild as she moved her hand from his ass to his balls and squeezed.

With a heave, Lex dropped her. "Damn it!" She crumpled to the floor while Lex joined her, cupping himself. "You bitch!"

"It was an accident." Gabi shrugged.

Sighing, I went over to help Gabi to her feet. "Look at the bright side. At least now, you won't constantly worry about him seducing her. It only took a day."

Gabi glared at both of us.

Lex used her head to help him stand, then limped toward me. "I think it's time to leave."

"Wait!" Gabi stood and held out the swear jar. "Two bucks."

"Are you shitting me?" Lex roared.

"Three." Her face broke out into a saucy grin as she shook the jar.

My eyebrows shot up in respect as Lex let out a string of curse words, then dumped a ten-dollar bill into the jar and pinched her cheek. "I hate odd numbers."

"Make sure you get tested at the free clinic, Lex. Who knows what you're carrying now."

"Don't worry. I'll be clean before I bang you." He winked.

She lunged again, so I pushed Lex toward the door. "Time to go, man." I waved at Gabi. "See ya next week for lasagna!"

"You can stick your lasagna up your—"

I slammed the door on her tirade.

"Dude." I chuckled. "You really need to learn when to stop."

"Can't." Lex pushed past me. "One day I really am going to kill her. Or she's going to kill me. Hope you don't mind bailing your two best friends out of prison."

"Is it really that impossible for you two to get along?"

Lex's sour expression said everything. And if that wasn't enough, he continued cursing Gabi's name as he got into his car and peeled away from the house.

CHAPTER ELEVEN

"Thanks for the coffee," Blake mumbled. "I'm not a morning person."

"I am." I casually sipped my black Pike Place Roast as we weaved a path through the weight machines. "Well"—I tossed my cup into the nearest trash can and grabbed a piece of cinnamon gum—"it's showtime."

Without asking, Blake stole the gum right out of my hand, then shivered. "It's freezing in here."

"Well, if you'd wear clothes . . ."

She elbowed me. "I wore what you said to wear."

"You're wearing a sports bra." I pointed to the black-and-pink bra that pushed the girls up high. "And tight spandex pants. So, basically, you're almost naked."

Blake pulled her thick hair into a ponytail holder and placed her hands on her hips. "Let's do this before I chicken out."

"Well, since I won't have time to actually work out today, we're going to do one of my WODs."

"WODs?"

"CrossFit." I shrugged. "Workout of the day. We'll do a quick warm-up, bust out an EMOM, and some max weight lifting, then end everything with an AMRAP and stretching."

Blake gave me a blank expression. "Are you speaking in code?"

"EMOM—every minute on the minute you do the prescribed exercise. AMRAP—as many reps as possible."

"Sounds fun," she said sarcastically.

I winked and slapped her ass hard. "Let's go, sweet cheeks. Weights to lift, guys to make jealous."

"All in a day's work." She rubbed her ass and glared in my direction, but I was already too busy getting our warm-up set together to care.

I grabbed two twenty-five-pound weights for her, and three for me.

"We'll do a two-hundred-meter jog and ten pull-ups, followed by hand-release push-ups and then plank holds, alright?"

Blake gave me a thumbs-down, then flashed me a beautiful toothy smile. "You're going to make me sore, aren't you?"

"So sore you can't walk," I said with a naughty grin.

"Double entendre?" She laughed. "Nice."

"Love coach. Kinda goes with the title."

"Does it?"

"On your hands and knees."

"What? To run?"

"No." I laughed. "I've always just really wanted to say that. You know, all dominating . . . Hey, can I tie you up later?"

"No." Blake's cheeks burned red. "I highly doubt that's part of the program."

"Don't knock it until you try it." I jogged away from her.

With a curse, she followed. "The answer's still no."

I sped up. "Blindfold?"

"No!"

I turned and started running backward. "I guess that means no costumes either, huh?"

"Client." She said the word slowly, then rushed past me. "That means the only man tying me up will hopefully be David."

Something pinched the middle of my chest as I tried not to allow what she'd just said to seep through the little rips she was making in my heart. What the hell was wrong with me?

David.

A man could really grow to hate that name, and the person. And every other male in the universe who played basketball.

~

"I know why Gabi says she wants to kill you all the time," Blake yelled hoarsely midburpee.

"Two more!" My chest hit the floor, and I pushed myself up to my legs and jumped into the air with a clap, then dropped again.

Blake was seriously holding her own. I didn't even have to slow down, which was impressive. She only complained once we started doing death by burpees, which basically meant you do burpees until you lose the will to live.

"I." She dropped to her chest. "Hate." She tried to push herself up. "Burpees."

"One more!"

Her arms trembled as she pushed herself up to her feet and finally managed to stand and do a weak jump. Her pretty face was dripping with sweat. With a wide smile, she held up her hand for a high five.

Was she high-fiving me?

After putting her through hell?

I hit her hand, then pulled her against my sweaty chest.

"Ahh!" She pushed against me. "Thanks for that. Clearly my workouts pale in comparison. You wouldn't . . ." She glanced away. "Never mind."

"What?"

"Do you work out like this every day?"

"Yeah." I tossed her a towel and checked my watch. David was late, not that I cared. I'd forgotten about him even working out during our time in the gym.

"You can say no." Blake put her hands in front of her. "But would you mind if I tagged along a few times a week? I can even pay you or something. My coach has really been after me to work on my cardio lately, and I think this will help."

I rolled my eyes. "You don't have to pay me . . . It's not like I'm a trainer. You can just do my workouts with me. I get bored being by myself, and for some reason Lex refuses to work out with me."

"Gee, I wonder why," Blake joked, tossing her sweaty towel at my face.

"Hey!" I reached for her, then pulled her into my arms and set her against the mat on the ground, my body hovering over her. "You tired?"

"Exhausted." She laughed. "But I love that feeling."

"It's the best," I said, my throat suddenly dry as her eyes fell to my mouth.

"So"—I put some distance between our bodies—"I'll help you stretch and—"

Blake's eyes widened as she jerked her head to the right, as if to say, *Look!*

David was making his way toward us, head bobbing to the hip-hop pounding from his phone. I'd always assumed guys like him listened to Josh Groban. Hell, he even looked like a taller version of him.

"Stay calm." I grabbed her leg and quickly pushed against it so that it was getting stretched toward her head, then placed my body over hers, my legs in between hers. Basically we were doing a *Kama Sutra* move with clothes on and no happy ending. Damn it.

Nodding, Blake closed her eyes and let out a little moan. "Ouch, that hurts."

"Sorry." My fingers fumbled as they moved down her calf to her thigh. "Shit, you're tight." Her muscles quivered beneath my fingers as I slowly massaged.

"Yeah," she breathed. "Right. There."

I dug deeper with my hands, then continued stretching her until we were nearly chest to chest. She arched as my hand found the knot.

"Sorry." I shared a wince with her as I continued massaging.

"Feels amazing." The knot relaxed, and I moved on to her next leg. "Oh." She nearly came off the mat.

"Doesn't the PT help you guys out with this?" I asked, trying to keep my hands focused on actually stretching her, instead of moving from her muscles to parts that didn't need stretching.

"He's groped me three times," she grumbled. "I think he takes his job a little too . . . personally."

"Kick him in the nuts next time. I'm sure you could blame it on your incredible reflexes." I pushed harder as I completely straddled her one leg while lifting the other high above her head. My body was really enjoying the stretch, but not because it was relieving tension. If anything, it was creating it, and it wasn't like workout clothing was very forgiving. All she had to do was look down and she'd see just how excited I was to help her out in any way possible, day and night, night and day.

"Blake?" A deep voice interrupted our stretching session. I glanced up and dismissed David with a quick smirk, the kind guys give each other when they know the other dude is jealous and can't do shit about it.

"Oh, hey." Blake leaned up on her elbows as I lowered her leg. "I didn't see you there, David."

"You look . . ." He pointed at her body and swallowed slowly, his eyes drinking her in with obvious interest.

"Exhausted," she said. She burst out laughing and grabbed my hand. "Ian really knows how to work me."

I nearly burst out laughing at the rage that crossed David's face. How dare I touch his friend! Just to piss him off, I kissed her hand and winked.

"You know"—David leaned down into our space—"if you ever want any extra help . . . at the gym, you could always ask me."

"Oh." Blake glanced between me and David. "That's nice of you to offer, but—"

"I think I've got it covered, David." I leered suggestively.

"Well, the offer still stands." David pushed to his feet and slowly backed away. "It was great seeing you, Blake. You look . . . really good."

She glanced down at her tits.

Which in turn made me and every other male within a fifty-mile radius join her in mutual admiration.

"Thanks!"

I nearly groaned when she popped her shoulders, making her chest bounce a bit. My hand twitched, along with my dick.

"Uh." Poor David looked about ready to swallow his tongue as he moved his hands to the front of his body and nodded. "Well, see ya."

Dirty little prick was covering his junk.

He immediately went to the bench press and loaded 275 on the bar. Really, dude? He was going to be in a world of hurt if he didn't at least warm up.

But the Jolly Green Giant was sneakier than I expected. He didn't pretend that we weren't watching. If anything, he knew we would be.

Sly Jolly Green Giant. I frowned as he started pumping the 275 like it wasn't a big deal. He stood, chest puffed out, and glanced over at us as if to say, *Oh, you're still here? Watch this.*

He added another thirty pounds.

He had no spot.

Had to hand it to him. He was an idiot, but he was a strong idiot.

"Wow," Blake breathed. I glanced at her wide eyes as they bobbed up and down with the cadence of his pump. Oh, hell no.

Grinding my teeth, I nearly mauled her right then and there. Was she seriously impressed with that douche? The line between personal and professional was blurring right before my very eyes, because I wanted nothing more than to pin her against the wall and sink myself into her.

I was caught in a situation I'd never been in before. A situation where the girl and the guy doing their natural *I'm man, watch me roar—oh my, look how strong you are* thing actually made my chest hurt.

I told Blake if it was necessary, I would kiss her.

Suddenly, it became extremely necessary.

To stake a claim.

So, without allowing my brain to conjure up logical reasons why it was a bad idea, I tugged Blake to her feet and kissed her.

The minute our mouths met, she gasped.

I expected her to completely shut down, which would mean I'd have to turn her back to David so she didn't give us away. Instead, she wrapped her arms around my neck, leaning her body into mine.

And opened. Her. Mouth.

She tasted like coffee and cinnamon. Holy shit. Someone should make a gum with that combo.

I invaded her mouth, plunging, pillaging, basically planting my flag and saluting it, all the while running my hands down her back, my fingers digging into her skin, willing the heat between our bodies to singe the clothes so that I wouldn't have to spend time ripping them from her body.

Her hands twisted in my hair as I angled my head differently, teasing her mouth. Making love to her lips.

A loud clang sounded.

We broke apart.

"Sorry," David called from his side of the weight room. "Dropped some weight."

Sorry, my ass.

Whatever. I didn't care. Because I was the guy walking out with the girl.

Not that she was mine.

Or that she wouldn't be his in a few days.

Shit.

"That was"—Blake ducked into my chest as I wrapped an arm around her—"a really great first kiss."

Damn it! I was ruining everything. I was her first kiss? Me? The certified whore? The guy she was paying? Not the one she was in love with.

And that was the kicker.

She was saving herself for someone important, while I'd never saved myself for anyone, ever.

The thought haunted me the entire walk to my car.

Chapter Twelve

Shell sat close to me while we pretended to study at the coffee shop. We exchanged a few hand grazes here, longing looks there, and a strategic pen drop, where it looked like I was staring down the front of her top.

And boom—like magic, Jealous Barista appeared. Tom. Shit, I hated Tom. Not because he was an ass, but because he refused to move past the bossy "I know what's best for you" face. And that was seriously starting to piss me off. It was the last phase, the one where the guy stopped being protective and moved on to actually doing shit about it.

Shell didn't deserve to be in limbo. She'd done a hell of a job, and if he couldn't see her for the woman she was, then she and I were going to have to have a heart-to-heart, and I'd only done that with a client once in my career. I didn't want it to start becoming a thing.

Plus, the sooner I finished with Shell, the sooner I could . . .

I frowned. What? Finish with Blake? Is that what I wanted? My teeth chewed the straw in my smoothie until it was useless.

"Can I get you guys anything else?" Tom referenced both of us. He used plural references and all, but he was completely ignoring my existence, his lazy-ass brown eyes fully focused in on Shell.

"Actually"—Shell yawned, stretching her arms above her neck and, like instructed, starting to massage the back of her neck—"I don't suppose you moonlight as a massage therapist?"

Well done. The line was delivered perfectly, like it had been rehearsed, which it was, considering the first four times she repeated it back to me she'd stuttered and nearly shouted "massage therapist," then snorted with a nervous laugh. I hid my smile behind my pen as I scribbled down more nonsense about business ethics. The irony wasn't lost on me, believe me.

Tom smiled brightly. "No, but I'm still good with my hands."

I glanced up at his weak-looking hands. Doubtful, very doubtful, man. I was pretty sure, given the chance to rock her world with said hands, she'd most likely cross things off her grocery list while he still fumbled to get a rise out of her.

Tom moved his hands to her neck and started massaging while Shell glanced up at me behind her long bangs and mouthed *Yay!*

I pretended to be too immersed in my studying to care.

Tom inched his way closer to her body, his chest pressed against her back. Then he leaned forward and whispered, "I'm clearing your schedule."

"You're clearing it?" Shell said, sounding surprised. "I don't understand."

"Look at him." I knew I was the "him" he was referencing. "I'm all over you, and he doesn't even care."

He was right. I cared more about the cramp in my hand from writing and the ache in my back from hunching over my book.

"Shh." Shell shushed him. "He's really great when you get to know him, and—"

Showtime.

"Shell," I barked. "Let's go."

I stood and started gathering my stuff.

"What if she doesn't wanna go with you?" Tom crossed his arms, just as expected, and his protective stance said it all: *Touch her and I'm going to rip your head off.* Or in his case, he'd conduct a poetry slam and use his words, because violence was so uncool. World peace. Save the whales. Soy milk. The end.

"Shell"—I furrowed my brows—"what's going on here?"

She stood on wobbly legs. "Ian, it's fine, we should go and—"

"Shell!" Tom grabbed her by the elbow and pulled her protectively into his embrace. "He's your study partner, not your boyfriend."

"Actually . . ." I smirked.

Tom's face turned a funny shade of purple. "Not anymore."

"Not anymore what?" Damn, my back ached. Why did it always take the guys this long to stake their claim? To finally plow the land, plant the flag, and sing the victory song.

His eyes darted between Shell's and mine.

And then the anger disappeared. There we go. In, three, two, one.

"Shell." Tom grabbed her by the shoulders and turned her toward him. "I like you. I've always liked you."

Thank God, a confession!

"Remember when you used to always order coffee but never tried it with a splash of milk and honey?"

And there's my exit. Someone save me from the "I've finally discovered it's been you all along" speech.

She nodded, tears pooling in her eyes.

"And when you stayed really late, fell asleep on your book, and I woke you up and you said—"

"Just one more cup!"

They laughed in unison.

Holy shit, pretending to be pissed was hard when I was on the verge of getting a headache as they traveled down courtship memory lane.

"He doesn't even know you like I do." He pulled her closer to his chest, his hands twisting around hers like his fingers were trying to mate with her palms. "Leave him."

Yes. Please. For the love of God. Leave me.

To her credit, Shell pretended to look torn as she lowered her head and then very slowly said, "Ian, I think you should go."

Triumph crossed Tom's features.

Victory pounded in my chest.

And so the last round went to Tom . . . The last round always went to the guy unless the computer program said the guy was a complete douche. But the program, so far, had been flawless in helping us separate the winners from the losers. And as much as Tom irritated me, I knew deep down he really cared for Shell, and that if they made it through the next few months, they'd most likely get married in a year or so. They were both immature freshmen, both selfish, and it made sense that it took a while for them to actually get over their own insecurities before they could be good together.

Six days in.

And Shell had her man.

"If this is what you want," I said to Shell, picking up my books and stuffing them in my shoulder bag, "then I won't stand in your way. Just remember, I'll be here when this douche drops you, which"—I eyed him up and down in challenge—"he will."

"You need to leave." He gripped her harder, tighter, his eyes possessive, furious. "Now."

And sealed.

Jealousy was one thing; saving her was another. But the minute his eyes shifted from saving her, into admission, and finally into the stance of possession? Well, I may as well tell them congrats on their newfound relationship. I'd forged it the best way I could. Planted the seeds, watered them, and allowed them to grow.

Unless a fire took hold and burned down the entire damn field, they'd be good.

Another satisfied customer.

I shoved past them and quickly got into my car, starting the engine and peeling out of the parking lot, to show how insulted I was at his stomping all over my territory.

My text alert went off at the stoplight.

Shell: Thank you, thank you, thank you.

The light was still red, so I texted her back.

Ian: No prob. Remember the rules, but,
    be yourself. Invoice in mail. Please
    delete this number and all emails. 2
    WM biz cards are in in your desk. If
    friends ask, you know what to do.
Shell: You're the best!

I threw my phone and chuckled. "I know."

My cockiness didn't last.

Because a brief vision of Blake sending me that exact same text buzzed through my mind like a bad high.

It would happen.

And soon.

We were four days in.

I'd told her I needed a week, maybe two, depending on circumstances. Shit, and she was making such good progress. She probably didn't even realize that she no longer hid behind her hair, or slumped in her chair during class. Her shoulders had straightened, she made eye contact regularly, and, damn, she looked hot.

She was even opening up more to me, sharing likes and dislikes, which I typically wouldn't encourage. But in her case she needed to learn how to get comfortable around guys, so I allowed it. It had absolutely nothing to do with the fact that I was eager to learn about her, or that the way she told animated stories that made me laugh.

Damn, I inwardly groaned. The way things were going, it wouldn't surprise me at all if David had already tried contacting her.

My mind went over all the scenarios. She hadn't texted me all day. Did that mean he was making contact? Did she even need me anymore? Why did it matter? Then again, she could be sick. Shit, she probably had the flu or something and was embarrassed because she puked all over everything and couldn't make it to the phone without the room spinning. And here I was, being an ass.

At the next stoplight I texted her.

Nothing.

Drumming my hands against the wheel, I cursed and made a U-turn toward Gabi's place. I was just going to check on her. Just once. And not because I was paranoid, but because I was worried.

An irritating voice inside my head reminded me that I'd never been worried about a client before; I'd never given them a second thought. But I ignored that voice, because it was in direct opposition to what I was feeling everywhere else in my body.

That maybe Blake needed me.

Or maybe . . . I needed her.

Chapter Thirteen

By the time I'd pulled up to the house, I'd convinced myself that Blake had only twenty-four hours to live, and the only way for her to survive was for me to have lots and lots of sweaty sex with her.

Somehow in my daydream I'd gone from washed-up NFL player to sporting a flight suit and aviators, like Tom Cruise in *Top Gun*.

And since she was a nursing major, a personal favorite when it came to my erotic fantasies, she was wearing a naughty nurse outfit, with thigh-highs and red heels.

My body tightened painfully as I tried in vain to keep myself from exploding from my own stupid fantasies. How had I gone from wanting to check in on her to wanting to be in her?

Damn, my imagination was graphic.

I jogged up to the house, let myself in, and yelled, "Gabi! Blake! Serena! Anyone home?"

"Geez." Gabi rose from the couch looking like a zombie. "Some people are trying to sleep."

"Sorry, sport." I walked over and ruffled her hair. "Didn't see you there. Cute hair. You joining the nice homeless people under the bridge later for an orgy?"

Her catlike eyes narrowed as she snorted in disgust and weakly pushed against my chest. "I'm sick, you ass."

I jumped to my feet and stumbled back, colliding with the lamp and sending it to the floor with a loud clang.

"Oh, please!" She blew her nose into a Kleenex, and the bun on the top of her head bobbed with a jerk. "You're lucky you don't have the clap from all the sex you have! And you're afraid of a little cold."

"I really hate germs," I pointed out, setting the lamp back on the table but still keeping a good distance between me and the diseased.

Gabi tossed the Kleenex at my face. I ducked and moved farther out of the way.

"Ian," she growled. "You sleep with germs all the time."

"I Lysol them before I sleep with them. It's part of the procedure before I bang them against the wall and allow them the honor of a blow job."

She scowled.

"Or bed . . ."

Her eyes narrowed even further.

"Though last week it was a door."

She groaned.

"We broke it."

"Enough!" More snot-rags flew in my direction. "Why are you here?"

"I, uh." Shit, I couldn't lie to my best friend. "I had an idea for Blake, and texting while driving is frowned upon. Haven't you seen the billboards?"

"You couldn't just call her?"

"I never call clients unless absolutely necessary."

I never do at-home check-ins either, but . . .

"She's upstairs. A pipe broke in the bathroom, and water was everywhere. I was going to call the plumber, but she said something about her friend's dad being a plumber, and suddenly some tall dude showed up and said he could fix it in a jiffy." Gabi lay back down. "Who says 'jiffy' anymore?"

"Good thing you can fix pipes!" Blake's voice filtered from upstairs.

"I clean them too." The familiar voice laughed.

"David." I spat his name.

"Who?" Gabi tried getting up, but I smothered her mouth with a pillow and shushed her. She flailed underneath it. "Can't. Breathe."

"Stop talking or I really will suffocate you," I hissed, dropping the pillow to the floor while I kneeled next to the couch, my ears ringing with static as I tried to listen to their conversation.

"I don't get what the big deal is."

I lifted the pillow and gave Gabi a threatening look.

She threw her hands into the air.

"So I think"—some sort of heavy tool dropped to the ground with a clang; a real tool, not David, damn it—"that should about do it."

"Why didn't you call me?" I smacked Gabi's head with the pillow.

"Gee, I wonder why," Gabi said in a mocking voice. "Because when the dishwasher broke, you said the only way to fix it was for me to dance in front of it topless, then shimmy across the floor in coconut oil."

I smirked. "Tell me you didn't at least consider it."

"And you wonder why I dream of your death."

I waved her off with the pillow. "You love me."

"It's always very vivid. Last night you were hit by a car."

"Nice car?" I asked.

She shrugged and snatched the pillow out of my hands. "Honda."

"Harsh. Must have been an ex-bedmate."

"Most of them drive Jettas."

"Weird, right? Every once in a while, a Honda pops up, though, or a cute little Nissan. But those girls tend to want more than one night, and I'm only one man, so . . ."

Footsteps sounded against the stairs.

I froze in my position on the floor, kneeling next to my sick friend as David's head appeared, and then his long, lean body. He was wearing torn jeans and a white T-shirt. I prayed he'd shown ass crack and had an unholy amount of crack hair waving in Blake's direction while he fixed the damn pipe.

Blake followed, her smile wide, excited.

Great. That was just wonderful. I was so pleased with my new client and her ability to attract Crack Man.

"Thanks again, David." Blake crossed her arms. Did she really not know what that did to a guy? Cleavage galore poured out from her tight black running top.

Wait, I hadn't bought her that. Where the hell did she get it?

I coughed.

Lame move. I knew it, and Gabi knew it by the arch of her brow. Even the damn pillow seemed to be judging me as it puffed out in my direction.

"Are you getting sick too?" Blake uncrossed her arms and made her way toward me.

"Very," I said with a nod.

Gabi opened her mouth in protest, then let out a little yelp while I pinched her leg.

"Oh no." Blake felt my forehead, and her hands were cool. Hey, maybe I really was coming down with something. Frowning, she leaned down, pressing her lips to my temple. Nursing majors. Freaking *loved* them.

"Blake?" David said from the door. "I'm sure he's fine, and the last thing you need is to get sick before your big test on Friday. Why don't we go get ice cream or something?"

Damn, he was moving fast.

Faster than I'd anticipated.

Damn it.

What? Suddenly he sees she actually has boobs and a guy that pays more attention to her and he wants to get ice cream? Like they're ten?

I coughed again, this time really selling it. Bastard wanted to play? I'd play.

I hacked and then gently pushed Blake away. "He's right. The last thing I want is to get you sick, and after . . . last night . . . you may already be coming down with something." My voice rasped, heated, wrapped her up in its sexual innuendo, and promised to never let go.

Blake's mouth dropped open. I gave a slight shake of my head.

"You're right." She sighed, defeated. "I'm probably already contagious."

"Most likely," I said and nodded, pretending to be sad. "I'm sorry, babe. If I had known, I wouldn't have put my mouth all over you like that. Damn, I'm such an ass."

David's hands tightened around the bag he was holding.

"Sorry," I mumbled toward him. "I forgot you were here."

"Rain check?" Blake said in a hopeful voice to David. "I'd hate for you to get sick and miss the big game."

Big game? What big game? I really needed to start paying better attention to his schedule.

But he was a basketball player.

Was he an athlete? Absolutely.

Did he get hit by three-hundred-pound men every few seconds? No.

So was he badass? Like me?

Not even close.

He dealt with sweaty men and balls.

I used to deal with testosterone-crazed linemen.

Used to.

Damn ache in my knee.

"You're right." David eyed me cautiously. "Well, you have my number now, so . . ."

"Yup." Blake stood, her boobs bouncing. I watched like a cat who'd just been given his first ball of yarn.

Want. To. Touch.

"I'll see ya around!" Bounce, bounce, bounce. Mother of—

I looked away. I had to. Otherwise, I'd have had to explain to everyone in the room why the plague caused erections. And that just . . . didn't seem like the best conversation to be having with a client.

A client. A client. A client.

Maybe if I kept repeating her status in my life, I wouldn't be so damn ready to turn her over the table and—

"Ian?" Blake was suddenly in front of me. Shit, had I said any of that out loud? I glanced to Gabi for help.

She was staring at the pillow, completely ignoring me.

Meaning she was pissed. She knew I wasn't treating Blake like a normal client. I'd have to be more careful in the future.

I jolted to my feet and started firing off the usual. "Next time he invites you over, you say you're busy. You're always busy until I say you're free, got it? Rule number three in the playbook clearly states this in painful detail."

Blake took a step backward and nodded seriously.

"And you don't let him call you or coerce you into hanging out, not when you're technically with another dude. It makes you look easy and doesn't make our relationship look real."

Gabi's eyes narrowed as she looked at us. "Is anything going on that I should—?"

"You're sick, Gabs." I shoved the pillow over her face. "You know what they say, 'Sleep, sleep, sleep!'"

"She can't breathe." Blake pointed at the pillow.

"She breathes through her hair." I nodded. "She's fine."

Gabi shoved both me and the pillow away and gasped.

"See? Totally fine." I cleared my throat. "I, uh, I'll see you guys later."

I ran out of the house, sweating.

And not because I was sick, but because I had a feeling I was about to be. Things were moving way too fast with her and David. I had a sudden desire to look more deeply into their program.

I just hoped Lex was home to help.

Chapter Fourteen

"Lex!" I shouted for him the minute I stepped over the threshold. "Emergency meeting. Now!"

Lex appeared a few seconds later, black-rimmed glasses sitting low on his nose, pen in his mouth. I was only slightly irritated that glasses made him look smarter than he already was.

"What up?"

And then he went and used phrases like "what up," and I felt so much better about my place in the world.

"David. What's his deal? She's working through the steps really fast, and he seems to be falling for it, but something just feels off with him." Actually, it was me, all me, but I'd die before admitting that. "Can you pull up his file?"

Lex's eyes narrowed. "David's file? You want to look at his file?"

"Why are you repeating what I just asked you?"

Lex leaned against the doorframe. "Oh, I don't know. Because normally you just look at the summary I toss in the packet. What gives?"

"Curiosity," I lied.

"Uh-huh." Lex smirked, then moved into the living room where his laptop was sitting. "And would this curiosity have anything to do with your inability to keep yourself from wanting to bang the client?"

I rolled my eyes. "I don't bang clients."

"Yet."

"The minute I have sex with a client is the minute this turns into a very lucrative prostitution ring, okay?"

Lex held up his hands, then leaned back in the chair as the Wingmen Inc. graph popped up on the screen.

David Hughes and Blake Olson match = 87% success past first 30 days.

"Eighty-seven?" I repeated. "Isn't that kind of high?"

Lex clicked down to the rest of the stats, mainly numbers that we'd plugged in after Blake's questionnaire, where Lex correlated with David's interests, background, grades, study habits, eating habits, relationships, and, yes, even his medical history.

Lex hacked.

Sure it was semi-illegal. Or maybe fully illegal. But we were helping people. I had my speech for the FBI all ready to go, if it ever came to that.

"Who the hell's allergic to raisins?" I blurted, reading through the medical history.

Lex slammed the computer shut and turned. "If I see a headline in tomorrow's newspaper about how the starting point guard for the Huskies nearly dies from anaphylactic shock, should I be worried? Or just give the police our address?"

I laughed. "Please, like I would stoop that low."

"Gabi called."

"Gabi never calls."

"She was worried."

"So she called you?" I fidgeted with my hands, then leaned back on the chair. "She hates you."

"Which she said at least ten times before finally getting to the reason behind her call."

"She yell?"

"When does she not yell?" Lex made a disgusted noise. "She thinks you're hooking up with Blake."

"No hooking up has taken place."

"Will it?"

I gulped. "No."

"Holy shit." Lex jumped out of his seat and felt my forehead. "Are you sick? Since when have you ever *not* hooked up?"

"Gabi's sick." I pushed away from him and started making my retreat into the kitchen. "Bring her soup. Be a good friend. I have work to do."

I thought he'd left me alone until I felt him breathing down my neck while I mindlessly rummaged through the fridge. "You like her," he said.

"I also like yogurt. You expect me to stick my penis in that too?"

Lex burst out laughing. "I never thought I'd see the day. And let me guess, you aren't even on her radar."

I slammed the fridge shut. "I shouldn't be on her radar, considering I'm her coach! I'm supposed to help her with David, not help myself to her goods!"

"She has nice goods."

"Shut the hell up!" I lunged for him, only to have his laughter stop me dead in my tracks.

"Oh hell, man, you've got it bad. And you don't even know why."

"Because she's a nursing major. And *you* know that ninety percent of male fantasies either include a sexy nurse, naughty cop, or sexually repressed schoolteacher."

"My man." Lex tossed me a spoon for the yogurt. "Just remember, they sign contracts. Keep your twitchy parts away from hers before you get into trouble. It says in the contract if you have sex with her, she can sue us. We did that on purpose, to gain their trust, but also to keep ourselves in check. It's never been a problem."

"And it won't be a problem." The yogurt tasted like shit.

My head felt hot.

And my skin was clammy.

Gabi!

In my mind I knew it was impossible for me to get sick from just seeing her today, which meant something was going around. Still, my patience was shot to hell, and I needed to blame someone.

"Why?" I threw the spoon against the sink and leaned against it. "One day, I'm going to kill Gabi and ask you to bury the body. Just don't ask questions when that day happens, alright?"

"Why one day? Why not now?" Lex looked confused.

My head started to pound. "Damn it! Are you sick?"

"Uh, no. But I take multivitamins. Your idea of a vitamin is eating a Flintstone once a week when you start to get itchy from having sex in the grass."

"Gabi must have gotten me sick," I grumbled. "I'm going to bed to sleep it off and hopefully not die. If I wake up a zombie, take at least a few cool pictures before you decapitate me. Cool?"

"You have my word." Lex nodded seriously as I stomped my way down the hall and slammed my door.

The last time I'd been sick was right before the draft.

Right before my life changed forever.

Being sick was a bad thing, because it felt like it was the universe's way of telling me things were about to go to shit.

Chapter Fifteen

I was having the dream again.

My brain was having a hard time keeping it repressed, what with my body shaking from the chills. Damn fever.

I rolled over and closed my eyes, only to be haunted by the little boy's face.

"Can I have your autograph?" he pleaded, jumping up and down.

I pulled out my black marker and crouched down to his level. "Dude, you can have my autograph and tickets for tomorrow's game."

"No way!" he shouted. "Dad, Dad, guess what?"

His dad mouthed a "Thank you" to me as a lone tear escaped his eye. I couldn't look away from the raw pain just that one tear elicited.

"What's your name?"

The little boy's blue eyes widened. "Tyson! Tyson Montgomery!"

It was cute how he shouted his name, like he couldn't believe he was actually telling it to me.

I quickly signed his Seahawks hat and then pulled out two tickets for the game. VIP. It was part of my bonus. I wanted tickets I could give out to people, but mainly I wanted tickets I could give to those who really needed to forget for a bit. Because that's what football did for me.

It helped me forget my insane parents.

My crappy and lonely childhood.

It helped me forget that I was still lonely.

"Here you go." I handed them over.

"Thank you." His dad pumped my hand as I stood to my full height. "You don't know what this means. His mom . . . she just passed, and . . ." His voice broke.

"It's my pleasure." I released his hand just as someone screamed in the distance.

"Watch out!" a man yelled just as a car came flying down the street, knocking over a hot dog stand and an NFL shop set outside the stadium.

I barely had time to react as the car made its way toward the little boy, who had moved down the line and was waiting for another autograph.

"Move!" I yelled.

My teammates ushered fans out of the way while the little boy stood dazed. The car made its way directly toward him.

"Move!" I screamed and then ran toward him, pushing him out of the way just as the car slammed into the left side of my body, lifting me into the air.

"Hey," a female voice whispered as something cold dabbed my head. "It's okay. You're just feverish."

I jolted awake, chest heaving, leg aching.

Blake pulled back a cold compress, her eyebrows knit with concern. "Are you okay?"

"You're here." Oh shit, oh shit, oh shit. Lex was going to kill me. She was at my house.

We never allowed clients to come to our house. Ever.

I was sick, but not too sick to remember the rules I'd established. The same ones I'd just preached to Lex that I wasn't breaking. And she wasn't just in my house; she was in my bedroom. On my bed.

"I texted you. I even called." Blake dipped the rag into ice water and wrung it out. "And you never responded. You've been out for almost twelve hours. I finally threatened Gabi, who then threatened Lex, who finally let me in the house after I threatened to burn it down."

A laugh escaped between my lips before I could stop it. "That worried about me?"

"You?" She blinked. "Oh, I'm doing this for entirely selfish reasons. If I lose my love coach, I lose my love. Simple as that." She winked.

Her wavy brown hair was pulled back into a loose braid. Soft pieces fell across her face, making me want to reach out and give them a little tug, or wrap them around my fingertips.

"Sorry." I touched my face. I was slick with sweat. My hands moved down my shirt.

It was missing.

"And sorry about the clothes." She didn't blush. She was all business as she started piling pillows around me, fussing over my positioning, and grabbing another blanket. "You were a mess when I got here. Lex said you were making the final transition into a werewolf and not to freak if you lashed out and bit me. I hope he was kidding, because you look rough."

I groaned. "I feel rough. And disgusting."

Smiling, she pressed the rag to my face again. It felt so good. I let out a little moan and grabbed her wrist before I could stop myself.

She froze.

And I immediately regretted my actions. "Sorry." I cleared my hoarse voice. "It just feels really good."

"I'm glad."

"You know what would make me even happier right now?"

"Soup?" she guessed.

"You in a hot nurse outfit. What are you? A curvy size four? Six? I think I have a few costumes in my closet if you want to—"

She flicked the rag at my face as water dripped down my neck. Chuckling, I tossed it off and was surprised to see her laughing with me.

Blake rolled her eyes. "You're kind of a pig."

"Right, but I'm more like one of those cute little pigs, you know, the teacup ones. Still a pig, but you can't help but want to keep it forever because it's so damn adorable."

"Not where I was going with it." She pulled off my blanket, exposing me to the freezing-cold room.

"Ahhhh," I groaned. "Why are you torturing me?"

"Take off your pants."

"What?" My body jerked with awareness so fast I nearly fell off the bed.

Blake sighed. "You're disgusting."

"Wow, thanks. I love you too."

"Take off your pants. Now."

"I'm disgusting, take off my pants. Can't say I've ever had that type of reaction from a woman before. In bed nonetheless."

Blake didn't answer. She just marched toward the adjoining bathroom and turned on the tub.

My head started to pound all over again. With a muffled groan, I pressed my fingers to my temples.

"We have to get your fever down." She was back in the room again. At least I think she was. Everything was going double. This was why I hated germs, and Gabi—in reverse order.

I waved Blake off. "Let me die." The pounding worsened as my head rushed with heat.

"Never leave a man behind," she joked. Then, with a tug, my jeans were off my body. Good. Not only was I helpless in front of the girl I wanted to get into bed, but she'd just stripped me naked and didn't even gasp.

I was freeballing.

And still, no appreciative "Oh my."

Damn it. I'd already lost before I even got put in the game.

"Up you go." She helped me to my feet. Thankfully, she was an athlete, so she was strong. I knew I wasn't helping her much, considering I kept stumbling as I tried to weave my way toward the tub.

"Why are you doing this?" I asked. Peering down at her, I saw three of her face. But she was still pretty, and in my feverish state I wanted nothing more than to kiss her, or just lean against her neck like a pathetic waste of humanity.

"Simple." She smiled up at me. "Despite your bossiness and crude humor, I like you."

Like "*like* me" like? Or just "hey, you're a good *friend*" like? I nearly groaned aloud at my inner narration.

Good job, Ian. Maybe during recess you can have Lex pass her a note and have her circle which one.

"I like you too." I smiled down at her.

"Then get in the bathtub."

I stared her down in what I hoped was utter defiance and strength.

"Get in—before I make Lex come in here and carry you. And I have a really good reason to believe his bedside manner is like a grenade going off in your face."

"How do you figure?"

"Easy. He went and checked in on Gabi once he found out how sick you were. He was with her all night, and there was a lot of shouting."

"Lex?" I made my way to the side of the tub. "My best friend Lex? You should have called the police. He's going to kill her."

"She texted that she's fine."

"She's feverish! Of course she's fine! I've seen two unicorns and a flying elephant since we've made the trek from my bed to the bathroom."

"Dumbo?" Blake laughed. "You saw Dumbo?"

"I was always terrified of big ears when I was little." Why was I saying this out loud? Why? Why? Why, God? *Why?* But it just kept happening. "I think it was because they used to call me Big Ears, and then once the kids discovered Dumbo . . . it was the beginning of the end. I refused to even eat elephant ears, because I assumed that meant my ears would grow more. How sad, to miss out on the best part of the fair."

"In you go," Blake said, ignoring my elephant-ear comment.

Slowly, I lowered myself, with her help, into the tub, and screamed out obscenities I'm sure no lady of her nature should ever have to hear.

"Son of a bitch!" I screamed. "I hate you. I don't like you anymore. I take it back. All of it. Get me out! Why is it so cold?"

"It's not cold." Blake held me down. "It just feels that way because you're so hot. We have to get your fever down."

"I'm always hot, Blake." I slapped her hand against my forehead. "See? Feel? I'm healed. Miraculous recovery." I winced as the throbbing pain continued, then nearly laughed my ass off as I saw an honest-to-God Dumbo fly out in front of me. "I just hate big ears. Why does nobody understand?"

"Big ears suck," Blake joined in. "And so do fevers. So I need you to cooperate while I keep filling the tub, okay?"

I leaned back, teeth chattering. "Worst moment of my life. This is a close second."

Blake turned to me, her eyes curious. "What's the first?"

"When I almost died."

She was silent.

"I just died in your arms tonight," I sang as my eyes started to close. "The tub isn't so bad, Blake."

"I know."

"I think we could be best friends. I only have two. I'm killing them off soon, though, so there's a vacancy."

"Good to know."

"But you have to cook for me."

Blake's musical laughter made my body clench tight, but the cold water prevented any embarrassments. Wait, why was I in water? Why was Blake here?

"I cooked for my dad and brother all the time."

"Really? Is your brother as pretty as you?"

Blake's eyes softened. "He's dead."

"I'm sorry." I reached blindly for her hand. I was so tired, but it was important to comfort her, just be there for her. I could tell in the way she suddenly slumped, as if forgetting all of the stages of her transformation from insecure to a confident woman. "Dying sucks."

I didn't know what else to say.

"Yeah." She let out a chuckle and shook her head. "It really does, Ian."

"Blake?"

"Yup." She turned off the water with her free hand. I was still clutching the other.

"I like you."

"I like you too."

"Despite my big ears?"

"Because of your big ears."

"That's what all the ladies"—I yawned—"say."

"Bet they do . . ."

The pounding started to subside. I don't remember getting out of the tub, but I do remember the feel of Blake's hand as I fell into a restful sleep.

Chapter Sixteen

My hand was touching something soft. Eyes shut, I squeezed, then squeezed again. Oh wow, good dream. Very vivid. Like her breasts were really there, in my room, in my bed. In my hand.

Well, since I was dreaming . . .

I climbed on top of Blake and used both hands, cupping their heaviness, giving another squeeze as my fingertips went to her nipples.

Her eyes flashed open.

"Clearly you're feeling better," she hissed, then with a grunt shoved me off of her.

"Nope," I said with a chuckle. "Still delirious. Where we at with that nurse costume?"

Blake quickly pulled on a hooded sweatshirt, covering up her white tank top and short black shorts. "No nurse costume. You're healed. And I have to get to practice."

"What kind of nurse are you? You sleep with your patient, then leave at first light! I should fire you." I grinned, then patted the spot next to me. "Five more minutes?"

"Hey, I'm just following the rules, coach! Doesn't it say in your contract that you can't legally sleep with your clients?" She winked.

Damn, she was adorable. I wanted to kiss that sexy mouth of hers.

"Sex," I said with a nod. "Not sleep. Sleep is encouraged. Did you know at least sixty percent of insomniacs turn to homicide?"

"That's a lie." She crossed her arms. "And I really do need to get to practice."

"Fine." I moved to get up.

"Wait!" She threw her hands in front of her.

But she was too late.

The sheet fell away, and I was completely naked, leaving me staring down at my own body and wondering if it was going to offend her that my little groping had clearly had an effect on my manhood.

"About that." I pointed. "It's morning."

"Sure." Her cheeks were bright red. "I'll just . . ." She backed up into the dresser, knocking over my cologne along with some ChapStick. She quickly bent over to pick them up.

I let out a groan as her ass waved in the air. "Not helping, Blake."

With a thump, she pushed the objects back onto the dresser and reached for the doorknob, only to miss it three times before yelling bye and slamming the door behind her.

The room fell silent.

I wondered if it was a bad thing that the sight of my arousal made her head for the hills. Never had that happened before. If anything, jaws tended to drop, parades started, lots of moaning commenced, and in two instances, bras spontaneously fell to the floor.

The door jerked open. "Sorry!" Blake stumbled through. "I just wanted to make sure you stay in bed."

"But—"

"In bed!" Nurse Ratched was back. She glared, her ice-blue eyes challenging me to argue further. I suddenly felt very, very mothered. Which was awkward, considering my dick hadn't gotten the message yet. "Take the Tylenol I left for you, and I'll stop by after practice with soup."

"Food?" My ears perked up.

"Food." Her eyes lowered briefly before she cleared her throat and pointed. "Shouldn't you take care of . . . that?"

"This?" Shit, talking about my junk just made it worse—the strain, the ache, the embarrassment—as my body clearly reached for higher heights. "Wouldn't a good nurse stay and help?"

She rolled her eyes. "You really are disgusting, you know that, right?" She was smiling, which led me to believe she was joking. Or . . . holy shit . . . was she flirting with me?

"I officially forbid you to hang out with Gabi anymore. What the hell has she said about me to give you such a low opinion?"

"What makes you think it's Gabi?" she said with a shrug. "Also. You're a whore."

"I'd be willing to amend my ways if you'd scratch the itch, doc."

"I'm leaving now."

"Was it something I said?" I laughed at her horrified expression, then ducked when the ChapStick grazed my ear, flying by with an impressive speed I hadn't been expecting.

"I'm spitting in your food!" she announced, slamming the door behind her.

The only reason I was able to turn around and climb back into bed, other than the fact that if I'd tried peeing it wouldn't have ended up in the toilet, was because she was coming back.

With food.

For me.

Damn it. Something was happening. Something . . . that I really didn't want to acknowledge. I always responded to women. Always. I appreciated them, thought all shapes and sizes were attractive. But I'd never responded to a client, crossed that line. With Blake it was more than that—it felt like more—because when we were together, I didn't want the time to end. I wasn't pretending to listen to her, and I didn't check the time and give all the nonverbal cues of needing to wrap things up.

I just liked her. Plain and simple. She was beautiful, but something told me that even if she was still wearing the baggy sweatshirts and sporting a scrunchie, it wouldn't have taken me a long time to discover the treasure that she was underneath.

She was fiercely loyal and hardworking. And she cared, even about someone who she really shouldn't care about—me.

Last night, while feverish, I'd had that moment. A moment of clarity. I was the Grinch whose heart grew three sizes. I looked down.

Or maybe it was just my cock.

Either way, it was no longer just this physical wham-bam reaction. There was something about her, something that made me want to punch David in the face and steal Blake for myself.

Food.

She wasn't bringing him food.

Food meant . . .

Oh shit.

It meant something.

Right?

And now I was acting like all of my clients—frantic, and desperate to win the attention of the person I was after. Fantastic.

I was still in the game, but I was warming the bench, splinters embedding themselves in my hard ass while David made a game-winning touchdown. Damn David.

With a sigh, I swiped my phone off the nightstand and sent off a quick text to Lex.

Ian: Where'd you bury her?

He responded right away.

Lex: I thought it best to leave you out of it just in case you have to testify.

Ian: You're a good friend.

Lex: Also, Gabi says sorry for getting you sick.

Ian: A true friend would apologize with cookies.

Lex: She said to go screw yourself.

Ian: She not up to the task? Still too dehydrated?

Lex: She said, and I'm quoting her, just FYI: Tell Ian that if I want to get syph I'll do it without hooking up with the campus bike.

Ian: Bike?

Lex: Because everyone's had a ride.

Ian: Unfair. It's me riding them, not the other way around. You know how I feel about lazy sex. *Cough, points finger*

Lex: Bite me.

Ian: Pretty sure Gabs already took care of that.

Lex: Remind me to get my rabies shot later.

Ian: Are you home?

Lex: On my way.

I frowned at the phone.

Ian: You're still at Gabi's?

Lex: I told you, I had to get rid of the

```
    body. Murder takes time.
Ian: Alrighty then. See you in a few.
Lex: By the way, I hate her. Just so you
    know. I only came over here because I
    was worried she had the plague and was
    about to start a citywide epidemic.
Ian: No need to defend yourself.
Lex: Good. See you in a few.
```

I set down my phone and smiled, imagining just how great of a doctor Lex had been to Gabi. I bet he threw the medicine at her, then yelled when she didn't suddenly just get better. He wasn't a patient man, not when it came to Gabi. I wanted to check on her too, but I was suddenly exhausted.

With a groan, I rubbed my eyes, quickly got under the covers, and went back to sleep.

CHAPTER SEVENTEEN

By the time Blake made it back to my house, I was showered and downstairs watching *Game of Thrones* reruns. When the knock sounded at the door, I knew exactly who it was.

I stood just as Lex went to open it.

Oh shit. I'd have to explain why she was back.

"Hey, Lex," Blake stood up on her tiptoes, kissed him on the cheek, and moved past him into the kitchen, like she was on girlfriend terms.

Curious, I watched out of the corner of my eye as she set two takeout bags down and started pulling out boxes.

Lex pouted, leaning toward her a little closer than I would have liked. "Please tell me you got food for me too."

I growled from my spot on the couch.

"Oh, hey, Ian. Didn't see you," Lex lied.

I gave him the finger while Blake continued piling an insane amount of takeout onto the table.

"I got your favorite." Blake grinned at my roommate like they were besties. What the hell? "Chow mein, right?"

"With pork?"

I choked on my bottle of water, then shot to my feet, dizzily making my way toward the bar.

"Of course." She scooted the tray over, while the smell of Thai food, Chinese, and . . .

"Panera Bread," I shouted, louder than necessary.

"Forgive Ian," Lex said. "Sometimes I think he loves food more than sex."

"And sometimes"—I sat—"depending on the girl, that's true."

Blake bit down on her lip, her face paling briefly before she scooted a black plastic bowl of soup in my direction.

She'd paled when I mentioned sex.

So that meant she was either jealous it wasn't her, or totally disgusted that I was the type of guy to go out and just have mindless sex with equally mindless girls.

I frowned down at the soup.

"Is it too hot?" Blake asked, coming around the bar and handing me a napkin.

She smelled like burnt vanilla. Her hair was pulled into a high ponytail, parts of the wavy golden-brown mess still wet. Face makeup-free except for eyelash stuff and some lip gloss.

I suppressed a groan. Damn, she really was pretty. All of her.

Even in the boyfriend sweats that I'd finally let her buy. In pink. Oh, her and pink.

I glanced down.

The flip-flops had made another appearance, though for some reason it was like as long as she was wearing them, in my mind, we were still on equal footing. Like the minute she was no longer comfortable around me was the minute I was going to lose my shit and just . . . I don't know. I hadn't planned that far, because I wasn't going to let it happen.

"Yes," I blurted. "The soup's freakishly hot." I leaned forward until my mouth was inches from hers. "Blow?"

"You want me to blow on your soup," she said in a deadpan voice. "Are you twelve?"

"Thirteen," Lex piped up. "Quick, tell her about the facial hair you just got. Oh, and his testicles dropped about two days ago, so if he's handsy, just know . . . he's brand-new and a bit horny."

"I'm sad"—I glared at Lex—"that Gabi didn't succeed in chopping your balls off."

"Not for lack of trying," he grumbled, his expression losing some of its exuberance.

"Also"—I grabbed my spoon while Blake handed me some French bread—"Gabi said next time you touch her tits, she's going to run you over with a lawn mower."

Lex snorted. "Like she could even start it. And I wasn't touching any part of her." He shivered. "Do I look like I want an incurable disease? Hell, I was trying to feel her forehead, and my hands . . . slipped."

"From her forehead." I grinned. "That's . . . wow . . . impressive. Must have been wearing a hell of a push-up bra."

I lifted the soup to my lips and dropped my spoon. "Shit, that really is hot."

Blake rolled her eyes, then leaned in and blew over the tomato soup, her plump lips forming the perfect *O*.

I watched.

Even Lex watched.

The room went dead silent.

She finally glanced up at us.

Lex turned around and started whistling while I continued staring. "You blow well," I said in my most romantic voice.

"Coming from you"—she shook her head—"I'll take that as the highest of compliments."

I kept my face impassive when really I hated that she thought of me that way. And I never cared what girls thought.

Because for the most part, the girls I was around didn't really do that often—you know, think about anything past having sex. There were no feelings involved, no sharing, just mutual pleasure. Up until now, I'd thought myself lucky to find women who only wanted to get off. Now? It felt like I'd been missing something. Something important.

"Eat." Blake winked and pulled out a chicken salad and started diving into it like she hadn't eaten in weeks.

Again, Lex and I paused.

Me because I was absolutely fascinated to see a woman other than Gabi eat food and not talk about dieting.

Lex because his biggest turn-on was Carl's Jr. commercials. It was his porn. Go figure.

I was never letting Blake eat burgers in front of him. Ever.

Not even the cheap ninety-nine-cent kind from McDonald's.

"Um . . ." I coughed into my hand when she glanced up and looked at us. "You have chicken just . . . right . . . there." I pointed to the side of her mouth.

Blushing, she wiped her mouth and shook her head. "Sorry. I'm always starving after practice. And I didn't have time to pack any protein bars, because I was too busy playing nurse all night."

"Without the nurse outfit," I complained.

"You still have that?" Lex asked.

"You guys are . . ." Blake stood. "Well, let's just say it makes total sense, what you do."

"What?" I ate more soup now that it was cooling off. "We save women from themselves. And more importantly, we help them get the men of their dreams. If that's so wrong, I don't wanna be right." I winked, and Lex held up his hand for a high five.

Blake moved back around the breakfast bar and pressed a palm to my forehead.

"Ouch." I nearly fell back out of my chair. "Kinda rough, Blake."

"Last night you said you liked it rough. Just following orders."

"I did?"

"Yup." She removed her hand. Despite the glint in her eyes, I couldn't tell what she was thinking. "Right before you told me to lick your ears."

"Erogenous zone," I offered with a smirk. "Don't knock it until you've tried it."

"Your fever's gone."

"Good." I stood and moved to grab my computer.

"Whoa, what are you doing?" Blake jerked the computer from my hands.

"Uh . . . working? I have a near-perfect GPA, and I need to keep it that way. I need to e-mail my profs, make sure we don't have any new clients that need interviewing, and—"

"Nope." She held the computer against her chest. "You're weak from the fever. Today you need to just chill. Then tomorrow you can work."

"I'm your love coach. If I chill, that means you aren't getting your man."

She chewed her lower lip and frowned. "I've waited this long. What's one more day?"

Sighing, I reached for my computer.

She pulled away.

"Blake."

"Ian."

I looked to Lex for help, but he'd already left the room.

"Fine." I sighed. "I'll just sit here and watch TV for the rest of the afternoon and evening, then go to bed at six."

"You're lying, aren't you?"

"Absolutely."

"Fine." Blake kept her death grip on the computer and made her way over to the couch. "So what are we watching?"

"You can't stay," I blurted.

"Why not?"

"Because!" I had work to do. I wasn't kidding about the homework or the need I had to make sure everything was on schedule. The sooner I got rid of her as a client and into David's stupid arms, the sooner she'd realize what a tool he was and come running back.

Right? All I knew was I wanted our time to be finished, so that it would actually be fair for me to join the game rather than watch from the freaking sidelines.

"We're friends," she announced.

I almost threw up. "What did you just say?"

"Friends."

That's what I thought. The f-bomb.

"I have two. Don't need another. You know, the whole third-wheel thing." I shrugged. "Now, if you want an upgrade, I can easily arrange more. Think of it as friends"—I held up one hand, then held up the other—"but you get benefits, like you'd get with a real job."

"You mean friends with benefits."

"Hey, you said it, not me."

"Ian."

"Yes?"

"Sit down, shut up, and try not to get delirious again."

Exhaling with frustration, I moved to the farthest end of the couch from her and sat. Not because I wasn't intoxicated by her presence, but because I was suddenly realizing that I had no self-control where she was concerned, and I didn't want her to realize how much she affected me.

How much I wanted to taste her again and again.

And how much I resented the fact that she would never want me in the same way.

For the first time in my life, I wanted a girl that wasn't mine to have.

And it sucked.

CHAPTER EIGHTEEN

"Ian?" Blake said. Somehow she'd managed to make her way from her end of the couch over to mine. Our leather couch was nice; one end of it had the longer side without cushions or whatever the hell you called it, so a person could lie back with their feet up and watch the movie.

"What up, sweet cheeks?" I yawned and wrapped an arm around her, then froze. Shit, it was too natural.

She cuddled into me.

My entire body seized with pleasure as she placed a hand on my chest and let out a heavy sigh.

"Out with it," I said. "And know the only reason I'm not pausing *Game of Thrones* is because I've seen this episode a thousand times. Otherwise, I'd duct-tape your mouth. You've been warned."

"Wow." She exhaled loudly. "Thanks."

"So . . ." I ran my fingers up and down her arm. It was instinctual; I couldn't keep my hands to myself and didn't want to. She was wearing a loose pink racerback tank top and a pair of spandex shorts that showed off a good chunk of her curvy ass and nice legs. "What's on your mind?"

"Do you ever . . . ?" She tensed a bit then, as if telling herself to relax, and leaned into me. "Do you ever think that what you thought you wanted isn't actually what you want anymore?"

"You mean . . . like you've lived your whole life in pursuit of one goal, and suddenly the goal changes?"

She jerked away from me and stared at me directly in the eyes. "Yes, that's exactly what I mean."

I sat up a bit. "Blake, that's life."

"But"—she ran her hands through her hair and retied it back into a low ponytail—"it just seems too wishy-washy, to go from one thing to another."

"That's part of what college is for." I frowned. "Discovering yourself . . . Realizing that, hey, maybe wearing Adidas flip-flops from 1992 isn't as cool as I originally thought." I smiled.

Blake burst out laughing. "They aren't mine, you jerk."

"So you stole a stranger's ugly flip-flops and decided, *Hey, let's bring these suckers back.*"

She scrunched up her nose. It was freaking adorable. "Not really. They used to be my brother's, and . . . after he died, I don't know . . . I just . . . wanted to be close to him."

"So you raided his closet?"

"Everything smelled like him." She glanced away, her face distant. "It was comforting."

"Until you had to wash them."

She burst out laughing again. "Until my dad forced me to wash them, yes. It's only been two years. I still miss him."

"How'd he die?"

"Car accident." She ducked back under my arm. "Drunk driver. The usual. Used to piss me off talking about it, but when I started wearing his clothes, it almost felt like this invisible armor."

"I hate to break it to you, sweet cheeks, but those shoes are anything but invisible."

A pillow flew at my face.

"Hey," I yelled as she tried to get up and escape from me. "Oh no you don't." I grabbed her by the waist and tossed her back onto the couch, then hovered over her.

"Stop!" She flailed underneath me, laughing her ass off. "You can't make me stay!"

I quickly leaned down and licked her cheek. "Sorry to break it to you, but if you lick it, it's yours."

Her laughter faded.

"Is that so?"

I nodded seriously. "First rule of kindergarten. Didn't you listen in class?"

"Must have missed that lesson."

I nodded. "It's right up there with fire safety."

She gripped my head with both of her hands and pulled. Our foreheads nearly touched. Breathing suddenly became extremely difficult as her eyes stared down my lips. And then very slowly, she turned my head and licked up my cheek.

Every single part of my body felt that lick.

And wanted to feel it a second time.

I closed my eyes and shuddered. "Thought I told you not to play a player?"

"Just following your rules."

"Sometimes"—I cupped her cheek with my hand—"I really hate my rules."

She swallowed. "Me too."

I wasn't sure who did it first, me or her, but suddenly we were kissing, or more importantly, I was straddling her, and kissing the shit out of her while she hooked her legs around my body and jerked me against her.

It was heaven.

It was hell.

Moaning, we both tumbled to the floor, her on top, then me, then her, then me.

She didn't kiss like she was innocent. She kissed like her mouth was starving for mine. And kissing her back was like finally finding the one girl I wanted to kiss, possibly even more than screw.

Because her lips felt so damn good that releasing them to take off her clothes would have been a crime.

Our tongues tangled as she ran her hands through my hair. I moved to her bra, and she kicked off her flip-flops, nearly hitting me in the head.

"Easy, tiger," I mumbled against her mouth.

She laughed, then kissed me harder, our teeth nearly knocking together as I deepened the kiss. Doubt became a fire alarm clamoring in my head, but I ruthlessly hammered it away, desperate for more of Blake. Her lips moved beneath mine—hot, wet, welcoming, and so demanding that she was nearly sending me over the edge.

The front door closed.

We stopped kissing.

But we didn't pull apart.

I knew there wouldn't be time.

"Whoa." Lex surveyed the situation. "Either he drugged you, or—"

"Training," I blurted, sharing a look with Blake. "We're setting up a date night for her and David. He's moving through the stages so fast I imagine he'll try something during the movie."

Blake's body went rigid, and she averted her eyes from mine, then gave Lex a forced smile. "I think I got it."

With a shove, she had me on my ass and was grabbing her phone and purse.

"Thanks, Ian."

"Blake—"

"Really." She turned, and her smile was so fake it hurt to see. "I, uh, I'll text you tomorrow about the details for the date."

Shit. I wasn't going to actually allow the date!

The door slammed.

I flinched.

Lex let out a low whistle, then patted me on the back. "Good job, dude. Why not just be honest? For once."

"She's a client." I was convincing no one with that convictionless statement.

"She's more."

"She's . . ." I punched the pillow, then threw it hard against the couch. "She's my client. If David's what she wants, I'll help her. She deserves at least that much."

"What if he isn't what she wants?" Lex asked quietly. "What will you do?"

"I . . ."

"That's what I thought." He walked over to the light switch and flicked it off. "See you on the other side."

CHAPTER NINETEEN

The next few days flew by. Blake answered my texts politely, and the kiss was never mentioned.

I knew I'd hurt her. When I closed my eyes, I still saw the look of disbelief on her face, which had quickly turned into anger as she hung her head and walked out of the house.

And that was why women weren't allowed in the house.

Why I had rules, damn it!

I stared at the couch. Like it was going to suddenly give me a replay of what had happened a few nights ago.

Her mouth had tasted so sweet, so luscious. Just thinking about it was making my dick strain against my jeans. My physical reaction was alarming enough without adding in the fact that I couldn't stop thinking about her, wondering if she was okay, and wanting to talk to her.

Just talk.

About nothing. I just needed to hear her voice.

Shit.

Lex waltzed into the room, took one look at me pouring myself a glass of orange juice, and smirked. "Oranges do it for you now?" he said. "Should I hide those orange-blossom candles in the living room, or is this just a stage?"

I rolled my eyes. "It's not the juice. Or the oranges." I sighed. "It's the couch."

"Uh." A perplexed look crossed Lex's features. "The couch?"

I nodded.

"So your new dirty words are big cushions? High thread count? Soft leather? Ikea?"

"Shut it." I covered my face with my hands and let out a few curses. "What the hell is wrong with me?"

"Dude, if a couch gave you an erection, you tell me."

"It's because of what happened on the couch."

"Ohh." Lex nodded and swiped his keys from the table. "You mean the practice kiss that really wasn't practice at all but you breaking your own rules, and had I come in, oh, I don't know, say a half hour later, said couch would be soiled with all the sex you're currently not having."

"Why are we friends?"

"See ya." Lex saluted me with his middle finger. "And not that I'm a relationship expert, since I'd rather bang 'em than lose 'em, but maybe you should talk to her." He nodded slowly. "Use your words."

"Bite me."

His laugh had me wanting to key his car.

Or maybe drive it into Puget Sound.

Fine. I could use my words. I could fix this. I *would* fix this.

I checked my watch. I had two hours before class, and Blake didn't have any morning classes.

"Words," I mumbled, reaching for my phone. "Use my words."

"This isn't coming out right," I blurted as Blake lifted a couch cushion high into the air, aiming for my face, and then, as if thinking twice about it, lowering it toward my groin.

I'd been at her house a total of five seconds before World War III broke out.

"You think?" she said, seething.

"I'm trying to make things better!"

"Is that what you're doing?" she screeched. "You apologized for kissing me, then kissed me again."

"About that." I winced. "I got caught up in the moment." Actually, she looked so damn pretty that I'd forgotten all about my huge speech. I'd just apologized for last weekend, then, two seconds later, fused my mouth against hers.

She kissed me back.

For around four seconds.

And then she shoved me back so hard that my coffee spilled and ran down my chest, probably leaving a burn trail all the way to my dick.

Wrong day to freeball it. That was for sure.

"Ian." Why did my name have to sound so good coming from those swollen lips? Probably because God was punishing me. The one girl I craved and she was ready to suffocate me. Great. "You're not that guy, the relationship one. That's what I want. Not fleeting kisses. Because"— she swallowed—"well, because it confuses me. And that's not fair."

I sighed, hanging my head. "I know, Blake. I'm sorry. I got carried away. You know the song 'Blurred Lines'?"

"Not helping your case."

"Sorry." I managed a weak smile. "Again." But what I really wanted to say? *Let me take you out on a date. Give me a chance. I could change.*

But I knew better than anyone.

Guys didn't just change. I mean, I'd never tried, but the thing about Blake? She was sweet, innocent, and what if I ruined her? What if I told her I wanted to commit, jumped in with both feet, only to cheat on her?

"I swear"—I gulped, hating every word I was saying—"I'll help you with David. And then . . . I'm hoping we can still be friends."

Her face fell. "Friends."

"Funny how words that are supposed to make people happy kind of make *you* want to punch a tree like Chuck Norris."

Blake burst out laughing. "Yeah, well . . ."

It wasn't awkward. If I had to describe the moment—me still dripping-wet with coffee, Blake holding a pillow to keep my mouth from assaulting hers—I'd say it was sad.

That's what I felt.

Sad.

Because I liked her.

Clearing my throat, I held out my hand. "Friends?"

She dropped the pillow, took a few steps, closing the distance between us, and shook my hand. "Friends."

"Good." I dropped her hand, flexed my fingers, gave myself an internal pep talk where her boobs weren't the main attraction, and stared her down. "Then let's get to work."

"Didn't you say you had class?"

"Skipping. We're going to basically bump into David all day long, and make him want to kill himself. You up for that?"

She nodded, but it wasn't an excited nod—more like she didn't know what else to do.

"You still want David, right?"

Dear God, please say no.

After a few seconds of hesitation, Blake answered. "David's . . . a good guy. He's the guy you marry, you know? The guy you take home. He's always been there for my family, and he's—"

"Safe," I finished for her, hating the word almost as much as I hated the word "friends."

Blake made a face. "Do you think that's wrong?"

Hell, yes. It was almost as bad as settling. But it wasn't my place to tell her that. Plenty of girls liked safe, only to fall in love with the comfort it brought later. Safe wasn't settling, but it sure as hell looked like it. Especially the way that Blake's shoulders suddenly slouched.

"Blake." I gripped her arms and pulled her forward. "Snap out of it. You're sexy as hell, know how to kiss so well that I'm pretty sure I'll never forget the way your mouth tastes, and you're sweet." I rolled my eyes. "Stop making that face. Sweet is good. You're the perfect balance of sexy and sweet. Think of your personality as catnip."

"Does that make David a cat?"

"Yeah." And I was a tiger, damn it.

"Okay . . . also, I never thought you'd ever call me sweet, especially with our first meeting not going so well."

I laughed. "But now we're friends, so you no longer want to gouge my eyes out."

The daggers she shot at me with her eyes told me to piss off. Obviously she didn't agree.

She held up a hand. "Only half the time. When you're asking me to play nurse and patient, or when you tell me to get naked, or when you grab my boobs without permission, or kiss me just because you have issues keeping your hand out of the cookie jar."

"Is that so wrong?"

"According to the contract . . ."

I rubbed my hands together. "I'm changing the subject now. Go put something on that screams sexy, and we'll get going."

Blake glanced down at her baggy black sweats and tight blue tank top. "What's wrong with this?"

My eyebrows shot up. "What's wrong?" I circled her, then slapped her ass and gripped it so hard she let out a little yelp. "There it is. Sorry. Couldn't find it underneath all that heavy black material."

Grumbling, she stomped away, then paused at the stairway and very slowly turned back to give me a coy gaze.

"Dude, hurry up," I said.

Her sweats dropped to her ankles.

Revealing ass cheeks with a string of fabric pressed between them. Sweet glorious Lord.

"Not funny," I growled. "I will seriously own your ass if you do that again, and I don't mean that in an 'oh, I'll just tackle you and spank you' way. I will breach my contract as many times as I can within a twenty-four-hour period. Now, if you're game for that, then by all means keep stripping. But if you can't hang with the big boys, I suggest you march that cute ass up the stairs, put on some clothes—ones that hide the white thong—and get back down here within five minutes. I still have to change, and you ruined our coffee." I hoped I still had something clean left at Gabi's house.

Her smile fell, and suddenly she was dashing up the stairs like the fires of hell were licking at her heels. Which, technically they were, since my tongue had fallen out of my mouth and a puddle of drool was pooling at my feet.

I took a deep breath, trying to soothe myself.

She wanted David. She deserved David. I'd get her David if it killed me.

While she changed, I pulled up Blake's profile summary and glanced at David's class schedule. He had a class in an hour and would most likely be hanging around the gym soon after for a light weight session followed by practice.

"Ready!" Blake appeared in front of me.

I lowered my phone, eyes narrowing as I examined her from head to toe. I circled her like she was my prey, and wished it were actually true.

"Who got you that tank top?"

"You don't like it?" She looked down and gripped the loose-yet-sexy tank top with a leopard print sports bra underneath. "Gabi loaned it to me."

That Gabi was really trying my patience. First, she got me sick, and now? Now she's loaning sexy clothes to her roommate?

"It's nice." With a shrug, I turned my head to the left, then leaned over, my face staring directly at her tight ass. "New spandex?"

Blake did a little wiggle. Or actually, her ass did.

When asses wiggled, I had a tendency to pet them.

Because really, that's what an ass shake was—an invitation to touch, and as a man it was my job to make sure that the ass knew that, yes, I would be paying a lot of attention to it later.

"Great," I croaked, peeling my eyes away from the gray-and-black tiger-striped spandex. "No."

"What? You just said 'great.'" She turned around, her eyes lowered to where mine were still fastened.

"No." I pointed at the offensive flip-flops. "If you want David, you have to give these to the Goodwill, or better yet, burn them, or"—I paused and added a small smile so she wouldn't be too offended—"leave them on your doorstep so I can steal them and stash them under my pillow. We'd always have the flip-flops."

I was turning into a lunatic.

Another reason she needed to get with David sooner rather than later. If I kept this up, I was going to grow ovaries and ask the clerk at Walmart where the tampon aisle was.

"I'm wearing them."

"No." I crossed my arms to match her stance. "You aren't."

"Make me take them off."

"You don't think I can?" We were chest to chest. I could smell her vanilla ChapStick. Her wavy golden-brown hair spilled over her shoulders.

The room was so tense I was surprised I could even breathe.

"Ian." She purred my name, and I was done for, seriously done for. Damn woman. "Please?"

"Stop that." I pointed at her eyes. "Stop batting your eyelashes. I'm immune!"

She kept batting them, her smile growing wider and wider, making her look more adorable than sexy. Which was a hell of a lot worse, because sexy you slept with, adorable you kept.

Forever.

I needed to look away. "Damn it." I rolled my eyes, breaking contact. "Whatever. Just remember, I warned you."

"Thanks." She slapped my ass just like I had done to her a few minutes ago. It tingled. It tingled hard. It tingled good.

With a groan, I followed her peppy steps to the door and mentally moved up the timeline. She wanted David?

She was going to get him.

By this weekend.

My heart did a little skip.

I brushed it off as heartburn and rushed her to my waiting SUV, my eyes lingering on her ass the entire way.

CHAPTER TWENTY

"You know"—I smirked—"this isn't a sting. You can take your sunglasses off. Plus we're inside, so it kinda makes you look like a loser. Just saying."

Blake elbowed me hard in the ribs and kept her sunglasses on, lifting her chin high into the air. "But you said not to make eye contact, and that's really difficult for me. Thus the sunglasses."

"Dude, just look at his crotch."

"His crotch?"

"Yeah, he'll eat that shit right up."

Blake burned bright red. "I'm not looking at his crotch!"

A girl hurried by us, nearly knocking over brochures for the business program.

Blake covered her face with her hands. "Please tell me I didn't just say 'crotch' that loud, twice."

"Say it one more time. I promise it will be worth it."

She lowered her hands and glared. "Any other pointers that don't involve me staring at his—" She motioned in the air with her hands and coughed.

"His . . . ?" I cupped my ear.

Blake licked her lips, her cheeks still stained red as she said under her breath, "Groin."

I kept my laugh in, just barely. "I think you can do better than that, Miss Nursing Major. I have an idea, let's play Name the Parts!"

"No," Blake hissed. "We aren't naming body parts in the hallway while waiting for David to just stroll by! What if he walks by when I say—?"

"Penis?"

Her hand slammed over my mouth. "Shh!"

I peeled her fingers away one by one. Strong grip—good to know. "If you can't say it, you probably shouldn't be playing with it, you know?"

Eyes wide, she gasped. "I'm not playing with anyone's"—she lowered her voice to a whisper—"penis."

"Isn't that a shame?" I sighed. "Hey, I've got one you can practice with."

"My face probably can't get any redder than it is right now, can it?"

"I don't know. Should we try?"

"Ian, I swear if you say one more word . . ." Her finger wagged at my face. It was cute, getting her all embarrassed. Almost like foreplay, only more fun, because she was so innocent.

"Penis." I said it again. "Just say it."

"No!"

"Tits."

"Oh hell," she muttered under her breath, then started marching away. I gripped her by the elbow and tugged her back against me.

"Come on, Blake. Eventually, you'll have to get past the point where you aren't afraid of your own sexuality. And something tells me that David's not going to be supergreat in bed, so you need to at least gain some confidence so you can tell him what you want."

"What?" Blake turned, hands on hips. "What makes you think he'd be bad? I mean, I'm a virgin."

"Yup."

She threw her hands into the air. "So . . . I'll suck."

"Not possible." I eyed her up and down. Not freaking possible. "Believe me. I know this shit. As for David? The last girlfriend who was interviewed stated that although he earned an A for effort, on more than one occasion she studied for a test during. You know? A test *during*."

"During?"

"Sex."

"How?"

"Well, the way she explained it was quite clever—she hid note cards in her pillow. Brilliant, right?"

Blake's mouth dropped open. "But, that's so . . . impersonal. And awful. Shouldn't you be putting your whole body into it? Your mind? Your soul? I mean, why *have* sex if you aren't going to give everything you are every single time?"

The more she talked, the harder it was to breathe.

Why indeed? Because sex felt good.

But lately, it had become monotonous, boring. And then Blake and I had kissed. And now, everything about her, even just conversation, was exhilarating and new.

Shit on a stick.

"Uh." I cleared my throat. "We're getting off-topic. The point is, you may need to give him direction. Meaning you may need to say words like 'penis.' The end."

"Fine." Blake closed her eyes for a few seconds, then opened them and whispered, "Penis."

"Louder." I grinned.

Her ears were as bright as a red crayon.

"Penis," she said loud enough for anyone passing by to hear.

Lucky for us, one of those people just happened to be David.

"Oh, hey man." I held out my hand for a good ol' friendly shake. "Didn't see you there. How's it going?"

David's mouth was open in, well, probably shock, that his good little bestie just uttered the name of a man part, out loud, in the business building hallway, like a pro.

"Blake?" He frowned.

"Oh, sorry!" Blake pulled off her sunglasses. "I forgot I had these on."

"You should never cover your eyes," he said in a low voice. "They're your best feature."

I laughed.

David glared.

"Oh, sorry. I thought you were kidding."

"What? I was just thinking that if we're naming her best feature—physical, that is, since we both know she has a killer personality—hmm." I gave her a once-over. "I'd have to say it's a three-way tie between her ass, tits, and hair. But hey, what do I know?"

Blake elbowed me hard in the ribs. I wasn't trying to be crude. In fact, my intention was the exact opposite. I said trigger words to get David to look. The power of suggestion, my friends.

I clenched my teeth as David, upon hearing me say each word, took inventory, slowly, methodically. Then like a lightbulb went on in his stupid-ass head, his eyes widened, perhaps opening the rest of the way, and he took a step backward, nearly colliding with a student rushing by.

"Yeah," he croaked and then coughed into his hand. "You're right. Everything's . . . perfect."

"And mine." I winked, stirring the pot of jealousy a bit more, trying to see how far I could push him while at the same time swelling with pride that for now, she was mine.

For now.

His head snapped in my direction. "I thought you guys were just seeing each other, nothing official."

"Made it official last night." I focused in on Blake's mouth as I brought her hand to my lips. "Right, sweet cheeks?"

Expecting Blake to nod and just go with it, I wasn't prepared for her to lean in and kiss my mouth, taking my head with both hands and forcing her tongue down my throat. But, not one to say no to kissing her, not ever, I kissed her back.

It ended too soon, once David cleared his throat.

"Sorry." Blake actually looked embarrassed as she tucked her hair behind her ears and then grabbed her sunglasses and forced them back on in one swift, sexy move. "It was just a really good night."

"It was," I said, leering.

"Well, good," David said a little too loud. "I'm happy for you, Blake. Really happy."

He looked anything but happy. In fact if that's what happy looked like, Blake was going to have the worst boyfriend in the history of boyfriends. The dude looked ready to puke all over us and burst into tears all at once.

"We should get going." I gave David a head nod and gripped Blake's hand as we left the building.

Once we reached the doors, I turned back to offer him my final acknowledgement, my final smirk. I knew he'd be staring at us, mainly her ass. He was, and when I gave him a challenging lift of my eyebrows, good ol' David gave me the finger.

"Hah!" I burst out laughing as I clutched Blake's hand tighter. "David's fun, isn't he?"

"What's got you in such a good mood?" she asked.

I didn't point out that she was swinging my arm and giggling with me. Damn, it just felt so natural, holding her hand, joking around.

"David flipped me off."

Her smile fell. "Seriously? That's kinda harsh, don't you think? Why would he do that?"

"Because his hands were free." I smiled down at her. "And mine"—I lifted our joined hands up—"weren't."

CHAPTER
TWENTY-ONE

Another three days went by. I expected to be finished with Blake in the next twenty-four hours. Not because I wanted to be done, but because I had to be done. Our client list was piling up, and Lex said if he had to kiss one more chick who tried to impale the back of his throat with her tongue, he was going to quit.

It was Saturday.

And David hadn't stopped calling or randomly dropping by to check the plumbing. Right. Good one, genius.

Hey can I look at your pipes?

What for?

To make sure they're clean of shit?

Some dudes really didn't know what the hell they were doing. At least come up with a good excuse the third time you drop by. I don't know, give yourself a flat tire, ask to use the phone, tell her you're dehydrated after your ten-mile run and need water.

But pipes?

Again?

She was going to be so bored with him. I knew it, and I hoped she was beginning to see it, but I had a promise to keep and a contract to shred once my job was done.

Then, and only then, would I sit back, let him crash and burn, then I'd swoop in and . . .

I hadn't really gotten to that part yet, ever.

I pulled up to Gabi and Blake's house and grabbed the snacks for our early spring barbecue out of the backseat. It was warm for March, around sixty-two degrees, meaning we wanted any excuse to be outside.

The door was already open when I glanced back at the house. A sexy-looking Blake was standing in the middle of the doorway, part of her stomach showing, compliments of her short white tank top and low-rise boyfriend jeans.

"Nice," I called out as I made my way toward her. "I like."

She turned in front of me, then blew me a kiss. "Good, because I haven't worn them in forever."

I walked past her and into the house, then she followed.

Out of nowhere, her smile fell and her eyes pooled with tears. Frowning, I dropped the groceries on the counter.

"Whoa, whoa, whoa." I gripped her face with my hands. "Hey, what's wrong?"

"It's, uh . . ." She gulped as a few tears splashed onto her cheeks. "He died two years ago today."

"Shit." I closed my eyes and pressed my forehead to hers. Then, without asking, I lifted her into my arms and hugged her.

Blake wrapped her arms around my neck in her typical choking fashion, but I didn't care. *Hold me tighter,* I wanted to say. Anything to make her feel better.

She sobbed for a few seconds before her body stopped shaking.

I set her on her feet but kept our bodies close. "I'm so sorry." I used my thumbs to wipe away the remaining tears from her puffy cheeks. "I know that doesn't make it better. Nothing I say will make it better. But I think he'd be proud of you. I can't imagine you growing up with some timid-assed brother who let you get away with anything." I squeezed her tighter. "You're an amazing woman. Funny, sweet, caring . . . There is nothing about you that I would change." I sighed. "You know, other than some of the clothing choices I'm sure he would have encouraged to keep all the guys at bay."

She burst out laughing. It was good to hear. Immediately, I relaxed.

"Yeah, he was . . ." She frowned. "Okay, don't take this the wrong way."

"I swear on guys everywhere if you say I remind you of him, you're going to see me freak out and do something stupid."

"As opposed to every other day?"

"Hey! I just comforted you. Now I'm stupid?"

A teasing smile lit up her face. "I wasn't going to say you were like my brother. Just that you tend to have a lot in common. He played football and was always trying to get me to jump out of my comfort zone. Thus, the jeans. I was wearing nothing but basketball shorts, and he finally told me I needed to start dressing like a girl. Shopping. It was one of the last things we did together before he died. I've never even worn half the clothes. I'm sure some are out of style, but"—her lower lip trembled—"I thought maybe if I tried . . . for him, you know?"

"Listen." I pressed a finger to her lips. "You are beautiful no matter what you wear. You could wear basketball shorts and those ugly-ass flip-flops every day of your life, and your brother would still be proud of you. I promise."

Tears filled her eyes again. "You think?"

"I know."

"How?"

"Because I'm proud of you. And I'm not easy to impress—you do know who I am, right?"

"Ian Hunter." She said my name with reverence. God above, I wanted to be worthy of the way she said my name.

"Guys," Gabi called from somewhere inside the house. "You just gonna stand there and eye-screw each other, or can we get the snacks?"

"Be right there," I yelled back, never taking my eyes off Blake. "Are you going to be okay?"

The light reflected off of her tearstained face. She was . . . beautiful. So beautiful it hurt. "As long as you stay."

"Done."

"Good." She reached for the bags, then blocked the door with her hand. "But I can't let you in unless you managed to get the chocolate Gabi and I begged for."

Sighing, I reached into one of the bags and pulled out two Hershey's Krackel bars. "You mean this chocolate?"

Blake swiped it from my hand and inhaled. "So good."

"Question." I leaned in. "If it was between me and a Krackel bar—"

"Krackel bar." She patted my shoulder. "Every time."

"Had to ask."

"Guys," Gabi yelled again.

"Coming!" we said in unison, making our way back through the house.

Gabi was in the kitchen prepping the hamburgers and hot dogs.

She frowned at us. "Blake, are you okay?" Her eyes fell on me in a crabby stare.

"Yeah." Blake touched her cheeks. "Let me just run upstairs real quick and get the mascara smudges."

I watched her run off.

Meaning I didn't duck and cover.

Gabi clocked me in the shoulder, then reared back like she was aiming for my face.

"What?" I stumbled back from her. "I didn't make her cry!"

Gabi didn't look convinced. "I told you to stay away from her!"

"And I did." I held up my hands in surrender. "Technically."

"Technically?"

"Shit, you have that look in your eyes again. Gabs, she likes David, I'm helping her with David. End of story."

"Did you have sex with her?"

"I wish," I grumbled.

Gabi frowned. "Wait, what?"

"Nothing. Hey, Lex is late—I'm going to go call him." I turned to leave but was tugged back by the loop in my jeans.

"Speak."

"Lex could be dead."

"Don't care."

"In a very serious accident, and we're running out of time."

"Out with it."

"Five seconds away from his last breath and you want me to gossip with you about my feelings?"

"Ian."

"Lex is dead. Hope you're happy."

Her grip on my jeans tightened, and then she tugged up.

"Whoa there." I jerked away from her and glanced behind me where the stairway was. "Okay, summarized version?"

She nodded and crossed her arms.

"I like her."

Gabi nodded more and then frowned. "Wait, that's it? That's the declaration I get after years of watching you screw everything with a pulse? You *like* her?"

"Yeah." For the first time in years, I felt myself heat with embarrassment.

"You. Like. Her." Gabi's voice was rising. I tried to shush her, but it was Gabi—that was like poking a grizzly. "Men are so stupid. Please tell me you didn't confess this out loud to her like a Facebook status. *I like Blake. Here's a picture of us. Oh, cool, five hundred shares.* Like we're in freaking HIGH SCHOOL!"

"KEEP YOUR VOICE DOWN!" I shouted.

"There we go!" Gabi slapped me on the shoulder. "A little passion. This is the first time you've admitted to liking anything in years!"

"Not true," I argued. "I adored that cute little gerbil you had."

"The one Lex killed? That gerbil?"

"Poor Arnold." I smirked. "Sore subject?"

"Bastard's going to get his balls cut off one of these nights, in his sleep."

"Don't sneak-approach him in his bed. He may think you want something you don't. And the last thing I need is to deal with Lex after he accidently grazes boob, only to realize it's yours. He'll cut off his hands, and I need his hands for my computer program and future lucrative business ideas."

"Back!" Blake bounced down the stairs.

Gabi gave me a look that said this was far from over before slowly unwrapping one of the Krackel bars and shoving the damn thing in her mouth.

"No sharing?" My eyebrows shot up.

"Nope," Gabi answered, mouth full of chocolate. "Get your own."

"I bought it."

"And we're poor college students, so . . ." Gabi grinned.

The front door slammed. Suddenly Lex appeared from the hall holding up two giant bags of groceries. "If you ever"—he swore violently—"and I do mean *ever*, send me to the store to get tampons again, I'm going to have sex in your bed with a complete stranger, take selfies, blow them up to poster size, and plaster them to your ceiling."

He dropped the bags onto the counter. A box of tampons fell out.

I smirked. "Errand boy."

"Suck it," Lex grumbled. "At least I know where they are. Last time Gabs sent you, you had to ask for directions, ended up hitting on the salesclerk, and never made it back to the house."

I stole a glance at Blake's expression. She was smiling, but it was forced, and suddenly all of my past bangs seemed more like past sins, past wrongs, something that made me less in her eyes.

"Thanks, man," I said under my breath.

"Any time." Lex rubbed his hands together. "Am I manning the grill, Gabs? Or did you grow a penis within the last twelve hours?"

Blake gave me a confused look.

I explained with a smirk. "Only boys can man the grill. It says so."

"Where?" Gabi asked, pulling the giant grill spatula from the drawer and hiding it behind her back.

"On the instructions when we're born," I said, faking a dumbfounded expression. "It's Life 101. Seriously, sometimes I wonder if you girls even went to elementary school."

Lex barked out a "hah," then stole the spatula from Gabi and marched outside with the plate of burgers and hot dogs.

"He's such a gem, that one," Gabi huffed out as she started pulling out all the condiments.

"A true gentleman," I said, just as a volleyball sailed toward my head. I barely ducked in time. "What the hell?"

Blake grinned. "You down for a little game, boy?"

Staggered, I stared at her dumbly. "Did you just call me . . . 'boy'?"

Another spike in my direction.

"That's it." I grabbed the ball and marched outside. "I didn't want to have to do this, but Blake, I was in the NFL—I can play all sports."

Lex coughed.

"Except golf."

He coughed again.

"And I think it's already been established that ice-skating shouldn't count."

Lex held up his hands, then went back to flipping burgers.

"Your serve." I bumped the ball in Blake's direction. "Ladies always first. I'm a gentleman on the court and in bed—lucky you."

"Oh wow. Thanks," Blake said sarcastically. "Let me just get comfortable." Her top came off.

I smelled something burning.

"Lex," I yelled. "Man the burgers. I got this!"

"Sorry." He turned back around.

I stared at her tan, muscled skin as she stretched her arms above her head and put her hair in a high ponytail. Her jeans were still on, but hanging so low on her hips a cop should ticket her. And the plain black sports bra just . . . for some reason . . . looked hot.

Damn hot.

"Ready?" she asked.

"Clearly someone's trying to cheat." I pointed at her stomach.

"Oh, this?" She shrugged. "Don't want to get sweat on my shirt. I'm sure you understand."

"Sure I do." I peeled my shirt off and tossed it onto the ground. "I understand perfectly."

I flexed what I'd been told on several occasions by numerous women, including a few professors, was my eight-pack.

Her eyes widened.

"Pissing match, party of two," Lex yelled.

Gabi came running.

Oh, good—an audience.

Chapter
Twenty-Two

"You know it's physically impossible to play one-on-one volleyball against me, right?" I smirked, tossing the ball into the air—once, twice—actually feeling a little sorry for her future loss. Maybe I'd buy her more chocolate, lessen the blow a bit.

"Sure. Okay." Blake's face was impassive. I couldn't read her at all. Was this what her opponents felt like all the time? My eyes narrowed. Not even a blink in my direction, or hesitation. Did she really think she was going to somehow beat me? For one, I towered over her; two, I was a guy; and three, I had balls, and I knew how to use them—well.

"Fine." I stretched my arms above my head, the ball traveling with me in my left hand. That's right, I was palming it.

Because I was a guy, and my hands were huge, and I could freaking spike it into her face so hard she'd probably need plastic surgery to get her nose fixed. But sure, yeah, let's play fair. "You can serve first."

"My money's on Blake," Gabi piped up from a lawn chair.

Lex closed the lid to the grill and pulled up a seat. With a snort, he pointed at me. "You do realize he was nominated for the Heisman, right?"

"Heisman Shmeisman," Blake teased as she bounced between her bare feet, her boobs joining in with the fun.

"Focus," Lex snapped.

"I am!"

Or at least I was trying. Really hard. To focus. Damn, they just never got old, did they?

"Twenty bucks says she knocks him out with the first spike," Gabi said in an amused tone.

"You've got yourself a bet." Lex shook her hand.

They were shaking hands. They were sitting next to each other, and World War III wasn't breaking out. I opened my mouth to comment just as Lex released her hand and rubbed it on his jeans.

"What? Afraid of girls now?" Gabi sneered.

"Just the ones who may be dudes." Lex nodded, then directed a pointed look at her crotch. "Hmm, I'm thinking fifty-fifty chance."

"Don't put it past me to dump lighter fluid on the barbecue."

"And burn down your own house?"

"Why else would I take out insurance?" Gabi said sweetly, smacking Lex in the arm, then grabbing his bicep and pinching.

Just kidding. All was right with the world.

"Are you ready?" Blake called.

"Yup." I tossed the ball into the air. "Service."

She returned with a simple bump, and I returned with a set. Really, it was kind of silly how slow the game was starting—

One minute, the ball was in the air floating in Blake's direction; the next, I was on my ass looking up at the sky and wondering if a tree branch had impaled itself in my neck.

"What the hell?" I croaked.

Blake stood over me, hands on hips. "Sorry, do you want me to warn you next time I spike it?"

"Nope." I grinned. "No mercy, huh?"

"Nope," she said in the same way I had.

With a coy smile, she offered her hand. I slapped it away and got to my feet under my own power. "Don't get pissed if I break your face."

"Likewise," she fired back, tossing the ball over the net.

"Careful, man." Lex laughed. "She's got a strong arm."

"You think?" I said.

Gabi kept silent. Smart girl.

"What is it?" I asked. "One to nothing?"

Blake blew me a kiss.

"That's it." I tossed the ball into the air and spiked it as hard as I could. She returned it just before it kissed the grass, causing the ball to float over the net. Cake. I jumped up to spike it down, but she blocked my shot, causing the ball to fall back onto my side. Quickly I stumbled backward and just barely caught it with my fist, bumping it up over to her side.

I let out a sigh of relief when it bounced on the grass.

"Aw . . ." I winked at Blake. "Next time, sport."

Her indifference shattered, Blake's face went from calm to "I may kill you in your sleep, then feed your intestines to the neighborhood cats."

I took a cautious step back.

"My serve." Her hips swayed as she moved back toward her side. "Service."

The ball came careening over the net like a bullet train. I had to dive to get underneath it, and even then it just barely grazed over the net.

We volleyed back and forth three times before she finally tipped it over and scored.

For the next hour, that was exactly how it went. We continued to volley back and forth while Gabi and Lex stuffed their faces. Neither of us wanted to quit, and every time one of us got to game point, the other was right behind. And Gabi said that the winner had to win by two, not one.

It was nearing ninety minutes.

I was hot as hell.

Starved.

And losing by one.

"Concede," Gabi shouted. "She's got you!"

"Never!" I jabbed a finger at Blake. "What if I let you win?"

"I'll know."

"Hmm."

"Besides"—she batted those damn eyelashes—"you're too competitive to lose that way."

Damn it. I took my stance and waited. So far, all of her serves had been brutal. Come morning, I would probably look like J. J. Watt had bitch-slapped me in the face—repeatedly.

The ball came flying over the net toward my left. I tried to move, but my knee caught, and the aching I'd been feeling for the past few weeks turned into full-blown bone-splitting agony. With a cry, I fell to the ground, my face slamming into the dirt and grass as the throbbing intensified.

It hurt too badly for embarrassment to be a factor. Shit.

"Oh shit." Lex called, and then he was at my side. "You okay?"

Damn, it hurt. Why did it have to hurt so much? Oh, right. Because I was missing some key tendons and ligaments, and a few metal rods were the only thing keeping my bones in place.

"Ian!" Blake stumbled to my side, her eyes wild with panic. "What happened? Do we need to go to the hospital?"

"No, no, no." I winced as I tried to sit up and stretch my leg out. Normally it was the only thing that helped. Well, that and pain pills, but I refused to take anything I could possibly get addicted to. "I'm fine."

Blake pulled up my jeans and started running her hands up and down the side of my left knee.

"But"—I cleared my throat—"that makes it feel so much better."

"Yeah, he's okay." Gabi rolled her eyes. "Come on Lex, let's go get an ice pack."

"Yeah, Lex." A smile spread across my face. "Run along."

He didn't argue. Probably because he knew I hated it when anyone hovered over me, or fussed, or just extended their concern or pity. It reminded me too much of that day; hell, it reminded me of that week, that month. Thirty days of hospital visits, surgeries, teammates with sad eyes that basically conveyed the truth I already knew, despite the doctors' optimism. I was done.

I would never play again.

"Here." Blake pulled her hand away from my knee and stood, then helped me to my feet. "Think you can limp over to the chair?"

I bit out a curse as I tried to put weight on the leg. It was still as sore as an abscessed tooth, but not so much that I was going to have to get it checked out. I'd experienced this type of pain before, when I tweaked my knee during box jumps. I knew it would go away, after an ungodly amount of anti-inflammatories and beer.

Body slick with sweat, I hobbled over to the plastic lawn chair and sagged into it with a sick thud, my legs sticking to my jeans, my jeans sticking to the chair, and sweat still dripping down my back.

Blake kneeled in front of me and frowned. "You need to take your pants off."

"I'm naked underneath."

"I'll close my eyes."

"I'm not taking my pants off and making a sweaty ass-mark on the plastic. I'm fine. I swear."

She didn't look convinced as she felt my knee from outside my jeans, her fingers lightly touching the swollen spot on the outer left, the spot where bone tended to still rub on bone. Some days, I could swear I still felt it.

Working out probably wasn't the wisest course of action, but my doctor had said I couldn't hurt myself worse. That was the good news. *Hey, kid, I know you've known only football your entire life, and I might have to amputate, but the good news is, you aren't dead!*

Might as well have been.

"It's starting to swell." Blake pressed a little too hard, sending renewed pulses of hot agony up my leg.

A hiss of pain escaped from between my lips.

She winced. "Sorry."

"Ice pack." Gabi opened the screen door and tossed a gel-filled blue blob at Blake. She caught it midair and placed it on my knee.

"I'm going to reheat the food," Gabi said. "Lex ran to the store to get some ibuprofen, since we're out."

"Thanks, Gabs," I called back, the cool pack already easing my searing torture.

"Yup." The door slammed behind her.

Blake didn't move from her position in front of me. Her eyes held worry. "What happened to your knee?"

"Easy." I leaned my sticky back against the chair and glanced up into her pretty wide eyes. "Some cocky topless chick tried to kill me."

"I'm not topless." She crossed her arms.

A groan escaped through my lips as my gaze zeroed in on her chest. "I stand corrected." I reached out and grazed my hand against her bare stomach. "Semitopless."

"I didn't mean, what happened just right now, where I literally handed you your own ass." She sat on the deck in front of me and hugged her knees. "I stopped following football after"—she shrugged—"after my brother. It was too hard."

"I get that." I exhaled loudly. "Believe me, I do."

"So?"

"Can you keep a secret?" I leaned forward just as she leaned forward, her eyes narrowing into tiny slits. Hah, she was already calling my bullshit. I loved it.

"Yes."

"I saved the life of two old ladies as they crossed the road. Didn't even see the cars coming. Did I mention they had cats with them? And

I managed to save all four lives. Possibly five, if you count the chicken that was crossing the road at the exact same time. The car ran me over. And well . . . they gave me the keys to the city . . ."

"Wow, just a regular crime fighter, aren't you?"

I nodded slowly, then crooked my finger. "So here's the secret part."

"I'm ready."

"I'm Superman."

Her eyebrows shot up as a patronizing smile appeared across her soft features, momentarily stealing my breath away. "Is that so?"

"Cross my heart." I winked. "Why else would my best friend, also known as my nemesis, be named Lex? I'll understand if you want proof. My cape's back in my room. Wanna see?"

"Superman had his cape on at all times."

"Right. The one I'm currently sporting's invisible, like my super-human sight. The only way to unlock your human eyes to my godlike strength is to have sex with me."

"Hah. And you were doing so well."

"Hey!" I held up my hands. "I don't make the rules, sweet cheeks. I'm just a regular run-of-the-mill hero."

"He really is," Gabi said. How long had she been standing there? "That poor little boy would have died. Can you imagine what that would have done to that father? After losing his wife? It was amazing, Ian. Don't sell yourself short. You saved his life, at the risk of losing yours. I still can't get over the phone call from Lex when he said to get to the hospital. They said you were hemorrhaging, and—"

"That's enough, Gabs," I said softly, though something that felt a hell of a lot like anger was burning me from the inside out, making me want to escape. But with a bum leg, all I could do is sit there and listen to her paint me out to be the hero I knew I'd never be.

Yeah. I'd saved that kid's life.

Yeah. They called me a hero.

But what kind of selfish prick's first thought after he sees his team-mates go to the Super Bowl is "I should have let the car hit him"?

"The drug dealer has returned." Lex burst into the yard and tossed a pill bottle into my hands.

"Don't you mean Lex Luthor?" Blake laughed, easing some of the tension. Her hand reached for mine and locked on.

She didn't let go.

She *should* have let go.

Because something, in that moment, snapped into focus. Even Gabi wasn't aware of the demons that still haunted me, but something told me Blake was more than aware of what it would be like to lose the very thing that had been holding you together your entire life.

Losing football was more than losing my identity.

Some days, it felt like I'd lost my soul.

"Gabs . . ." Blake cleared her throat. "Is the food ready?"

"Oh!" Gabi shot to her feet. "Sorry, guys, yeah—the plates are inside. You want to eat out here or at the table?"

"Outside," Blake and I said in unison.

Gabi was silent, like she was examining both of us and about ready to come up with some stupid conclusion about the reason we were both acting funny. Thank God for Lex.

"Woma-an," Lex growled. "Stop being"—he shoved her toward the door—"you. Just for, like, two seconds. Food. It's only food. *They* want to eat outside, we let them eat outside. Also, you promised pie. I don't smell any pie."

"Correction. I said I'd *buy* you pie, not bake one for you. If you want to marry your mother, just do it, Lex."

"It better be apple," he grumbled before the screen door slammed behind him. He returned quickly with both of our plates and whispered under his breath, "I'll take care of the terrorist, but you owe me."

"Thanks, man." I laughed as he disappeared back into the house and screamed, "Stella!"

CHAPTER

TWENTY-THREE

We finished our food in silence. The painkillers were starting to kick in, making it easier to enjoy my meal without grimacing every time I shifted my leg. Layered clouds in pinks and reds streamed across the sky.

"It's getting late." Blake took my plate into the house and returned with a giant piece of pie.

"I think"—I took the plate from her and basically shoved half the pie in my mouth before finishing my thought—"I may get hurt again if this is the response I get."

"Hah." Her eyes homed in on my mouth. "You have some . . . apple . . ."

"Saving it."

"Then it's in the perfect spot, Superman."

"God, I'd kill for a woman to call me that in bed."

"How about you lie on your bed . . ."

A smile so wide it hurt spread across my face.

"With your clothes on . . ."

The dream popped, and my smile left. I pointed a finger at her. "You're no fun."

She smirked. "And when I call you Superman, you pretend that it's because of your amazing sexual skills and not the fact that you really are a hero."

"Not a hero." The pie suddenly went dry in my throat, and I had to work to get it down. "I think that's the worst part. People called me a hero, still do sometimes. It makes me feel . . . guilty. And pretty unworthy. Here I am, bitter about not being able to play football, and the kid could have died."

"In a way," Blake said, her voice just above a whisper, "*you* sort of did."

I jerked my head in her direction. "What did you say?"

She took my plate and sighed, her shoulders hunching a bit, like she did when she felt nervous or embarrassed. "You lost part of what made you you. That would be like me working my entire life to go to the Olympics for volleyball, only to get hurt the day before the plane was supposed to take off."

"Yeah." I swallowed the giant ball of sadness lodged in my throat. "I've worked past it, you know? I don't want you to think I'm one of those broken guys still stuck in the glory days of 'if only I'd been able to stay in the NFL.'" I shrugged. "I dealt with that particular feeling for one day. When the Hawks went to the Super Bowl for the second time. And then, I was just . . . over it. All of it. I wished I hadn't saved the little boy, I wished I was a more selfish person, or slower." I laughed and shook my head.

"What made you get over it?"

I looked up. "He stopped by the hospital that very next day."

Blake leaned in. Damn, I wanted to swim in the depths of those eyes. She was just so . . . open. "And?"

"I called him by his last name—Montgomery, or Little Monty. He was really little. Apparently still afraid of the dark . . . He, um, brought me his stuffed bear, very smartly named Bear."

Blake laughed, her eyes filling with tears.

"His mom had passed away from cancer earlier that year. It was the first father-son outing he and his dad had gone on since her death. She gave him the bear exactly twelve hours before she breathed her last breath. He was a guard bear, Monty said, and he was supposed to keep him from being afraid." I gulped. "He said it was a bravery bear."

A tear spilled over onto Blake's cheek.

"He gave it to me, said he didn't need it anymore because he had me. But that I might need it since I still had another surgery." I sighed, trying to keep the emotion from my voice. "That damn bear lives the high life in my room, let me tell ya."

Blake laughed softly. "And Monty?"

"Monty's going to be one badass football player one day." I chuckled. "His dad sends me his practice and game schedule. I've been to a few of his practices, which basically means his friends think he's way cooler than he really is. Or so he says."

"So"—Blake leaned forward—"moral of the story . . . you really are Superman."

"Hah!" I laughed. "To one person, yes."

"Two," she corrected. "And sometimes, that's all that matters, isn't it?"

"Yeah," I croaked out. "I think so."

She moved closer, and I captured her lips with mine as her arm wrapped around my neck. I massaged my tongue against hers, savoring her sweet taste.

The light above us flicked on.

We broke apart like two kids on curfew.

"Guys?" Gabi poked her head out the screen door. "You up for a movie?"

"Sure thing." I didn't take my eyes off Blake.

"You think you can make it?" Her lips were still wet from my kiss. I had to look away before I did something stupid. Again.

"Sure." I stood on my good leg. "I'll just lean heavily on my badass opponent. I claim rematch by the way."

"Wouldn't expect anything less." She pressed her body up against mine as we awkwardly made our way into the house.

Lex yelled at Gabi that she picked the movie last time.

They stopped arguing when we made it into the living room.

"You guys." Gabi scrunched up her nose. "No. Just not happening. Shower, or no couch time."

"Gabs," I whined. "I smell awesome. I always smell awesome. Tell 'em, Blake."

Blake glanced up at me with guilty eyes. "You smell like . . . grass."

"Well, you smell like . . . dirt."

Lex burst out laughing. "Good one, man. You gonna make mud pies later or—?"

I flipped him off. "Fine, we'll go shower."

"Not together!" Gabi frowned.

"Don't worry." Blake laughed. "I'm more of an archvillain type of girl. Who wants the hero when he won't even get her dirty?"

I stumbled against her and nearly face-planted the wall with my mouth while Lex howled with laughter.

"You got my number, baby," Lex called, then started yelping. "Ow, stop scratching me like a damn cat!"

I suppressed a smile. Gabi had most likely attacked him with her nails. She was good with those things.

Blake went up ahead of me. I followed, hopping up one stair at a time and using the railing for help.

I purposely bumped into her once we reached the top of the stairway, and whispered in her ear, "Heroes get dirty too, sweet cheeks. It feels so good it must be bad."

An erratic pulse beat in her neck as she leaned back against me. Like a heat-seeking missile, my mouth found it and settled there. The ragged throb against my lips gave my body vivid ideas. My mouth was just getting used to the idea of marking her when the doorbell rang.

"Ignore it," I hissed, my teeth nipping at her neck while my mouth sucked hard. She let out a little moan, her hands blindly reaching behind her. Not that she had to reach or feel far. I was right there with her, hard, waiting, straining against my jeans just to feel her.

"Hey, is Blake here?"

It was David.

Blake froze, her hands slowly returning to her sides.

As I slowly deflated.

And the moment was gone.

"Hey, Blake?" Gabi called up the steps. "David's here to see you!"

I stepped out of Blake's way, and with a voice I didn't even recognize, I said, "Well? What are you waiting for?"

Indecision crossed her features, followed by hurt, as she stepped away from me and ran down the stairs.

"What the hell am I doing?" I muttered under my breath, aching for her touch. And not just for the release.

For her.

CHAPTER
TWENTY-FOUR

The bastard stayed for the movie. Best part? Because of my leg, I couldn't really maneuver myself in between them, and because my job was technically to bow out and let him have the girl once he passed the last few stages, I was stuck anyway.

At least his excuse was better this time.

He was asking her out.

Technically, it was a dinner date with him and his dad. Apparently, they all went way back. If I had to hear one more story about how Blake and David built their own damn tree house, I was going to shit a brick and knock him out with it.

So far, I hadn't noticed any sly movements from him. He didn't glare at me, didn't flip me off again. If anything, he was trying to be too nice. Something wasn't quite right, but it took me a while to put my finger on it.

Befriending the enemy.

I knew it well.

Because in the end, it would prove to the girl that the guy wasn't really jealous anymore, he just wanted her happiness above all else, blah, blah, mother-effing blah.

And the real catch? No matter the girl, she always—and I do mean always—believed the guy she was after, because he seemed to be the one who practiced more self-control, whereas my job had always been to push that control so that the girl got noticed. True colors are very rarely shown during the courting phase—I knew that better than anyone. He was putting his best foot forward, capitalizing on whatever weaknesses he saw in me.

I had never cared until now.

Now it just seemed unfair that by being good at my job, I was losing someone I really liked.

"I'm going to make some popcorn." I stood.

"But your leg," Blake said.

At least she was still concerned. Though she didn't stand to join me, so I wasn't sure how far that concern stretched. She was freshly showered, her mop of wet brown hair was tied into a knot on her head, and she was sporting a loose-fitting tank top that revealed way too much cleavage. Something good ol' David noticed right away.

"I can limp." Jealousy surged through me as I noticed David's hand on her thigh. I needed to get out of there. Fast. "It's only a few feet."

Amongst everyone's protests, I made it into the kitchen, bracing myself against the countertop.

After a few seconds of inhaling and exhaling like I was a newborn babe and just learning how my lungs worked, I reached for the snack cupboard and pulled out a bag of microwave popcorn, just as footsteps sounded in the kitchen doorway.

"Blake, I'm fine. Go watch the movie."

"Not Blake." David's deep voice jolted me out of my pity party.

With a very forced, sly smile, I pressed "Start" on the microwave and turned around. "Something I can help you with?"

"I get it." He nodded. "She's yours for now. But we have history. Something you can't compete with. Not now, not ever."

"Aw, shucks, how will I ever compete with the tree house?" I tapped my fingers against my chin. "I bet the fact that I have a bigger dick helps."

David took a menacing step toward me, his fists clenched. "If you touch her, I swear I'll—"

"Make a fist?" I pointed down at his hands. "Dude, I get it. You can't have her, so now you want her. But she's not yours. She won't ever be yours. Not unless you kill me, which you're welcome to try now that it's a fair fight and I only have one leg."

"You smug bastard." He sneered, all politeness gone from his countenance, like he'd peeled back a mask and revealed that he wasn't exactly what he seemed. "What the hell does she see in you?"

"Oh, I'm sorry. I thought we already went over this. Should I just take off my pants and show you? Heard you may be into dudes, but I wasn't sure it was true until now." I was trying to goad him, push his buttons, and see if, maybe, just maybe, good ol' David wasn't as good as we suspected.

David's chest brushed mine like he was ready to body-slam me back against the kitchen counter, then pummel my face in. He could try. He would fail, but he could try. A good fight was just what I needed.

I'd never pushed any of my clients' love interests this far, never made it about me, or took it this seriously.

Because, up until that point, I didn't realize I'd been fighting him. But I was. I was fighting him.

No. I shook my head. "You don't deserve her. You never will."

"And you think you do? A washed-up has-been who can't keep it in his pants?"

"No," I answered quickly. "I won't ever deserve her either, but at least I know it. At least I wake up with absolute certainty that I'm the lucky one."

"Hey . . ." Blake strolled into the kitchen, her sweats riding low on her hips, revealing a tease of tan skin. "Wasn't aware making popcorn took this much brainpower."

"Yeah, well, all those drugs in my teen years fried mine, so David offered his help, but he was struggling to read the word 'Start' on the microwave. Thank God you're here now." I smiled smugly at the dude while he forced a similar smile on his face, then backed way off.

"I gotta run, Blake." He reached for her and kissed her head. "Next Thursday night, seven—don't forget. Dad's really excited to see you."

"Great." She beamed as he left the kitchen.

Her expression went from elated to detached. "I think I'm going to head to bed."

"Blake—"

"What?" She was turned away from me. "What do you want, Ian?"

You. That's what I should have said. Instead, I opened my mouth and nothing came out.

"That's what I thought." She snorted. "Just know, I may not be here by the time you figure it out."

The microwave dinged.

"Yeah." I leaned back against the counter. "That's what I'm afraid of."

CHAPTER
TWENTY-FIVE

"I hate mornings." Lex let out a loud yawn and e-mailed me the client list for the next two weeks.

"You always say that." I lifted my cup to my lips and sipped while I scrolled through the list. "What the hell is this?"

"A swap." His face was serious. "I wasn't sure you could pull off the more difficult ones, so I gave you the clients who should only take a few days. Besides, you're still balls-deep with Blake."

"I wish," I muttered.

"Hah." Lex rolled his eyes. "Poor bastard. Can't plow the field or even get close to it, hmm?"

"Close enough." I ignored the blatant stares in our direction. Girls. Sometimes there were just too many of them. Damn, if I closed my eyes I could still feel Blake's fingers grazing the front of my jeans. Her nimble hands just needed to reach a bit farther.

I was nearly arching off the bench when my text alert went off. Shit.

```
Blake: FREAKING OUT!
Ian: Inside voice. Lex can hear you, and
     he hates mornings.
Blake: Dinner date this week--his dad
       bailed. It's just us. I've never been
       on a date.
```

My stomach recoiled. "Well, shit."

"Something wrong?" Lex glanced up from his phone, thankfully missing the giant erection I was sporting by just thinking about Blake. I'd never hear the end of it if he thought her texts were enough to get me going.

"Yeah." I sighed and sent a text back to Blake. "I've gotta fake a date with Blake so she doesn't puke all over David."

"So what?"

So I'll wish it was real. That's what, jackass.

For once, my brain and my body were in complete agreement.

"Nothing. Just . . . a lot on my mind."

Good timing that a girl with a huge rack just happened to mosey on past us, gaining Lex's attention, and adoration. He barked out, "I know exactly what you mean."

Two weeks ago I would have waved the girl over and then proceeded to bend her over as fast as possible, preferably against the closest and most sturdy object I could find. But now? The idea of sex did nothing for me. Her fake tits were just that: fake. Her smile was the same. And, damn, did every stupid girl really have to wave with all five fingers? It was like she was wiggling worms in my direction and I was a bird just waiting to take a bite.

The girl stopped midstride, turned, and eyed both me and Lex in a come-hither stare that had Lex sucking in a deep breath and standing. "I'd ask if you wanna join, but something tells me you won't be able to get it up."

I guess that made Lex the peacock in this scenario.

"Funny." I snorted. "Try to let her down easy afterward, Lex."

"Please." He started walking away, and his ridiculous swagger had its desired effect. The girl checked him out, then started breathing way heavier than necessary for doing nothing but standing with her mouth hanging open. "I always do. And when that doesn't work, I just give them a fake phone number."

"You're such a good guy. Seriously," I called after him. "A saint!"

"Hear that?" he said, approaching the girl. "I'm a saint. Care to confess your sins?"

I choked on my laugh as I pulled out my phone and sent a text back to Blake.

Ian: I'll be at your house tonight at 6.
    Have Gabs help you get ready. What she
    says goes. No arguing.

Blake: But her idea of a date includes
    very tight dresses.

Ian: I'm sorry, were you trying to
    tease me? Make my mouth water while
    simultaneously seeing if you're good
    at flirting via text? What's the
    problem?

Blake: They're tight!

Ian: And?

Blake: I can't eat in tight dresses.

Ian: Try.

Blake: But . . .

Ian: You want my help or not? I'm your love
    coach. Stop being so argumentative.
    Oh, and wear your hair up.

Blake: Fine, but if I end up passing out
     because I can't eat anything out of
     the bread basket, I'm blaming you.

I sighed, and with a smile texted her back.

Ian: Might be worth it, to see your tight
     ass in a tight dress with your tight
     tits and tight . . . Oh, I'm sorry,
     lost track of where I was going with
     that.
Blake: You really are a pig.
Ian: Teacup. Don't forget.

She didn't text back after that, and I had work to do if I was going to pull off the perfect date. My heart raced in my chest as I quickly searched through my catalog of restaurants. Oh shit. It wasn't a real date. It was a fake date. I'd done it a million times. I liked to call this one the "Let's get it all out of your system" play. You do a practice run with the chick before her first date with the guy she really likes; that way, she doesn't have any surprises. Most girls build up the date so much in their minds that they can't relax enough to eat a leaf of lettuce, let alone hold a conversation. Lex and I figured that if we made the practice date feel as real as possible and added in possible scenarios—basically doing a test run before the big game—it would help ease their nerves and make them less likely to choke on a peanut or accidently snort while laughing.

Even though it wasn't a real date, the smile wouldn't leave my cocky-ass face.

Well, that was new.

I scrolled through the restaurants, but nothing sounded good or even remotely interesting. Blake wasn't the type of girl you wanted to impress with expensive prices and pretentious company. She genuinely liked food, and I imagined she'd probably yell at me if I took her someplace where the idea of food was one carrot with balsamic drizzled over it.

My stomach growled at the thought. I don't care what guys think girls want; there is nothing sexy about a chick eating a lettuce leaf while chugging a vodka soda.

First off, the lettuce almost always gets stuck somewhere, usually between the front four teeth, and the vodka soda gets them tipsy so fast that by the time you want to order dessert, they've already lifted their foot underneath the table and tried to get you off with their big toe.

Not gonna lie, it's happened a dozen or few times. Meaning I know what small amounts of food and large amounts of alcohol do to the dumb ones. And the sad ones are no better. If anything, it's worse, because they're too nervous to drink, spill water all over you, and when the night's over, when you've finally finished coaching them on why it's smart to eat rather than starve themselves all day, they're suddenly ravenous.

I had one chick steal a couple's bread basket.

Another ordered so many desserts she puked on me.

Hmm. I continued scrolling through my phone and grinned when I found the perfect place. It would be . . . interesting, that's for sure.

Lex let out a loud laugh. I glanced up and wasn't surprised at all that Big Tits was already fondling his ass and whispering sweet nothings into his ear. Twenty bucks he was doing chem homework in his head while she touched him. Another hundred that during sex, he'd be organizing his notes for his test. Sometimes I wondered why he even bothered.

He was a bastard. But I loved him.

A week ago, I would have given him a high five.

Now, it just felt . . . sad. A bit empty.

I heard more laughter from Lex as they sauntered off.

I needed to clear my head, and fast. Lex said I had another chick who was meeting me in a few minutes, but she'd yet to show, and typically if they were going to show, new clients were really early, spying the bench, waiting, watching, in the creepiest of ways.

But today? I had shit to do. So I quickly glanced around the area, left to right, right to left. Bingo!

Aw, poor sad, confused single woman wearing Keds, ripped boy-friend jeans, and a white T-shirt. Shit, was that a red headband? Was it the Fourth of July? Damn, at least bring a hot dog if you're going to dress like a barbecue.

You, I mouthed at her, then crooked my finger.

She paled, looked behind her, then back at me.

"Yes." I nodded. "You."

She looked behind her again.

Oh good Lord.

Was I seriously going to have to get up?

Finally, after a few minutes of hesitation, she hung her head and shuffled toward me.

When her small body cast a shadow over the bench, I leaned back and took inventory.

A-line haircut. Brown hair. Cute body, but very small, almost pixie-like. Zero self-confidence, considering she was hunched, and something about the way she dressed told me she didn't actually dress herself, meaning her confidence had never been . . . poured into, if you will.

My bet was . . . she was still hiding underneath the shadow of her mom and was ready to break free and live. It was in the way she carried herself, the way she dressed, very prim and proper, like she was ready to go to Sunday dinner instead of class.

Too bad her parents were . . . hmm, I was guessing . . . local.

"You live on campus?" I asked.

She shook her head no.

"Still with the 'rents, huh?"

A small nod.

"You have friends?"

She nodded vigorously.

"They live on campus?"

Another nod that had me feeling like I was pulling teeth.

"Great . . . Are you poor?"

Frowning, she finally lifted her head so I could see her deep-green eyes. "No."

Thank God. It spoke.

"Good." I stood but quickly backed away, since she literally only came up to the middle of my chest. "Your first assignment is to tell the parents you're moving out. The next is to find housing on campus or near campus. Cut the apron strings . . ." I tilted my head. "What's your name?"

"Who are you?" She frowned. "I'm supposed to meet—" And she clammed up again.

I held out my hand. "Name's Ian Hunter. I'm your new wingman."

She stared at my hand, then placed hers across it, shaking it in such a wimpy, weird way that I shivered a bit.

"Assignment number two." I gripped her hand hard. "Guys like soft bodies, not soft handshakes. Shake my hand the way you'd"—I coughed—"*shake my hand.*"

"What?"

"To quote a popular song, guys want 'a lady in the streets but a freak in the bed.' Judging by your shaking skills, I'm assuming you wouldn't know the first thing about handling any part of me in bed. Firm grip, always important. Guys read into shit like that. I'll send you the schedule later. Look over the information packet Lex sent you, and be sure to fill out the questionnaire. No calling. Only texting and e-mailing. Gotta run."

"But—"

"Nice meeting you . . . ?"

"Vivian," she yelled, a smile curving her lips.

I saluted and jogged off.

CHAPTER TWENTY-SIX

"It can't be that bad," I said through the door. My forehead was about to get a splinter if Blake didn't hurry up.

"It is." Her words were muffled. "It's . . . very bad."

"Bad as in so bad I may keep you locked in your room with me inside? Or bad as in the guy who works at Asian Fusion, the one with the unibrow, would reject your V card?"

"Bert?"

"His name is Bert?" I laughed.

"He's supernice," Blake said loudly, and then she cursed. Something hit the door, and it creaked open, revealing one hand, with fuchsia nail polish painted flawlessly across the nails.

Rolling my eyes, I pushed the door open. Blake stumbled back. The first thing I saw was hair. Tons of thick, wavy, glorious I-may-actually-sell-Lex-so-Blake-can-move-in-with-me hair.

"Damn," I muttered, reaching out for her. "You wore it down." It was a statement of appreciation.

Blake took another cautious step back. Her eyes were smoky, not overdone, just perfect, her lips, a pale shade of pink.

The dress was black.

And to her credit, it was tight.

I'd never been a fan of knit dresses; they reminded me of grand-mothers who crocheted on the porch, and that visual was enough to make sure nobody ended the night on a satisfied note.

But on Blake?

This knit dress was . . . stunning.

The dress hugged every curve of her body, just barely covering her ass. It was sleeveless, with a higher neck than I usually like to see, but when she turned, I saw that it was completely open in the back. Have mercy, I loved the girl's back.

I braced myself against the door. "Are you sure you wanna go out tonight?"

Blake stopped midturn, pressing her hands down the fabric cur-rently mating with her thighs. "Is it that bad?"

"Yes," I growled, closing the distance between us. "It's . . . horrific. Ugly, terrible. Gross. How could you possibly attract men in this"—my hands roamed from her arms all the way down to her hips, and then I couldn't help it and just pulled her against me—"monstrosity?"

"Monstrosity, huh?" She let out a breathy laugh. "Is that why you keep staring at it? It's like a car accident you can't look away from?"

"You've got one thing right." I massaged her hips with the pads of my thumbs. "I literally can't look away. Not sure if I'm even capable of it."

"Date." She stepped out of my embrace. "Remember? This is a fake date so I don't make a complete fool out of myself when David and I go out this Thursday.

"Who dates on a Thursday?" I griped. "Dating on a Thursday's like ordering from the early-bird menu or bringing a coupon."

"Ian"—Blake waved in front of my face—"that's why you're upset? Because I'm going out with him on a Thursday?"

"Yes," I said slowly, blinking even slower, trying to come up with a better reason why she shouldn't go out with him, one that didn't include me being twisted in jealous knots or possibly falling head over heels onto my ass for the girl. "I hate Thursdays the way Lex hates mornings. Nothing good ever happens on Thursdays."

"Oh, really?" Blake grabbed a small, slinky black clutch and put it under her arm. It looked perfect there, way better than the giant Caboodle-looking thing I noticed lurking in the corner. Holy shit. Was that a sticker?

I pointed at the Caboodle.

"Ignore that." She smacked my hand, but I couldn't help it. Like a tractor beam, it pulled me toward it.

"This is amazing," I whispered reverently. "Almost better than the shoes."

"Ha ha." Blake tugged my arm. "You were saying? Thursdays?"

"Easy." I flipped open the lid to the Caboodle. I was imagining myself as Captain Jack Sparrow, discovering hidden treasure, when an honest-to-God banana barrette popped out to greet me. "I judge days of the week based on TV shows. Nothing good is ever on Thursdays. Believe me. In a very weird twist of fate, *TV Guide* is more of a life guide. Hey, look, more scrunchies."

"Okay." Blake tugged me away as I tried to grab at the giant white—yes, white—scrunchie, but her grip was too damn strong. "Show-and-tell is over."

"You would make a killing on eBay." I got to my feet. "And because you showed me"—I glanced back—"that, I'll take you on this fake date so that you can have a blast on Thursday and gain true love's first kiss."

"Not really . . . my first kiss . . . now." She stumbled over the words a bit.

Tension pounded between us, like a heart that was beating outside my chest. I wanted to kiss her again, taste her . . . forever.

"Ian?" Blake broke the mood. "Don't we have reservations?"

"Yes." I swallowed and offered my arm. "From the minute we leave the house, imagine it's a real date. I'm going to coach you, you'll listen carefully rather than take notes, and hopefully by Thursday"—I'll hear that David was in a tragic accident where he loses all use of his penis—"you'll be confident in your abilities to woo the one you want."

"Okay." Blake huffed out a nervous laugh. "And you promise I look okay?"

"No, Blake." I lifted her hand to my lips and pressed a kiss to the inside of her wrist. "You look phenomenal."

She blushed bright red.

"And if that bastard doesn't come out and say those exact words or better ones—hell, if he doesn't write you a sonnet—he's undeserving, got it?"

"Okay." Blake jerked her hand away and crossed her arms. "So where's my sonnet, Ian?"

"Damn you for listening *too* carefully." I winked and led her down the stairs and out into the brisk night air. "Fair lady of . . . black," I said in my loudest voice. "Beauty you do not lack."

"Ohhh, now you're rhyming."

I laughed and opened her door. "But treasure these words when we part." I tilted her chin toward me. "I will always keep you safe"—what the hell was I saying?—"in my heart."

Her mouth dropped open.

I wish I could say I just thought of that shit in my sleep.

I didn't.

I never had.

I was a doer, not a talker.

Hell in a freaking handbasket, I was pretty sure I'd just written my first love poem, to a girl who wasn't even my date, a few days before I was supposed to encourage her to walk off into the sunset with some other douche.

"That was nice, Ian." She cupped my cheek.

I jerked back. "Yeah, well, you know me. Nice is what I'm good at when there's something I want."

Her smile faded.

Asshole, party of one? Oh, look, a table!

～

"Okay, it's time for me to break down the rules of dating. You'll note that in the playbook this is labeled 'Sex God Ian's Rules for a Successful First Date.'"

Blake rolled her eyes. "Funny, because when I glanced at the play-book this morning it specifically said 'Ian's Rules for a Successful First Date.'"

"Hmm, must not have given you the updated copy."

"Yeah, that must be it." She let out an airy laugh that by all means should have floated right out the window rather than hitting me square in the face, stealing the air from my lungs and making me want to burn my own playbook, forget the rules, and just keep her to myself.

"Rule number one." I started driving toward campus, trying to shake thoughts of Blake on top of me out of my head. "Never touch a man's stereo. I don't care if he has a thing for Enya and you're ready to catapult yourself from a moving vehicle. Music is not a deal breaker, unless you make it a deal breaker. If he asks you what you want to listen to, always default to what's already playing, got it?"

Blake was silent and then, seriously, like she hadn't been listening at all, touched the controls and changed the station to techno.

"What the hell," I yelled.

"Not buying it," she shouted back as the music got louder. "You listen to classical?"

"Sometimes," I lied. Really, I only kept classical music on because studies showed it helped women relax when in a tense situation, and since I usually helped the girls who weren't the most confident, I figured if Mozart worked on pregnant moms, it would work on college girls.

"But this"—Blake laughed and pointed at the radio; "Beautiful Now" by Zedd was blaring through my speakers, making my ass vibrate with the bass—"is way better. Admit it. Stop being an ass, and wave your hands around like you just don't care, yo."

"Wow. Okay." I burst out laughing. "First off, you're white—sorry to break it to you. Second, if a dude was hard of hearing and only had his sight and was freaking color-blind, he'd know you were white based on the fact that you honestly just thrust your arms into the air while simultaneously sticking your tongue out—oh God, did you just snap your fingers?"

Blake kept dancing, or doing what I can only assume she thought was dancing, her body moving back and forth in the seat.

It was cute as hell.

So I turned up the music once we were at the stoplight.

"Do it," she yelled as she rolled down her window.

"No." I crossed my arms.

The light was still red.

"Do it!" Blake laughed and then reached across the seat to tickle my sides. "Come on, dance for me, Ian."

With a sigh, I lifted my hands above my head and then burst out laughing. "Hell no. No hands above the head. At least try to keep your business in your business, like this." I showed her how to jam out in the car.

"Nope." Blake shook her head. "Try harder. My turn for the rules." She raised my hands above my head, her lips so close to mine I could smell her bubble gum. "Now, snap them, and move."

I did. Looking like a complete poser.

And she laughed.

Our mouths almost met.

A horn honked behind me.

With a curse, I glanced at the light. It was green, and for who knew how long. Quickly I sped off toward the place we were going.

"Cute lesson," I said once the song ended.

"I thought so." Blake winked. "If David doesn't want me based on the fact that I'm trying to help him expand his taste in music, then he can just . . . suck it!"

"Hah!" I burst out laughing. "Great, but maybe don't say 'suck it' while looking that hot. He may take you literally."

She made a face, and then more techno came on. Blake danced in her seat the entire way to the water.

"We having a picnic or something?" she asked once I turned off the car.

"Nope, but we do have to work for our food. Are you okay with that?"

"Sure." Her eyes narrowed. "You promise you didn't just take me out to the docks to make out?"

"Rule number two." I shoved my keys and wallet in my pocket and held out my hand to her. "When a guy wants to surprise the shit out of you, don't question him. Just tell him how awesome he is."

"You are"—she stood on her tiptoes and kissed my chin—"the best fake date ever."

I growled out a curse and tugged her against me. "Remember, you need to pretend this is real; otherwise, what's the point?" My body buzzed at her nearness.

"A fun night? Good food?" she offered.

I smacked her on the ass.

"Ouch!" She pushed away from me, laughing. "I'm pretty sure that's not allowed on first dates."

"Ah, she can be taught." I released her and gave a little clap while Blake rolled her eyes at me.

"Behold." I held out my hands. "Our ride."

Blake eyed the dock, then me, then the dock. "We're canoeing?"

"Toward our restaurant, yes."

A smile broke free across her face. "I have to give it to you—that's pretty cool. Though I don't know how much help I'm going to be in this dress." She looked down at the short piece of fabric hugging her thighs, hugging the exact spot where I wanted my fingers inching, digging.

"Cross my heart," I hid my other hand behind my back and crossed my fingers. "I won't look up your skirt."

"Rule number three?" Her eyebrows shot up.

"Men always lie," I said through my laughter.

After fifteen minutes of intense struggling, I decided helping a girl who was wearing a short dress into a canoe should be counted as an Olympic sport. What was supposed to be romantic was taking a turn for the worse. Maybe this was why Agua Verde didn't rent canoes in the winter time? Thankfully, Lex had helped me rent the canoe so that we could still have the same ambience.

Blake grabbed her paddle and eyed me. "I would have been a fantastic rower, just so you know."

"Oh?" I flashed her a smile and grabbed my paddle, then propelled us out of the cove and toward Agua Verde, the restaurant I was taking her to. "And why do you say that?"

"Long arms . . ." She shivered a bit. I stopped paddling and handed her my suit jacket. "Thanks." Another shiver. "Long legs . . ."

I couldn't help but stare at her legs. Keeping my mouth from watering took a gargantuan effort.

"Trying to tempt me, sweet cheeks?" I joked, even though my body was already painfully reminding me that it wanted to get to know hers in a very up-close and personal way.

"Do I?" she asked, her voice losing all trace of humor.

With a gulp, I turned away, putting more effort into the paddling so I could focus on the strain of my arm muscles rather than the one currently taking place somewhere else. "Always."

"I thought all men lied."

"Not all men," I answered truthfully. "At least not about something like that."

The restaurant was just coming into view. It was a local favorite, something you had to experience at least once if you were in Seattle, but because she'd just moved here, I assumed she hadn't had a chance to go.

"Look!" She pointed as someone from the dock waved at us. I quickly steered us into the spot while one of the employees grabbed the canoe and tied it up.

"Mr. Hunter, right on time." He held out his hand to Blake, helping her onto the dock. "We have you seated outside. The heaters have been placed near your table so your date shouldn't get cold, though we do have blankets to offer you if it gets too chilly."

"Fantastic." I slipped him a twenty, patted him on the back, and turned to Blake. "Shall we?"

Her eyes freaking lit up like I was sunshine. "Why, yes, Mr. Hunter."

"Mr. Hunter was my father." I shivered uncomfortably. "And if rumors from my nanny are believed to be correct, he was a horny bastard. To you, I'm always Ian."

"Hah!" Blake laughed. "Rumor has it so are you . . ." With a sigh, she whispered my name again. "Ian."

The way she said my name always had a dizzying effect on my senses. Funny, because for years I'd been surrounded by hot chicks who freaking shouted it from the rooftops, yet it never reverberated in my chest the way it did when Blake uttered it.

A tiny moan crossed her lips. "This place smells so good."

The waiter stopped by, his eyebrows shooting up into his hairline. Back off, dude.

"I'm Julio. I'll be your server this evening. Can I get you started with anything?"

"Two lime margaritas on the rocks," I said before Blake could open her mouth.

"Salt on the rim?" Julio asked.

"Sugar." I licked my lips while staring at Blake's mouth.

"Got it." He walked off.

"Rule number four." Chips and salsa were placed in front of us. "Two drinks. Never three . . . or four. You may be nervous, but if you go past two, you start to lose your inhibitions, and things can easily go downhill really fast. Two is a safe number, but only if you've eaten normally that day."

Blake shoved a chip into her mouth. "Do I look like one of those girls who doesn't eat normally? I eat, Ian. I can't help it."

"Don't want you to." I laughed as she hungrily grabbed another chip. "Plus, you need food with all that cardio you'll be doing later."

The chip paused midair. "Cardio?"

"Sex." I nodded. "Isn't that what you want to eventually do with David?"

Her face paled. "I, uh, I haven't really thought about it."

"Come again?" I was in dangerous territory. She was my client, and I should have been worried that she hadn't thought about it rather than elated.

"I don't think about David and sex."

Our drinks arrived. Julio cleared his throat. "Tonight's special is—"

"Give us a minute."

He walked off while I was still staring at Blake like she'd lost her mind. "Sweet cheeks, it's going to happen eventually."

She shifted in her seat, tucked her hair nervously behind her ear, and then leaned forward. "I don't want to think about it, because it makes me want to puke. I'm going to be horrible, he's going to hate it, and I'm going to make a fool of myself."

"Rule number five." I shook my head slowly. "Guys never hate sex. If they don't get off, it's either because they mistook numbing cream for K-Y, or they're gay and you lack the goods to get them there."

"K-Y?"

"Still need a minute?" Julio asked.

I glared.

He held up his hands and walked off. What, were we his only table or something?

Blake started downing her drink.

"Blake"—I grabbed her wrist and helped her set her drink down— "if you can't think about sex with him, should you be . . . going on a date with him? I mean, why use my help?"

"It's just moving so fast." She grabbed another chip and chomped down. "I wanted him to notice me, not take me to bed two weeks after your little plan worked."

"Okay." I leaned back. "So tell him no."

"I can do that, right?"

"Rule number six," I said softly. "You can always—and I do mean *always*—say no. In fact, when it comes to David, I strongly encourage it. Who knows where his dick has been. Maybe he has herpes. How would you even know?"

"Okay, now you're freaking me out."

"Good, no sex. Go to a nunnery. Lex and I will sneak in chocolate and wine for you every year on your birthday." I reached across the table and patted her hand. "Blessings, child."

Blake glared, but she was laughing all the same. "Stop!"

"Okay." I grabbed a menu. "Let's order before Julio spits in our tacos."

Our drinks were already empty. Huh, when did that happen? We both quickly decided on a variety of tacos to share and ordered another round of drinks.

"To our first date." Blake lifted her glass into the air and clinked it against mine.

"To our first date," I repeated. But my mind kept reminding me that it was also going to be the last.

CHAPTER TWENTY-SEVEN

"We broke a rule," Blake announced. "You had two margaritas and a tequila shot."

"Because"—I laughed and tugged her against me, burrowing my face in her neck—"you'd never done a tequila shot. I felt sorry for you. Besides, aren't rules meant to be broken?"

Blake glanced up at me, tilting her mouth so close that I had no choice but to lean down.

"Your paddleboards are ready," the employee announced.

"Wait, what?" Panic crossed Blake's features. "We just had a ton of food, not to mention a tequila shot, and we have to somehow paddle our way back?"

"It's a half mile," I said. "You'll be just fine. Just, you know, try to stay on the board."

"Hah!" Blake shoved me hard and grabbed her paddle. "I've never done this before, so if I drown, it's on you."

"Mouth-to-mouth. Thank God for CPR." I gave her a serious nod. "Do what you have to do, just don't get pissed if I have to save your life."

"Enjoy!" The man handed me my paddle.

I pulled off my shoes, put them in the bag that the attendant had, which I'd made Lex swear to pick up later, and then hurried over to Blake. "Give me your heels." I held open my hands.

"My heels?"

"Yup." I pulled them from her feet. "Lex is picking up our stuff later. Going barefoot will be easier. Besides, you'll be too busy staying upright with your puffy life jacket."

"Alright." She wiggled her toes, crouched down on the dock and slid to the board on her knees.

"Balance is key," I called.

"Oh man." Blake huffed out a curse. "I'm going to ruin Gabi's dress."

"Hmm, Blake in a wet dress, me giving mouth-to-mouth—you sure this isn't a dream?"

"Not funny, Ian!"

The attendant chuckled while I handed him the rest of my stuff and quickly got on my board. "Follow me, sweet cheeks."

It was a struggle for her at first, but within a few minutes, because of the athlete she was . . . it was a race.

It was one of those unspoken races. The type that happens without anyone having to say anything.

I pulled ahead, and then Blake, and then me again.

"What do I get if I win?" I teased.

Blake barked out a laugh. "Please, when have you ever beaten me?"

"Sure, talk down to the hero, sweet cheeks. It won't work! I'm still kicking your ass."

Blake's laughter was like a caress as she nearly rammed me with her board and then flew by.

"Shit," I yelled, putting my back into it.

"Neck and neck," Blake said when we were a few feet from shore.

"Winner takes all!" I shouted.

Blake was ahead by one inch.

So I did what any sane man would do.

I pushed her into the water.

It only came up to her waist, but it was enough to completely soak the dress.

"I can't believe you did that!" She slapped the water.

"Rule number seven," I called back once I reached the shore. "Never trust a man during competition."

"Noted!" She flipped me off, then used the ladder on the dock, climbing up it. "You win."

"That's right . . . I win." I turned, my mouth dropped open, and some foreign-sounding moan emerged from between my lips.

"What are you staring at?"

"Damn, you're even more beautiful wet."

"You're such a guy." She rolled her eyes and made her way toward me, her legs and feet dripping with water.

"Yes." I couldn't help it anymore; I tugged her against me and kissed her hard. "I am."

She shivered in my arms; whether it was from the cold or the kiss I wasn't sure, and I really didn't care.

I didn't stop.

"Rule number eight," I whispered against her mouth. "If he goes in for the kiss, let him."

"Mm'kay." She kissed me back, wrapping her arms around me, her cold body rocking against my heat. She may have thought she was going to suck at sex, but I knew, right then, her body was very much aware of what needed to happen.

Her tongue flicked mine lightly as she rubbed herself against me.

Shit.

It wasn't that it had been too long without a girl.

It was that it'd been a lifetime without the right one.

We kissed for mere seconds, minutes, before she withdrew, not just physically but emotionally. And I knew I only had myself to blame, for blurring the lines so freaking well.

For making her believe it was all just a game, when it was so much more.

"So, almost done." Blake nodded, then wiped her mouth with her hand. "How am I doing so far?"

My heart cracked a bit. "You're doing fantastic."

"Good." She gave me a light shove. "Not only do you owe Gabs a dress, but I'm going to kick your ass for pushing me into the water. Who does that?"

"Conceited bastards who like to win?"

"Oh, so only Ians. Gotcha."

I smirked and pulled out my keys. Once the SUV was unlocked, I grabbed a blanket from the backseat and handed it to her.

She stared at it. "Do I even want to know why you have a blanket in your car?"

I rolled my eyes. "Not for the reasons you're assuming."

"Oh, so you don't screw girls in the backseat?"

"Can't say that I have." I wrapped her tightly in the blanket. "Then again, there's always a first time for anything."

"No," she said quickly.

"Ah." I stepped back. "Good, you're listening to the rules."

"Yeah," she whispered. "Thanks for the help . . ."

"Anytime." The date was ending. Why the hell was I allowing it? We drove in silence back to her house.

I turned off the car and stared at the porch light, willing the electricity to go out, or for her house to suddenly get burglarized so I'd have an excuse to go with her inside.

"Final rule," I muttered under my breath. "If you're feeling that the date's gone well and you want it to continue, it's up to you to invite the guy in."

Blake chewed her lower lip and nodded. "Alright."

Shit. I wiped my face with my hands, then gripped the steering wheel. So that was it. I guessed. There was nothing left to say.

"Ian?"

"Yeah?" I croaked, not looking at her.

"Do you want to come in?"

My heart stuttered in my chest as I slowly turned my entire body to face her. "That depends."

"On?" Her smile was confident, sexy.

"Do you have refreshments to offer me? That's kind of the next unspoken rule—don't invite them in assuming something will happen. Invite them in for a drink, coffee, late-night movie."

"All of the above," she said with a nod. "How's that?"

"Well, then." I shut off the car. "I accept."

CHAPTER
TWENTY-EIGHT

The door shut behind us, blanketing the house in silence except for some engine-revving in a car commercial playing on the TV. I tried to even my breathing, but it was damn near impossible.

Blackness filled the small hallway.

"Gabs must be sleeping," I said, mainly to fill the awkwardness with my voice.

"Serena and Gabs are at a movie," she whispered back.

"Oh." I clenched my eyes shut. I needed to seriously back off.

Blake dropped the blanket to the floor and turned in one swift movement. Her eyes searched mine.

I reached for her, needing to just touch her. One last time. Just one last time before I let her go to David . . . Just once before . . .

But her eyes were so hopeful.

And she was just so damn sexy.

More than that.

I'd gone from being the coach to the damn client . . . wanting so desperately for the girl to notice me that I'd go to any lengths to get her attention.

Blake's eyes met mine. She didn't turn away.

Life is full of choices. Some good, some bad. I wasn't sure, in that moment, if I was making a bad choice or the first good choice in a really long time.

Tension hung in the air while we both continued to stare at one another.

When my eyes locked in on her mouth, she moved, ever so slightly, toward me, her body giving me the tiniest hint that I wasn't going insane, that she wanted me just as much as I wanted her.

Without thinking it through any further, I slammed my mouth against hers, coming up for air only long enough to utter, "Screw David. You're mine."

My hands flew at her dress, tugging the wet material down her legs. She stumbled out of it, her wet body sliding against mine. My fingers fumbled for her hips, and I lifted her into the air while my mouth was still fused with hers, tongues twisting, entwining. I wasn't sure where she ended and where I began. She let out a loud moan that reverberated through the nearly silent hallway.

Her hands dug into my back, gripping me tighter, harder. Control long gone, I swept my tongue across her lower lip, then pulled back and glanced at her swollen mouth and attacked it again from a different angle. My dick strained against my jeans as her core rocked hard against me.

"Damn it." I stumbled back against the wall with her in my arms, then slowly started taking the stairs one at a time. And with each step, another kiss to her mouth, then one to her neck. Her soft moans were going to be the absolute death of me as I made it to the landing and charged toward her room. The door slammed behind us.

The room was quiet.

Except for my heavy breathing.

And hers.

Slowly, I slid her down my body, growling in pleasure as the friction from her legs caught on my jeans, making me mindlessly thrust toward her.

Blake's eyes zeroed in on my mouth. I licked my lips in anticipation, still tasting her, my body so hot I felt like I was going to explode. When had it ever been like this? When had I ever been so . . . obsessed?

She reached for me.

I leaned back and wagged my finger.

Blake's eyebrows shot up. "Too fast?"

I burst out laughing as the warm light from the lamp illuminated her perfection. "Yeah, something like that. As in if we don't slow down, it's going to be over way too fast."

I couldn't tell if she was blushing; the room was too dark. But what I could tell? She was mind-numbingly beautiful with her wavy hair sticking to her neck, her perfect, nearly naked body beckoning me to take a little bite wherever I wanted. To mark her as mine.

"You about ready now?" she teased.

"Sweet cheeks"—I reached for her hands and tugged her roughly against me—"I've been ready since I saw those sexy flip-flops."

Laughing, she pulled back, or at least tried, but I started moving my lips across her neck, sucking, licking, just freaking tasting, as if I'd never been with a woman before. And maybe I hadn't, at least not a woman like Blake. One who drove me insane by just breathing.

Blake was in the sexiest damn lingerie I'd ever seen, and my hands ran down the red lace in appreciation as she deepened the kiss. Her chest heaved, splaying her breasts against my chest. I could feel her nipples harden.

I was mindless, an animal, consumed by the feel of her.

Knowing she wanted me as much as I wanted her.

I released her so I could fully admire the red lingerie, desperate to see what I had already felt.

Her gaze heated, but then insecurity washed over her features.

"Oh no you don't," I growled, reaching for her again, my mouth angling harshly against hers, my kiss more aggressive than gentle, because, hell, I felt aggressive, like I would die if I couldn't be inside her.

"I think I need more rules," she whispered once our mouths broke free. "So I know what to do."

"No more rules." I traced my finger down the curve of her breast and gave her bra a little tug. "Rules in the bedroom only lead to confusion and lack of orgasms."

"How do you figure?"

Shit, I knew that look: she was starting to think. And thinking was always frowned upon. Thinking meant she was going to be the sane one, the one who said, 'Let's just be friends,' when I really wanted to get her naked and fill her to the hilt again and again, until I was dehydrated or near death.

"I figure"—I slid my hand down her arm—"because women concentrate way too hard on *thinking* their way through sex rather than *feeling*."

Her lower lip trembled as I reached behind her back and undid the clasp, my hands skimming over her bare skin, memorizing the smoothness. I pressed a kiss to the place where her shoulder and neck met.

"Feel," I whispered, "all you want. And if you say no . . . mean it."

"What do you mean?"

I pulled back and cupped her chin between my fingers. Damn it, now she was making *me* think, and that also wasn't a good idea. I'd never been guilty of developing a conscience, until now. "The minute you say no, I'm covering you in as many layers of clothing as I can, and getting as far away from you as physically possible. So don't say no unless you really mean it, because I won't be coming back if you change your mind."

"Yes," she whispered.

"I don't believe I asked you a question, sweet cheeks."

With shaking hands, she touched my sides, then my hips, where my jeans were already hanging painfully low, and then she reached for the button. She made new definitions for torture as she slowly played with the zipper and then said, "I'm saying yes."

"You'll have to be more specific."

My dick jumped to full attention as her fingers grazed the front of my jeans.

Gritting my teeth, I hissed. "You can do better than that."

I didn't expect her to slip a wicked little hand into my jeans and grab me.

But she did.

And the small part of my brain that told me this was a bad idea, that it would change things forever, died as she squeezed.

"Better?" she asked.

"Don't stop touching me," I said through clenched teeth. Her innocence was staggering, but more than that, the innocent way she explored my body was enough to set me off before any sex even took place.

There was something to be said about being with the right girl.

Waiting for the right moment.

She grunted and then pulled her naughty little hand back. "I think you should take off your jeans."

"You think?" My eyebrows rose.

She leveled me with a glare, then gave my jeans a damn hard tug. "Take them off."

"Did you just boss me around? In your bedroom?" I smirked, enjoying the way her cheeks reddened.

She reached for me again.

"Whatever you say," I groaned. "I'm yours."

I slid my jeans off slowly. I wanted to do everything slow, to give her time to change her mind but also to make sure she knew without a shadow of a doubt what she'd be saying no to.

She sighed loudly. "I'm disappointed."

"What?" I had to fight to keep myself from yelling. When had a girl ever said that to me?

She gave me a teasing smile. "I thought for sure you wore an old-school Speedo."

"That's it." I grabbed her by the ass and tossed her over my shoulder, marching her over to the bed. "Teasing time's over . . . at least for you."

I flopped her onto her back and crawled up her body, my erection painful, my vision blurring from want.

Blake licked her lips.

"Do that again," I instructed.

"What?"

"Lick your lips. While I lick you." I winked and lowered my line of sight so she'd get the idea of exactly where I was going to lick her. "Trust me."

I could still make out the blush on her cheeks in the dark. Damn, I wanted her response to always be one of wide-eyed innocence.

"What do you mean when you—?"

I ignored her embarrassed protests. They died across my lips as I worked her into a heated frenzy that had her reaching for my hair and tugging it so hard that I growled. My mouth trailed up and down her neck, then lower, and finally, I got the first taste of her—the first real taste. Her hips bucked.

"What are you doing?"

"I should think that would be obvious." I pressed my hands against her hips to keep her from somehow giving me a black eye. "I'm making love to you—with my mouth."

Another moan from Blake as her body writhed, and then her hands were tugging against my head so hard I started chuckle against her, which of course made her moan louder.

"Of course you'd be demanding in bed," I muttered after she floated off into orgasmland. I moved up the bed and eyed her with amusement. "Are you still saying yes?"

"What was that?" Her eyes were glazed, her lips swollen. God, I could just devour her—in fact, I was planning on doing that very thing as soon as she was ready.

"Oh, that?" I winked, then kissed her sensuously across the mouth, still tasting her, not wanting the taste to go away, afraid that after tonight it would. "That was round one."

"How many rounds are there?" Her eyes were hopeful.

"For you?" I pulled back. "As many as you can handle. And then . . . more."

"Ian?"

"What?"

"I want to make you feel that way."

"You do." And that was the truth. I was nursing an erection, a.k.a. blue balls of steel, and she did make me feel that way, just by allowing me to pleasure her, to bring her to the brink of madness.

Blake leaned up on her elbows, then reached for me. "I want you to feel that way . . . right now."

"Blake . . ." I wanted sex. I always wanted sex. From her? I wanted endless hours of sex. But . . . somewhere along the way, I'd completely fallen for more than just the promise of filling her tight body. I wanted more. I craved something beyond the physical, and it was scaring the shit out of me.

Because she *should* say no to me. I didn't deserve her. Maybe that was it—I knew I didn't deserve her.

"Now." She tugged me against her, and my body bucked in response. I nearly impaled her by accident, something that had never happened to me before.

I settled between her thighs, every part of me throbbing, aching.

"Blake . . ."

She was grabbing for me, touching me everywhere, driving me insane as she kissed along my neck.

I hovered over her, positioning myself, alternating between wanting to fill her to the hilt, and wanting to back off and lock her in the bathroom. "You have to be sure."

"Please." She bit down on my lip. "It's you, I want you." Her hands tugged my hair as she pulled my head down, capturing my lips between hers. Damn, she was a fast learner, considering she hadn't been able to kiss a few weeks ago. "Ian . . ."

"I hate David," I admitted. Why the hell was I saying his name in bed?

"Okay." She kissed me again and again and again.

I lost myself in her kisses.

I allowed it.

Our mouths fused together as I bruised her lips over and over. The sensation of her nails running up and down my back was the purest ecstasy. I reached between our bodies, pressing my palm against her core.

Blake let out a little moan.

I jerked back and looked into her eyes. "Rule number nine."

Hazily, she stared back at me. "I thought you said rules in bed prevented orgasms?"

"Rules," I said, my voice husky as I racked my brain for a way to ask her about condoms. I'd never been in a situation like this before, and it's not like I was still in high school and had my very first condom purchase just hanging out in my wallet.

Blake was so wet, ready for me.

"Blake, I need . . ." Swallowing my absolute *need* to be already inside her, I cleared my throat and tried again. "Condom?"

With a lazy smile, she pointed to the nightstand. "I didn't presume, I mean, ever, but this used to be Gabs's room, and—"

"Stop"—I jerked open the drawer—"right there."

She giggled as I ripped open the wrapper and covered my length. Eyes wide, she reached for me, but I batted her hand away.

"If it's your first time," I whispered, ignoring her confused look and slowly inching myself into her, "make it count. And focus on me, only me."

With clenched teeth, I pushed forward.

She let out a little gasp and nearly fell off the bed. Her eyes fluttered closed and then opened again. "If protection's rule nine, what's rule number ten?"

Slowly, I started to move. "Never forget it's me who makes you feel this way."

"That's a rule?"

"My new rule." I arched back and then slammed forward again. "You're mine, Blake, you hear me? Mine."

"Yes." She gasped, pulling my head down, her lips meeting mine with desperation. "Yes."

CHAPTER TWENTY-NINE

I wish I could say that I was a gentleman, that I let her sleep it off and then very tenderly drew her bath and asked, "Where does it hurt?"

Instead, I'd officially lost my damn mind.

And made love to her three more times before finally collapsing halfway on top of her.

I was in such a deep state of exhaustion that I'm sure if the world had somehow ended between five and six a.m. and the only way to save it was to join forces against the zombies with Channing Tatum, I would have said, "Pass," yawned, and turned on my side to get a few more minutes of sleep.

Hours later, the sun was starting to seep into the room. I stretched across the bed and felt an empty cold spot beside me.

Another first.

I jerked up and came face-to-face with a very pissed-off best friend, who was holding a pillow above her head as a look of pure hate crossed her features.

"Gabs." I held up my hands. "Were you going to suffocate me?"

"Thought about it," she said through clenched teeth. "For at least ten minutes."

"Shit." I rubbed my eyes, my voice hoarse from sleep. "Are you telling me you hovered over me with a killer pillow and contemplated murdering me for a whole ten-minute period?"

"Yes." She didn't look apologetic. Her eyes were wild; her auburn hair was pulled back into a baseball cap. She looked like she'd just returned from her morning run.

I glanced down at her pink Nike Frees. "Cool shoes. Those new?"

"Don't!" Her nostrils flared. "Don't you dare change the subject."

"Ah, yes." I sighed. "My impending death. Well, get it over with."

"How could you!"

"How could I . . . live? Breathe? Well, it's simple. I'm sure our mutual best friend, Lex, could explain the mechanics behind the human body if you're so inclined."

"Ian." Gabi slammed the pillow into my face.

Repeatedly.

Every time I tried to get a word in, she slammed me again.

"Stop!" I tackled her against the bed and tossed the pillow to the side, only then realizing that I was still naked.

"NO!!!!!" Gabi shouted so loud my eardrum nearly burst and fell out of my ear.

"Oh, please!" I hurried to cover myself. "Like you've never seen a penis!"

"It's yours!" She pointed.

My lower appendage had the good sense to be mortified that it was getting yelled and pointed at.

"Gabs . . ." Once I was safely covered, I tried again. "Why are you pissed?"

"*My* roommate!"

"You do realize Lex screwed Serena within twenty-four hours of her moving in, right?"

"But that's Lex! He's a horrible human being!"

"I'm sure he'll be happy to know you approve."

"Blake's a friend." Gabi sighed. "And now it's going to be awkward. Not to mention she's your freaking client! What the hell were you thinking?"

"Easy."

"She's not easy!" she shouted.

"Let me finish." I leveled her with a glare. "I was thinking, easy, I really like her, I care for her, David's a freaking douche, and I'd rather die than let him even touch her. And if you must know, I was also thinking, 'Damn, she's hot. Hell, I want her—'"

"You mean you aren't bailing?"

I frowned. "Do I look like I'm jumping out the window and making an excuse about my sick dog right now?"

"You don't have a dog."

"Even so, if I regretted last night, which I don't, I'd be in a hell of a hurry to make sure old Fido made it after that Honda hit him overnight."

Gabi was still frowning at me. "She likes you."

"Oh, thank *God*!" I shouted. "And here I thought she hated me when she started screaming my name—"

Gabi glared.

I stopped talking to offer her a teasing smile. "Say, where is Blake?"

"Baking," Gabi muttered. "She got up at the ass crack of dawn and went for a four-mile run, then decided to make pancakes for the slut in her bed."

I was already out of the bed before Gabi could yell about my nakedness again. I dressed in record time, then launched myself down the stairs and into the kitchen. "Pancakes?"

Blake was facing the stove, her hair pulled into a wet knot on her head while she hummed and flipped a pancake into the air. "Only if you save some for Lex. I told him he could have one after he called Gabi this morning freaking out about you missing your normal meeting at the bench."

"Shit!" I glanced at the clock on the microwave. "I didn't mean to sleep in."

Blake turned, her face flushed. "Sorry, you just looked exhausted."

"Sweet cheeks." In two steps, she was in my arms. "I *am* exhausted, but in the best possible you-should-probably-take-a-week-off-from-school way."

"Why would I take a week off school?"

"Think of the possibilities—spending your days and nights in bed. It might change your life."

"Hah," Blake wrapped her arms around my middle. "Maybe it already has."

I smiled down at her. It was a new feeling. Not waking up in a panic to leave, but in a panic to see her, to make sure she was okay, to kiss her again and again.

"I could get very addicted to your taste." I kissed her lightly on the mouth. Blake moved her arms so she could wrap them around my neck and pull me closer.

"Not in the kitchen, guys," Gabi said from the doorway. "We have to eat here."

"I love eating," I murmured against Blake's lips. "And pancakes? You know that's how Gabs kept me around, right? She fed me. That's what you do when you want to keep a man. If you give him food, he's yours for life."

"Why else do you think I went to the store and bought sausage to go along with the pancakes?"

I groaned and kissed her again.

"I will seriously grab the pillow from upstairs." Gabi's irritated voice pierced my good mood. "Now break apart." She clapped. "For once, I'm not cooking, so I want to sit and have my coffee without watching real-life porn."

"Who has porn?" Lex waltzed into the kitchen, his grin lazy as he eyed Gabi. "Looking good, Gabs. Run out of makeup this morning, or are you trying to look twelve so you can pay less for a movie ticket?"

Gabi glared, continuing to sip her coffee. The glare had me stepping out of the way just in case she'd somehow discovered a way to kill people with a look.

Lex didn't seem the least bit affected. If anything, he seemed to enjoy her hate.

"So who got laid last night?" Lex asked once he'd grabbed a cup of coffee and was sitting at the breakfast table.

Gabi pointed at me, while I pointed at Blake, who pointed back at me.

Lex frowned. "So you either both got laid or you hooked up. Which is it?"

"Uh . . . hooked up," Blake announced, casting a shy glance my way and then winking. "And it was everything the girls write about on the bathroom stalls."

"Ha ha." I smacked her ass and started pulling out plates.

"Um . . ." Lex coughed. "You do realize you can't hook up with clients."

"Oh, that." I nodded. "I'm pretty sure our contract was terminated the minute she screamed my name."

"So"—Gabi eyed both of us—"no David?"

"No," I said while Blake said, "Yes."

All talking ceased.

I whipped around so fast I nearly collided with the open fridge door. "What the hell do you mean, 'yes'?"

"He's still a friend!" Blake laughed nervously. "I need to at least meet with him for dinner. Like I said, he's a friend."

"Um, I was a friend and we ended up screwing four times last night. Sorry if I'm not exactly confident in your ability to keep friends at arm's length!"

Blake gasped.

Lex muttered an "oh shit." And looked like he wanted to high-five me, or bow down to me, or maybe just challenge me to an endurance run.

Gabi cackled behind her coffee cup.

"Is that all it was to you? Blake crossed her arms. A quick hookup?"

"Hell no," I yelled, stalking toward her. "Which is another reason the last thing I want is for you to hang out with Douchepants!"

"He has a name!"

"Yeah, it's Douchepants!"

Blake rolled her eyes. "I've known him my whole life. It would be rude to suddenly cancel. Tell you what. If it makes you feel better, you can drop me off and pick me up."

"Oooo, rent a minivan like a soccer mom!" This from Lex.

"Lex, not helping," I said quickly. "Ask Gabs about getting fired."

"How do you even know that?" Gabi yelled while Lex turned on her with venom in his eyes.

"Sleep with the boss?" Lex said in a harsh voice.

"Ah! I hate you guys!" Gabi smacked Lex on the arm while I turned back to Blake.

"Ian." She said my name like she was disappointed in the fact that I was jealous. "I promise it will be fine, okay?"

She reached for my arms.

I didn't budge.

With a sigh, she whispered in my ear. "You know I could take the day off . . . but I do still have to go to volleyball practice." She finished the whisper with a slight lick on my ear.

The lick decided it for me.

I was locking her in the room with me.

And I was going to do everything within my power to make sure that when she did meet with David, my name was the only one on her lips.

"We'll be back!" I yelled loud enough for everyone to hear and then tossed her over my shoulder and carried her up the stairs into her room.

CHAPTER THIRTY

"Must. Get. Water." With a hoarse groan, I shuffled toward the bathroom and turned on the faucet, splashing my face, then cupping my hands underneath so I could drink.

"Your cardio needs work." Blake came up behind me and turned on the shower.

I glowered at her in the mirror. "I kicked your ass!"

"Oh, is that what you did? When you said you had to stop because your ankle hurt?"

With a yelp, she moved out of the way as I snapped a towel in her direction. "Just because I suck at sprints doesn't mean my cardio needs work. Maybe if you wore more clothes while working out, I wouldn't get so distracted."

"So you almost coughed up a lung because you were distracted?"

"Right." I nodded and pulled my shirt over my head, tossing it onto the floor. "Distraction messes with my breathing, and if you don't breathe right, you gas." I winked.

She rolled her eyes and pushed me out of the bathroom.

"Hey!" I yelled when the door slammed in my face. "I thought if I went on a jog with you, I was allowed shower time. Wasn't there a sticker chart? With sexual favors each time I hit a goal?"

The door cracked open. "You're insane, you know that?"

"Insanely hot?" I crooked my eyebrow at her and inched the door open farther. "Insanely . . . satisfying? So insane that you had not one, not two, but three orgasms, all within a five-hour period, was it?"

Her face blazed red.

I smirked.

The door slammed back against me again, and this time the lock turned.

"Fine," I said against the door. "A girl needs some privacy—I get it. I'll just be out here sitting in my own sweat while I wait!"

"You were complaining about being behind." Blake's voice carried through the door. "Get some work done! Sit on the floor and stop complaining!"

I loved that bossy attitude.

After spending that first day in bed together, we decided that we needed to venture out into society and actually go to school. I told her I was 90 percent sure we could still pass all our classes even if we just stopped going halfway through the semester, but Blake was on scholarship, and honestly I really did enjoy school. So I decided the best way to go about it was to go for a run with her, placate her with coffee, then explain my Wingmen Inc. schedule to her, as well as my duties, in a way that wouldn't make her fly off the handle.

Blake didn't want me to terminate her contract, because technically I'd held up my end of the bargain. David had noticed her, and in return, she could have had him.

If I hadn't stood in the way.

She only had two days left, since we had changed the contract end date to her actual date with David to keep my record pristine.

Well, not exactly pristine. I did have a black mark, since I'd done the unthinkable and slept with her.

But being with her now was different.

She was different. My end goal wasn't to hook up with her and leave. I wanted her for as long as she would have me. Hopefully forever.

Shit. I was already in deep.

I quickly grabbed my phone from her nightstand and started poring over e-mails from the last few days.

Vivian wanted to meet.

She had been in love with a guy named John since her freshman year two years ago, and Lex sent me his schedule.

And it looked like I had one more client starting the following week, who had spent the last three years pining over . . . yup, you guessed it, her study partner.

Seriously, nine times out of ten it was either the study partner or someone in their class that they'd creepily stalked. I was cool with it, but it usually meant I had to do a lot of groundwork. Getting the girl from being essentially nonexistent to suddenly on the guy's radar was no easy task. And doing that while seeing Blake?

Well, let's just say my methods were going to have to change, because no way was I going to be that guy. The one who pretended to be dating other girls while I actually had a legitimate girlfriend.

My hand froze over the text I was just about to send Lex. My breathing slowed. My chest tightened.

The shower turned off.

I stared at my phone harder.

And tried to remember to breathe.

Suddenly, Blake's feet appeared in my line of vision. She waved in front of my face. "Ian? What's going on? You look like you're going to puke."

"Are you my girlfriend?" I blurted.

Blake joined me on the bed, towel wrapped tight around her body. "If that freaks you out—"

"No," I said. "That's just the point. It doesn't. Shouldn't it?"

Blake shrugged. "Well, it's not like you've been afraid of commitment. Up until now you've just been"—she winced—"screwing anything that breathed."

"Nice, and here I thought you were going to lay me down easy and say something like 'Oh, Ian, you were just waiting for the right girl to sweep you off your feet!'"

"Girls don't do the sweeping. Surely *that's* in your rule book."

"Why do men have to do all the work?"

Blake smiled and then slowly untucked her towel and straddled me. "Is that what this is about? You want me to do some work?"

I nodded, afraid that if I spoke, it would somehow spook her into running away. I didn't even touch her. I just . . . stared.

"So in order to be okay with being my boyfriend . . ."

Damn, the word sounded good on her lips. I was a possessive bastard like that, knowing that she was mine, that nobody else got to see her naked, that no other guy had pressed his mouth against hers. It was enough to make me want to shout in triumph.

"I need to . . . earn my keep?" she said.

"Your words, not mine," I whispered in a cocky voice. "Hey, you wouldn't happen to have any maid outfits in that giant closet of horrors, would you?"

"Nope."

"Damn." I sighed. "Janitor outfits? Fast-food? Tell me you at least have a McDonald's uniform, and I will bang you so hard you're going to call me Ronald for a week."

"You're really weird."

I gripped her by the ass and tossed her onto the bed. "Yeah, but you fed me, so remember what that means."

Blake ran her hands through my hair. Her fingers went to my lips and lingered as she whispered, "I get to keep you."

"Yeah." I kissed each fingertip reverently. "I sure hope so."

"Feeling insecure?"

"No," I lied. "Just . . . different. This feels different."

"Sometimes different is exactly what we need."

"Yeah." I kissed her soundly. "It is."

I finally left Blake's house two hours later, freshly showered and ready to meet Vivian at the HUB. It was our second meeting, during which I'd go over the schedule and see if she was okay with it. Hopefully, getting a good look at the guy she was interested in would help me gauge how fast he'd make it through the steps.

Vivian was sitting in Subway, chewing her fingernails and staring hard at one of the employees. He was a bit on the short side, wore his Subway visor backward, and said "yo" more than anyone should ever say within a five-minute period.

"Yo," I teased, taking a seat across from her.

"He doesn't even know my name," she mumbled under her breath.

I ignored that. "Did you move out of your parents' house?"

Her attention still fixed on the guy, she nodded and kept talking to me without making eye contact, which was borderline creepy. "I moved in with a good friend right off campus. I even cut my hair."

"I see that." She'd also discovered red lipstick and all the ways one could get it on her teeth by not properly applying it. "Vivian . . ."

She was still staring at John.

Fine. She wanted his attention? I was going to get his attention.

"You bitch!" I jumped to my feet and tossed my chair to the floor. Stunned students glanced at us. "I can't believe you slept with him! At my party? At my house! IN MY BED!"

Vivian's mouth dropped open as she looked between me and the suddenly very still Subway line. Sandwich artistry had officially stopped.

"Ian, what are you doing?" she hissed.

"Um, breaking up with you. What does it look like I'm doing?" I waved my hands around in the air. "You slept with my brother!" I had no such brother. "During my birthday party!" My birthday was in November. "What? You didn't think I would find out?"

Tears filled her eyes.

"Ian . . ." They started spilling onto her cheeks.

"Hey, man." John walked over and put his hand on my arm.

"Don't touch me!" I jerked away.

"Chill, yo, just chill." He offered a calm smile. "It's just that, Vivian here"—I *knew* he knew her name—"looks pretty scared. And whatever went down, it's not cool to air it out in front of an audience."

"You know what else isn't cool?" I was seething. "Her." I pointed a finger in Vivian's direction. "Making me want her so desperately that I was even thinking of forgiving her for doing the unthinkable. She's just . . ." I looked away. "She's beautiful."

John glanced at Vivian. I prayed she'd keep her mouth closed, because lipstick on her teeth would do the opposite of attract him. Then again, maybe he was into train wrecks. "Yeah, she really is," he said.

I knew what he saw, the girl next door plus a little bit of red lipstick. Her face was still flushed, making her lips plump. Her eyes were wide—they looked huge—and the fresh haircut made her look like she'd just gotten done having sex, which is of course what had given me my brilliant idea.

It wasn't just jealousy that got a guy going.

It was the simple fact that another dude had discovered a treasure that had been walking past him for years, and he'd never even given it a second glance.

All guys wanted to be first.

We wanted to be Christopher Columbus, Lewis and Clark—you get the picture.

He would always be second to me. Or so he thought. Meaning he would try twice as hard to erase the memory of her first.

Damn, I *was* brilliant.

"Look." I ran my hands through my hair, trying to look stressed. "Viv, can we talk outside?"

She nodded, slowly standing to her feet. I was glad to see that she'd taken my advice and at least dressed her age. Nice skinny jeans and a black racerback tank top made her look older than twelve.

"Hey." John grabbed Vivian's arm and whispered something in her ear. She nodded, ducked her head, and walked out with me.

Once we were outside, I steered her toward the bench and sat.

"That was—"

"Shh." I held my finger to my lips. "Give it a few minutes. He's going to be looking out here, and if we talk right away, it will look like we're fixing things. If we stay silent, we both look . . . hopeless. We need to look hopeless."

Vivian nodded, even crossed her arms.

After five minutes, I turned to her. "Sorry for embarrassing you."

She shrugged a shoulder, then smiled to herself. "He told me to meet him when he gets off work. Said he cheated on his girlfriend in high school and knows how bad it sucks to feel guilty for something that's entirely your fault."

"Hmm . . . interesting. That wasn't in his folder, which basically means I'm more brilliant than I originally realized."

She scooted closer to me.

"No, no." I laughed and created more distance. "From here on out, we're chilly, distant. Still semitogether but . . . only for appearances."

"Right." She folded her hands in her lap. "So do I meet him?"

"Sure. Bitch and complain, tell him it's not true, because it isn't, but say I refuse to believe you because I have trust issues. Tell him it's most likely over, which really frustrates you, since I was the best sex you've ever had."

"What?" She blushed bright red. "I can't say that."

"We did things backwards." I shrugged. "Usually I make them jealous first, then they offer a shoulder to cry on when things go to hell. But we're switching things up. Tell him you're upset because you're going to miss me in your bed. Say I was incredible. Say at night, you scream my name, only to wake up alone."

"I can't believe we're having this conversation." She started rocking back and forth, her eyes darting between me and the grass, cheeks still flushed. "I can't . . . say those things."

"You can." I checked my phone. "You will. And once that's over with, you leave, tell him you're exhausted, haven't been sleeping well. He'll want your number. Give it to him. He'll text you good night. Don't text him back until about three a.m. He'll text you back, believe me. And when he does and asks why you were up, say you're restless."

I scrolled through John's background. They had around an 80 percent chance for a good match. That is, if he stopped pissing around during class and actually finished his homework and turned it in on time. Vivian studied a ton.

"You have any tests coming up?"

"Yeah, in bio."

"Great. He's in bio, right?"

Another nod.

"Tell him that the only thing taking your mind off everything is studying . . . He'll offer to come over and study with you. Give it a day, then let him. Text me the minute he comes in the house, and I'll text you during the study session so that you seem distracted. Laugh at some of my texts, and then sigh and slam your book shut. He'll tell you that you deserve better and ask if you've ever considered being with anyone else. And this is where it's very important that you listen to my every damn word."

"I feel like this is happening really fast." Her breathing picked up speed, like she was ready to pass out.

Oh, good, another hyperventilater. I didn't have time for this shit today. Blake would be getting out of volleyball soon, and I had plans for that mouth, those legs—well, every single part of her.

"You want him, right?"

"Yes."

"Good, so tell him you've never been with anyone else. Tell him you've only kissed . . . ?" I waited for her answer.

"Two guys," she nodded her head confidently.

Good, she was getting the hang of it.

"Great," I said. "The first was in high school?" I was guessing.

A nod and then a shrug. "Well, we both were in high school. I haven't dated much since coming to college."

"Sorry."

"Overprotective parents," she huffed. "They control everything. It's just easier sometimes to lie down and let them."

"You've moved out, so now you're good, right?"

"Yes." She beamed. "Okay, two guys, and then what? How do I know if I'm any good at kissing? What if I'm not good enough?"

The girl had a point.

I held up a finger. "Hold that thought."

Gripping my cell with my hand, I dialed Lex's number. He answered on the first ring. "Tell me you're walking by the fountain in a few seconds."

"I see you right now."

"Need you."

"Great."

He hung up.

Vivian frowned as Lex made his way around the fountain and stalked toward us. I loved watching girls' reaction to him. He was built like a football player but had the brain of . . . I don't know, an evil genius? It was almost like he knew exactly what chemicals were firing off in their hormonal little bodies when he smiled in their direction, and knew just the amount of pressure to add to each kiss to cause an explosion.

Right. In the past, I'd had times where I wanted to kill him and dissect his freaky little brain. Now it was just interesting to watch.

"You called?" He shoved his hands into his pockets.

I gave a nonchalant nod toward Vivian. "She needs to know how to hook a guy with the gentle kiss."

"Right on." He set his bag down. "We doing this here?"

I glanced around. "Yeah, but maybe stand back more by the trees so John doesn't see."

He pulled Vivian to her feet and led her back toward the trees, then placed both hands on her shoulders. "You ready?"

"Wait." She looked back and forth between us and whispered in a shaky voice, "What's happening?"

"First day of the rest of your life." Lex nodded seriously. "Think of it as sex ed, only . . . better."

"I know about the birds and the bees."

Lex smirked, eyeing her up and down in disbelief. "Sure you do."

"Who are you?" she demanded, putting her hands on her hips.

"The second half to his whole." Lex pointed at me.

"You're gay?" she said.

He tugged her close to him. "Rub against me and find out, sweetheart."

I rolled my eyes. "Viv, just let Lex teach you how to kiss. I can't do it, because . . ." I frowned. Technically, I could do it. I just . . . didn't want to. It felt like cheating, even if it was just a job. Shit, I wondered if strippers thought the same thing every night they got ones shoved down their panties.

"He grew a vagina," Lex said helpfully. "Besides, he may get more tail, he may even have me beat in bed—we haven't really done a survey as of late—but this? This I know I excel at. So pucker up, buttercup, because I'm about to change your life."

"The survey was falsified," I argued.

Lex pressed his mouth against hers softly, then pulled back. "Now, before I go in again, I'm going to lick my bottom lip. Note I said lick, not slobber. A light lick, so that our lips slide across one another. And then just a small tease." He licked his lips and kissed her again, this time lingering at her lower lip before another kiss. Then his tongue slid out, meeting the entrance of her mouth before he pulled it back.

Her eyes were closed, and she leaned forward as Lex started talking again. "Now, once you have the correct pressure down, make sure you keep your hands above his waist. They are never down, they are never tugging at his head, simply touching his biceps lightly, almost like you're trying to control yourself. Got it?"

Vivian didn't look confident, but she nodded and then leaned in and kissed Lex.

When she was finished, she took a step back and waited.

"Good." Lex frowned. "Maybe hesitate a bit more, make sure you're touching at least one erotic point on my body."

"Erotic point?" Vivian frowned.

Lex sighed as if he were teaching math to a first grader. "Pecs, dick, hips, elbows, shoulders, thigh. But in this case, I said no below the belt, so touch my elbow. Or if you really want to go big, go ahead and touch his thigh."

"His thigh." She nodded. "Okay, so we're sitting?"

Lex groaned. "Dude, I really don't have time for this."

I intervened. "Viv, if you're standing, go for the bicep. Like this." I pulled her into my arms. "And if you're sitting, yes, graze his thigh. But don't grope. A graze is how you touch a flower; a grope is how you grab a stress ball."

"Flowers, not balls." She nodded. "Got it."

Lex burst out laughing. "Alright, my work here is done. Have fun, kids."

He walked off whistling while girls stared after him.

"You think you got it?" I crossed my arms. "Because we're running out of time, and I have things to do."

"Yup." If she nodded one more time, her head was going to fall off.

"No more nodding, no more short answers. Say 'yes' instead of 'yeah.' Always answer with full sentences—you aren't sixteen anymore. And don't nod. If you nod, he can't hear your voice. And we need him to hear your voice. We want it to torture him when he's in bed. Alone. Got it?"

She nodded, then stopped and said, "Yes."

"Good girl. You have my number. Text soon."

I walked toward my car. I was going to be late for dinner, but that didn't matter. I just wanted to see Blake.

Hell, I didn't even need sex.

Which meant something was seriously wrong with me.

CHAPTER THIRTY-ONE

"I think you should fake the flu," I said while Blake rushed around her room to get ready for her dinner with David. I'd stalled her as many times as I could. First in the shower, then before she got dressed. And now, as she slid on heels, all I could think of was her wearing those heels with me, naked. "On second thought." I tilted my head. "Wear those for me tonight?"

Blake laughed and stood on wobbly legs. "So how do I look?"

I sighed and closed my eyes. "Gorgeous."

"You're not even looking."

"Because looking at you pisses me off. It reminds me that he's going to be looking at you, and every time I think about him in the same damn room as you, I want to cut off his shooting hand and bury it in Gabs's yard."

"That's really graphic."

I groaned. "You have no idea"—I stalked toward her—"how graphic I can really be. Care for an example? I have several." I nipped her lower lip and tugged the strap to her slinky black dress down her shoulder, kissing the spot the strap had just occupied and trying to shove the material farther down.

"Oh no you don't." Blake wagged her finger at me. "Think of it this way—the sooner I go out with him and tell him how blissfully happy I am with you, the sooner we can get this whole David thing behind us. Besides, like I said, he's a friend."

"My point exactly. You sleep with your friend every night."

Blake sighed. "Ian, trust me. I want you. Not him."

It was in that moment that I realized she had me by the balls in a very disturbing way, because for the first time in years I was insecure. Fearful that our relationship was too new and that she'd default to what was comfortable.

Fearful that she would settle.

Then again, what made me better than David?

Shit. What if she was settling by being with me, not him? What if I was holding her back? What if . . .

And this is why guys like me should never date, because guys like me have way too many thoughts. Guys like me help girls get guys like David. I knew exactly what he would do to woo her. I knew exactly how he'd respond to every laugh, every sigh. Damn it. It was like sending her out unarmed. She wasn't ready for battle, not when it came to the stacks of childhood memories David had against me.

I really should have read through the compatibility results that Lex had given me. At least then I'd know who was the better man, even though the very fact that it could be him made my chest tighten with rage.

If she was meant to be with him, she would be.

But she was with me.

"Ian?" Blake waved in front of my face. "Are you okay?"

"Go," I huffed. "I won't drive you to dinner like the crazy-ass boyfriend who can't trust his girl. Seriously, go. I'll, um, I'll see you tonight?"

"Yeah." She frowned. "I'll stop by your house afterward. Is that still okay?"

"Of course." I forced a smile, then kissed her briskly on the cheek. "Just don't let him touch you. Anywhere. Not even your back, which means he's thinking of touching your ass, alright?"

"Promise." She held up her hand. "Go watch a movie, relax. Maybe do some homework."

"Hah." Like I wanted to do statistics while he was looking down her dress and imagining her naked. Like hell. "Great idea."

"Trust me?" she said in a hopeful voice.

"Yes."

She left me standing there in her room, wondering how the hell I'd gone from being a guy who was confident in every area of his life to a guy wondering if I'd made a huge lapse in judgment by giving her a chance. Because the minute you're in a relationship, like really in it, you have the potential to fail.

And I didn't fail.

That was why after my injury I'd pushed myself so hard.

It was also why I didn't take risks, why I didn't date. I loved women. Loved them. And I enjoyed sex immensely.

But sex had always been just sex.

Now it was attached to Blake.

Shit.

First thing on the list? I was going to open that damn folder, check out the stats, look at the breakdown, and make a decision, even if it killed me. Besides, how bad could it be? I wasn't a horrible guy, and things were going great with Blake. I was sure the program had matched us at a high percentage. Hell, maybe even somewhere in the nineties.

But would I continue dating her if I found out that we were doomed from the start? Even if I really cared for her?

The thought haunted me the entire way home.

CHAPTER THIRTY-TWO

Lex had left the results in the living room, where he normally does his work. The dining room table was clear except for a few stacks of file folders and Lex's ever-present MacBook Pro.

I pulled out one of the metal chairs and sat, my eyes never leaving the stack. Shit, it wasn't like it was paternity test results. It was just a number.

A number that would tell me once and for all if I was the settler or the settlee.

Damn it.

I tapped my fingertips against the table, then with a curse pushed back the chair and stood, looming over the laptop, still staring but having second thoughts. What would this really accomplish? If I was wrong, if she really was better off with David, then . . . if I really cared for her, I'd let her go, right? Why would I want to hurt her? I had started Wingmen Inc. for people exactly like her.

To protect her from guys like me, guys who were players. Is that what was really happening right now?

"Oh shit," I grumbled.

I was turning into a chick—thinking of every possible outcome, analyzing every angle of the situation. So basically I was like Lex with tits.

"So you are going to read it?" Lex's voice interrupted my stare down with his laptop, causing me to curse again and nearly push the computer to the floor.

"Haven't decided yet." I crossed my arms. "What are you doing home?"

"I live here." Lex's face was tight. "Unless you're kicking me out, which you may do after you take a quick read through."

"That bad?" The files mocked me with all their organizational brilliance. There was a tab for each client, and I could see my name. I really didn't want to see my name.

"Two-shots-of-whiskey bad." Lex started moving around the kitchen, cupboards slammed, and then suddenly a glass of whiskey was thrust into my hand and he was pulling out the stack of papers labeled "Ian Hunter."

"Have a look," he said. "Don't say I didn't warn you. But if this helps, then I'm all for it."

"How the hell is this going to help?" I tossed back the entire drink, wincing as the dryness burned like fire down my throat. "Bring the bottle."

Lex exchanged my glass for my file and walked back into the kitchen. The file was thick, and holding it made me think back on all of the shitty things I'd ever done to girls. I couldn't believe my sneaky roommate had kept a running track record just in case I ever decided to be stupid enough to fall for someone.

"Tell me the truth," I said once Lex returned with the bottle as well as a full glass. I ignored the glass and swiped the bottle away from him before he could argue. "Did you record all this shit knowing that one day I'd finally jump off the ledge into commitmentland? Or are you really just looking out for our clients?"

"Odd." Lex pulled out a chair. "Because it seems like you're asking me if this is personal or business."

"And every single business ethics class has suddenly thrown up inside my head. Thanks for that."

Lex smirked, jerking the bottle out of my hand. "To be honest, I did it for our clients, because at the end of the day it's about them, not us. I input your information the minute I saw things start to change between you and Blake. Hell, the minute I noticed the linger."

"Come again?"

"Don't play the dumbass. It doesn't look right on you." Lex rolled his eyes. "The linger. You lingered. You leaned. Every single muscle in your body tensed when she walked into the room, you clenched your fists when David walked into the room, and your eyes did that weird narrow thing where it looks like you're just trying to concentrate or maybe do statistics homework in your head when really you're just doing everything in your power *not* to kill the unlucky bastard you happen to be glaring at." Lex tilted back the bottle and took a giant swig.

"I mean this in the most complimentary way possible, Lex, but if you were a chick, I'm pretty sure the knowledge you have on me alone would constitute stalker-like tendencies."

"Don't I know it?" He barked out a laugh. "I can't help that I'm a genius. My blessing, my curse."

"Right." A headache started throbbing between my temples. "Fine, it's like a Band-Aid. I'm just going to rip it off and look."

"I can read the results out loud in my sexy voice if that helps."

"You have a sexy voice? No shit?" I laughed, stealing the bottle again and taking a smaller sip this time.

"Yeah, one of my conquests said that just this morning, though I think she was just trying to get me to come back to bed rather than jump out her window because my house was flooding."

I glanced around. "Wow, yeah, I see what you mean. So much water. Good thing we have insurance."

"Hey, that's exactly what I said."

"You're a bastard—you know that, right?"

"Says the guy whose dog's died how many times in the past year?"

I scowled. "No more than ten. Totally different."

"Dude, you kill imaginary dogs. At least I make up an excuse about a very possible home disaster."

"Fine." I held up my hands. "I'm not going to argue with you. I'm just going to read, process, and then"—a deep sigh shook my whole body—"get drunk."

"Right on." Lex stood. "Maybe wait to drink more out of the bottle until you've read and fully understood all the calculations, alright?"

I nodded and pushed the bottle away. I'd had maybe two swigs, hardly anything noteworthy, but still, maybe I'd want to go for a drive afterward—you know, off a cliff.

The first page wasn't so bad.

Then again, it only had my name, age, height, and weight. Shit, wouldn't surprise me at all if Lex had my social security number too.

Next page had Blake's information, everything I already knew.

And the third page had our results.

Her match with David had been in the eightieth percentile. I had *that* freaking number memorized. Hell, the stupid bar graph was cemented in my mind like a nightmare that came back every time I closed my eyes.

Fifty.

The number was daunting. Our match was in the fiftieth percentile. Numb, I continued reading.

I scored below average in the following areas: ability to commit and relationship history, and above average in sexual promiscuity.

Swallowing the giant lump in my throat, I kept reading.

> *Stats show that if Client A were to embark on a rela-*
> *tionship with Client B, there is a 50% chance one or*
> *both hearts will be broken and that the relationship*
> *will end within two months once the honeymoon stage*
> *is finished.*

Two months.

Our program even gave a freaking timeline of the relationship demise.

I shoved the papers to the side. I didn't need to read anymore. Curiosity was an evil bitch, so I grabbed David's info and read.

> *Stats show that if Client A were to embark on a rela-*
> *tionship with Client C, there is an 88% chance that the*
> *relationship will bloom into success. The relationship*
> *will have an even higher chance of success once passing*
> *the three-month mark.*

No shit.

I shut the folder and checked my watch.

She'd been on her date for one hour. And I was sitting at home, well on my way to getting drunk and feeling sorry for myself because of a few stupid numbers.

Without thinking, I grabbed my keys and marched toward the door.

"Oh no you don't." Lex's voice echoed through the hallway. "I'll drive. I had one drink. You had . . . who knows how many. Where are we going?"

I refused to answer.

"Oh, good, so a stakeout? Sounds fun. I'm in."

"Don't you have homework or something?" I pushed past him and grabbed my jacket. "Anything?"

His smile fell. "No."

"What?" My eyes narrowed. "You're never home on a Thursday night, or any night for that matter. What's going on?"

"Nothing." His answer was quick, and his jaw ticked into place like he was trying to crack an entire row of teeth. "Drop it."

"Okay." Pain pounded through my head. "And we're going to U Village. He took her to dinner at Pasta and Co."

"Hah." Lex laughed, then sobered. "Oh, you're serious? Pasta and Co?"

"Not everyone's an expert in seduction, thank God."

"Pasta. Hands down the worst date food next to ribs."

"Again, thank God for that."

Lex paused in the doorway. "Look, do you really think this is a good idea? As much as I'm against any sort of relationship where you hang up the cape and actually stay committed to one person, this could end badly, you spying on her."

"Superheroes don't spy. We . . . check in."

"And as the villain to your hero, I would just break in, so who am I to talk?"

"Exactly."

CHAPTER

THIRTY-THREE

Spying didn't feel wrong to me until we rolled up in my SUV like two dudes trying to scope out a bank.

"Far corner," Lex said lowering the binoculars. "She's facing him, not sitting across but to the side. Bastard may have skills after all. Wanna see?"

"No." I stared straight ahead. "The absolute last thing I want to see is how close he's sitting to her, or if he's strategically dropping his napkin on the floor so he can have an excuse to scoot his chair closer."

"It's scary," Lex said in a low voice, "how well you know the male gender."

"Napkin drop?"

"Yup."

"Chair scooting?"

"Hell yeah."

"Shit." I rubbed my eyes, my vision blurring from the headache. "He's probably going to lean in and say he can't hear her very well because of the crowd. There will be another chair scoot until they're thigh to thigh, giving him a one-inch walk for his hand to cover her bare leg. Best erotic zone for a date."

Lex was silent. And then, "Shit, man, you should write a book . . . He's frowning, he just looked apologetic . . . Another chair scoot, but I can't see under the table."

"He's touching her. Of course he's touching her."

"Don't assume."

"Because I've been wrong up until now?" I snapped.

Lex didn't answer, and I still couldn't bring myself to look. Looking felt like the final straw, a betrayal. I'd said I trusted her, so at least by using Lex I was keeping my promise. Sort of.

"So, Superman, what's the next move?" Lex asked after a few seconds of silence.

My phone buzzed.

It was a text from Blake.

Frowning, I opened it up and felt my entire body tense.

Blake: Dinner is over. Ordering dessert,
    then I'll be home. Don't worry.

"Lex?" I grimaced at the phone, rage pumping through my system as I contemplated slamming the phone against the dash. "Have they eaten yet?"

"I see bread on the table . . . but no main dish. Wait, hold on." He was silent again, and then continued, "The waiter stopped by, but David waved him off."

Nodding, I fired a text back to Blake.

Ian: Is the food good? What did you order?

I got a response right away.

```
Blake: Food's great. I got chicken pad
    Thai.
```

"Lex . . ." I seriously needed to leave before I barged into the restaurant and raised hell. "Are you sure they haven't eaten?"

"Almost positive. Why does it matter?"

"I guess it doesn't." Except she was lying to me about something small. Which meant if something big took place . . .

Why tell me what she ordered and say it's good if she hadn't even eaten yet? Why make up a lie? Why the hell was I being so paranoid?

"We should go," I said. It wasn't like I could confront her now, and it was just food after all.

"Yeah," Lex said, quickly putting the car into drive and tossing the binoculars in the backseat. "Great idea."

"Whoa, suddenly in a hurry?" I laughed as Lex turned the car around so that my window was facing the restaurant.

It was a glance.

One freaking glance.

That I would regret for the rest of my life.

Blake.

David.

Kissing.

I held up my phone, unable to stop myself from taking a picture of the lip-lock, thinking at any minute she was going to push him away, slap him, stand up, and leave.

She didn't.

I snapped the photo.

And when Lex peeled out of the parking lot, I hit the final nail in our relationship coffin. Hey, look at that—we made it to three weeks.

Apparently, our matchmaking program needed a bit more work.

I clicked "Send" with the caption Hope you enjoyed dessert.

"Lex," I mumbled once we got back to the house. "Get me drunk. Now."

He stared at me, his face unreadable, which wasn't like Lex. We'd been friends for years, and he'd never, in all our time hanging out, looked at me like that, not even when I was injured and in the hospital.

For the first time in my adult life, my best friend looked at me with pity.

It sucked.

∼

"We don't have enough to get you drunk, that's the bad news," Lex announced once we were back at the house and I was staring down at the countertop, my mind a blur of anger and disappointment and, if I was being completely honest, a lot of sadness.

The sadness I refused to deal with.

Because dealing with sadness meant mourning, and that was stupid. Why would I mourn something that I barely even had?

But anger? I could completely work with that. How the hell did someone like me get in this position? Granted, we were doomed to fail. Fine, I got that part, but why lead me on?

"How's it feel?" Lex poured me a glass of whiskey and sat across from me in the barstool.

"Um, getting my heart broken? Gee, I don't know, Lex. It kinda tickles, like a feather getting stuck up my ass. What the hell, man, are you serious right now?"

"I mean, being on the other side." He looked honest-to-God curious. "The one who gets rejected even though clearly he's a better choice."

"Oh, please. You saw the numbers."

"Right. The numbers. Don't tell me you really believe that shit. Yeah, we based our company on it, fine. And yes, for the most part it works. But it never takes into account chemistry. You get that, right? A computer can't do that."

"And the day it can . . ."

"Right, we're screwed, because robots will be taking over the world. Lucky for you, I'll be heading up the takeover, so I'll save you a spot on the mother ship." He rolled his eyes. "Seriously, I can't believe I'm having a chick-talk with you, but there is no mathematic equation for chemistry. At all. You can't force it, and you can't predict it. She and David may look good on paper, but does he turn her on? Do his smiles make her want to die inside? His kiss—is it panty-melting? Isn't that what chicks say?"

I held a hand up like a stop sign. "I think we need more alcohol if you're going to use words like 'panty-melting,' Lex."

"Pretend I'm a chick."

"I'd rather not. Since I hate all women right now, I'm bound to do something stupid, like kiss you in hormonal confusion, then try to slam this bottle over your head in rage."

"First off, don't kiss me—it will ruin our friendship." He held up one finger, then another. "Second, we're both into girls, so I think it goes without saying that the experimental stage passed around the same time we went through English 101." Another finger flipped up. "And third, if you hit me over the head with a bottle or even a pillow, I'll probably take you down like I did in the sixth grade when you told Amanda that all the metal in my mouth made it so that aliens could see me from space."

"You want me to talk?" I laughed bitterly. "About what it feels like to watch a girl you've just been screwing kiss another guy? Or the girl you care about lie to you? How about this?" I held one finger at a time as I made my own list. "It sucks. I want to kill David. I want her to hurt just as bad as I hurt. I want the pain in the middle of my chest to alleviate enough so I can freaking breathe. I want to slam the door in her face, then apologize and pull her into my arms and beg her to choose me." I stared at my hand, all fingers extended, then shook it as though doing so would cross the items off my list. "I want so many damn things and I'm so confused that I think my only option is to drown myself in the whiskey we apparently don't have enough of. That's the truth."

Lex was silent.

The kitchen clock ticked in the distance, grating on my already-frayed nerves.

"Well." Lex cleared his throat. "You have two choices. Tell her you saw her and confront her face-to-face, or just . . . let her go without explanation. One's easier on you, and the other is hard on you both. Think about it, and don't make the douche mistake of being dramatic about it. Remember, we have dicks."

"Could have fooled me, since it seems like she just kicked mine clean off and laughed while doing it."

"That was your heart, not your dick. You know the difference, so stop being an ass and drink the rest of that whiskey."

"Two drops left. Think if I close my eyes and click my heels together, it will turn into two bottles?"

"Do it and I'm calling you a chick again."

With a frustrated sigh, I tilted back the bottle and tossed it in the trash, then pulled my phone out of my pocket.

Seven missed calls.

All from Blake.

"What's it gonna be?"

"I'm a fixer," I said, still staring at my phone. "So I'm going to fix it. We're still under contract, but as per our agreement stated in the last section, at least for Blake, if he takes her out on a date and kisses her, the contract is complete." I glanced over at his laptop. "Terminate it."

"Uh." Lex shoved to his feet. "Are you sure that's a good idea?"

"What?" I sneered. "That's what she wanted at the beginning, and regardless of how she got it, it happened. Terminate the damn contract, ask for payment, and delete her information from my schedule while you're at it. I have to meet with Vivian in the morning, and then I have a new client next week."

"Ian, think about this." Lex started toward me. "By ignoring her, you take the chance that—"

"That what?" I yelled. "That she'll be gone forever? She already is. She made her choice. She's been in my bed every freaking night for the past damn near two weeks, and still she kissed him back. She kissed him, Lex. I'd almost rather she slept with him." He knew as well as I did how personal a kiss could be. Sex could be mindless, but kissing? It never was. Thousands of thoughts led up to the kiss, millions of sensations took place during, and it was the only act of foreplay that replayed in women's minds, most of the time more than sex, for years to come.

You remembered every moment of your first kiss with someone.

Your first time having sex? In a lot of instances, it's cringeworthy, not notable, embarrassing, not good enough.

Kissing, though, was always remembered.

And there was always a reason for it.

"Ian, I'm going to ask you one more time—are you sure?"

"Delete the file, Lex. I'm still your boss, technically, right?" It was a low blow. Even though we were partners, I had a slightly larger stake in the company—60 percent. I knew my bringing his attention to it stung.

He looked pissed, ready to punch me in the jaw. "Yes."

"Then do it."

I left him in the dark living room and stomped my way up the stairs. When I was halfway up, the doorbell rang.

Lex answered it, like I knew he would.

"Is Ian here?" Blake asked.

I paused on the stairway, lingering in the shadows, eavesdropping.

"No," Lex lied. "Blake, you should go."

"No!" she yelled. "I can't. He doesn't understand what he thinks he saw. I just—I need to explain."

"Fine." Lex crossed his arms, bracing himself in the middle of the doorway. "Explain to me. Why the hell was some other guy kissing you?"

She was silent for a few breaths. Then she said, "I'd rather talk to Ian about that."

"Tough shit. You've got me. Talk or leave, I don't give a damn."

"He kissed me!"

"Tale as old as time." Lex sneered. "And you kissed him back. Am I missing any important details, where you pushed him away, kneed him in the balls, screamed at the top of your lungs?"

"I did . . . push him away . . . after a bit."

"And you hesitated. That doesn't speak well for you, or for the way you think about my best friend. The same best friend that I'm pretty sure is going to want to quit the most lucrative business concept I've seen in decades, all because some girl who doesn't even know how to dress without his help thought she would aim a bit higher and cheat." I clenched the wood stairwell so tight my hands hurt. I was torn between wanting to defend her and wanting to yell at her like he was.

"Aim higher?" She laughed. "With David? Are you insane?"

"You must be so proud of yourself," Lex said in a low voice. "The one girl to take down Ian Hunter, and you didn't even keep him. You just tossed him aside once your childhood crush looked your way. Do you think David would even care about you if Ian hadn't put you on his radar? Do you think he cares about you now?"

"We're friends. That's it."

"And you and Ian were . . . what?"

"Dating! We *are* dating!"

"You kissed another dude. That means whatever you and Ian had is over. Be expecting the contract termination in the morning. I'm tired of talking to you, and honestly, I think you're a bitch. There. I said it. Go cry into your pillow about how horrible men are. Better yet, I bet David would love to comfort you. Spread your legs for him. We're done here."

The door slammed.

Stunned, I waited for Lex to say something to me, but he was silent, scary silent, as he paced in front of the door, then kicked the wall with his foot.

"Heard that?" Lex asked in a hoarse voice.

"Hard not to."

"I didn't mean to call her a bitch. I got caught up in the moment." Lex suddenly jerked his head up and smiled. "You can thank me later."

My eyes narrowed. "What do you mean, thank you later?"

"You ever wonder why you do dates so well?" He gave a careless shrug. "Why I've always been happy to let you train the clients in the art of seduction while I only work on kissing techniques and breakups?"

"No, but I feel like you're about to reveal some hidden talent." The pain was less severe when I wasn't thinking about her voice, about how sad she sounded.

"My specialty? Breakups. I've been meaning to talk to you about it, but . . . I think we can add that specialty to Wingmen Inc. We help people break up, we can also help them get back together. If she cares for you, she's going to be back, in three, two, one."

A knock sounded at the door.

Lex lifted an eyebrow at me, then jerked the door open. "Didn't I tell you to run along?"

"Just"—Blake pushed against Lex's chest—"stop talking for two seconds so I can speak without having to defend myself. Tell Ian I'll be back. And if he doesn't answer his phone, I'm going to climb into his window. And if he locks me out, I'm going to break it with my Caboodle, or something equally as heavy. I won't stop until he hears me out. And I think . . ." She was silent. Was she crying? "I think I love him."

My world stopped spinning.

I slunk to the floor, nearly tumbling down the stairs as I waited in stunned silence for Lex to say something.

"Good answer. We'll be in touch." With that, he slammed the door in her face, gave me a cocky grin, and said, "Told ya so."

CHAPTER THIRTY-FOUR

My bed freaking smelled like Blake, which was really ironic since I knew firsthand what smell did to the memory. It's why I used only certain body washes around the clients, certain colognes, creating an attachment yet making sure that attachment wasn't so tight that they felt like they were more in love with me than the guy they were chasing. I needed to earn their trust, but not so much that they attached emotionally.

Never, in my wildest imagination, did I think it would backfire on me, that the roles would be reversed and I'd have to sleep in a hellish combination of lavender and vanilla-scented shampoo, with my body strung so tight that I was afraid of too much friction from the sheets while I dreamed of her at night.

She'd said she loved me.

I wasn't sure I believed her.

Everyone loved me, or everyone thought they did.

And love didn't mean you went and allowed another guy to kiss you, or worse, kissed him back.

Groaning, I slammed my hand into the pillow next to me, then fluffed it up again, only to be paralyzed by the onslaught of lavender and vanilla all over again.

"Damn it." I shoved away from the bed and glanced at my nightstand. It was six in the morning, a better time than any to go work out, especially since I knew that David would be long gone from the gym by the time I got there. I wasn't entirely sure I'd be able to keep myself from kicking his ass if I got the chance. At the very least, I might offer to spot him on the bench only to let all the weight fall onto his chest—or his neck.

Good to know I was contemplating murder.

A vision of his arms wrapping around Blake made me clench my fists tightly at my sides. Right. It would be worth it, just to see the dumbass helpless look on the bastard's face.

~

"Two more," David's friend DJ said, his fingers lightly touching the bar as David made a loud, giantlike moan and thrust the weight up. "One more!"

David's legs nearly came off the ground.

Was the entire basketball team that inept at proper lifting? Or just David? It looked like he was using every cell in his body to try to will the bar back up. It would seriously make my day if the bastard let out a fart and someone just happened to tweet it. Oh, the hashtags I could come up with. I was already irritated that David had gone off-schedule and was working out during my time, but whatever.

I returned to my push ups and heard more yelling from David's general direction.

"Good burn, good burn," DJ said. I heard backslapping, and probably ass-slapping. I didn't miss that part of organized sports—the culture, the way weight lifting and training ended up almost being a religion. It wasn't healthy, and it was one of the things that made me thankful that I was on a different path, even though it wasn't the one I would have originally chosen for myself.

I had finished my last push-up and collapsed onto the mat, evening my breathing, waiting for my heart rate to come down, when a pair of flip-flops stepped directly in my line of vision.

Black-and-white 1992 Adidas flip-flops in a size nine.

Slowly, I raised my head, then pushed myself to a sitting position on the mat. "Yes?" I kept my voice curt, irritated. That wasn't hard to pull off, since I was exhausted from my workout and extremely pissed off. Love or no love, she'd still kissed another guy.

Cheating was cheating.

Period.

Blake's wavy hair was pulled into a low ponytail, and she was sporting black-rimmed glasses. I'd had no clue she even wore glasses. A generous amount of midriff was showing, compliments of her low basketball shorts and her very high and tight pink sports bra.

I could only imagine how many guys in that exact moment started stacking on the weights in hopes of impressing her, not realizing she wasn't the type to be impressed by that. I should know.

Athletes saw through shit like that, especially when you couldn't even pull the damn bar off the rack.

"Blake," David yelled across the gym.

I clenched my teeth and tried to keep myself from seriously losing my shit. Why the hell was she here?

"Listen." Blake ignored David and leaned down, her voice low. "I need to talk to you alone."

"Didn't you get my e-mail?" I stood abruptly and toweled off my neck. "We're done."

"No, we aren't." Her lower lip trembled as she placed a hand on my forearm. "Ian, I love you. I'm sorry about the kiss. I can explain. It wasn't about you. I was confused."

"No shit," I said with a hollow laugh. "Look, you did us both a favor."

"Oh?" It was her turn to look pissed as she jerked her hand away and crossed her arms, pressing her tits high enough to give any dude looking our direction sexual fantasies for hours.

"Yeah." I quickly tugged her arms down and pinned them at her sides. Better. "Our projected success rate . . . it wasn't good. So unless you want to take a fifty-fifty chance"—I shrugged and nodded toward an approaching David—"you should go for the one you've wanted all along."

Damn, how had I never noticed how stupid his walk was? Straight lines, amigo, straight lines.

Blake's eyes narrowed. "All of that's changed. You know that."

"It's the sex," I explained. "A chemical reaction occurs that bonds you to a person emotionally when you have sex. Give it a few days before it'll wear off. So will I."

"Ian," she said again, this time with more desperation. "I'm telling you I love you, and you're pushing me away. Don't you care about me at all? Maybe even a tiny bit?"

Yes. I cared too much. And in that moment, regardless of what she said, regardless of how she felt about me, I knew I was going to have to make the choice for her.

Because it wasn't worth the risk. She was worth it, absolutely. But me? I wasn't.

It sucked to actually have zero belief in myself, but what if I hurt her? What if, in this situation, I was her Jerry, my sister's husband? The guy she settles for, only to pine for someone else ten years down the road?

"Ian?" Tears pooled in her eyes.

"Go." I stepped back. "Your boyfriend's waiting for you."

"My boyfriend's standing in front of me."

"Not anymore," I whispered, taking one last lingering look at those lips, those eyes. I had to look away. "Be happy."

"Are you?"

"Am I what?" My head snapped to attention. David was only five feet away from us now, and gaining.

"Happy?"

"Does it matter?" I asked while David snaked his arm around Blake and tried pulling her in for a kiss.

"To me, yes."

"Ian!" David held out his free hand. "Good to see you, man."

I stared at his hand, then blankly met his gaze, blatantly ignoring his supposed offer of friendship, because all he was doing was trying to give me the winner's shake. The one that said, *Oh hey, sorry you lost, you pathetic bastard, but here's a participation medal for all your trouble. No hard feelings, right? Oh, PS—did you teach her that arch thing in bed? Thanks, man. Thanks a lot.*

"Hell," I said under my breath and faked the best smile I could muster. "See you guys later. And David?"

Unbelievable. He was still smirking. "Yeah?"

"Treat her well."

"Oh." His eyes lowered as he kissed the top of her head. "I already did . . . last night."

Blake's eyes widened.

And before I knew what was happening, I was launching myself across the mat and pummeling his face with my fist.

Repeatedly.

"Ian," Blake shouted as strong arms wrapped around my chest and jerked me away from David's body on the floor. I tried to go after him again.

"Dude." DJ gripped me harder. "Let it go, man. Just let it go."

"You bastard!" I yelled. "Disrespect her like that again and I'll kill you!"

David sneered through bloodstained teeth. "I was kidding." He patted his already-bruising nose. "Geez, man, take a joke."

A joke? Who joked about having sex with a girl in front of her? Guilt gnawed at my chest, because really, how many times had I done the exact same thing?

"Ian," Blake called after me.

I couldn't even look at her.

With a curse, I left the weight room amidst the crowd watching with horrified curiosity.

"Ian!" Blake reached me and grabbed my arm. "It's not what you think."

"Tell me." I didn't even recognize my own voice anymore. "Was it before or after?"

"What?" She looked confused.

"You told Lex you loved me—was it before or after you screwed him?"

"Never!" Blake shoved me. "Are you serious right now? How does it go from kissing to sex?"

"I don't know. You tell me. I basically walked you through the steps, Blake."

"Unbelievable!" She shoved me harder. "I tell you I love you, and not only do you push me toward him but you accuse me of sleeping with him too?"

"It's not like you didn't want it, I'm sure," I muttered.

A stinging sensation knifed through my cheek as her hand went flying across my face.

"We done?" I asked, sidestepping her.

"So. Done." She jogged back into the weight room, and I continued my walk of shame all the way to my car.

Funny, a few weeks ago what just happened would have been the perfect setup to get the guy to finally notice the girl. Hell, even I couldn't have written such a good ending.

The only problem?

It wasn't fiction.

It wasn't a setup.

It was life.

Whoever said "if you love something, you let it go" clearly had never been in love before. Yet that's exactly what I was doing.

Letting her go.

To the better man.

Which, for the first time in my life, I realized . . . wasn't me.

CHAPTER THIRTY-FIVE

"Ian? Are you even listening to me? We kissed. It was amazing . . ."

Hell, even if it was the worst kiss of her life, it would have still been amazing, because when you're in love or when you really like someone, you can damn near justify anything.

Well, of course he had coffee breath. He works at Starbucks! Duh, he drinks coffee!

Silly Ian. Oh, no, he meant *to hit my teeth!*

He said he'd been pining for me for years. Years! Can you stand it?

No, I really can't. Please stop talking.

Or my personal favorite: He said more spit makes things better, because a dry mouth can kill you during oral. I swear.

Right, and balls fall off if you don't have sex before forty.

No, really. Look it up.

"Ian!" Vivian snapped her fingers in front of me. "After the kiss, how do I still keep him interested?"

Yeah, I needed to stop daydreaming about a certain girl and a certain guy who I could see were currently walking hand in hand toward the HUB.

"You . . ." Frantic at the sight, I reached for Vivian's hand. "Shit, Vivian, one kiss is fine, but the second kiss is the one that tells them the first wasn't a fluke. So this time, let him kiss you, but give him some mixed signals. It can't be too easy."

"Okay." She frowned. "So maybe sit farther away from him?"

David laughed at something Blake said. She was wearing jeans and a short top that showed off her tan skin, damn it!

"Ian," Vivian growled.

"Right." Without thinking, I pulled Vivian into my lap, blocking my view of David and Blake. "Get playful with him, and when he leans in, pull back, like this." I leaned in, she pulled back and smiled.

I felt hollow. Empty. "Good job, Vivian. Just make sure that it's a playful kiss, and then it can turn passionate. But don't make out—that's not for the second kiss or even the third. Keep him wanting. When do you see him again?"

"Well." Vivian squirmed on my lap. Damn, her butt was bony— give the girl a cookie or something. I love women's bodies, but eat, for God's sake. "We're supposed to study tonight."

"Public place. Then go somewhere for drinks afterward, tell him you need a break."

"Got it." Vivian squirmed more.

Blake and David must be gone.

"Okay, off you go." I heaved her off my lap and stood just as David and Blake turned toward me. By the looks of her mouth, he'd been kissing her, or trying to pry her lips from her face. But she didn't look satisfied; if anything, she looked pissed.

You're welcome for giving you your heart's desire, princess. Now stop glaring at me.

"Old client?" Vivian nodded over at them.

"Sort of." I frowned and grabbed my phone. "Text me with the location tonight, and I'll hang out in the background to make sure you don't need a wingman."

"Hah." Vivian nodded. "You really take your job seriously, don't you?"

David gave me the finger behind Blake's back. I knew there was something wrong with that bastard!

"You have no idea."

"Thanks, Ian!" Vivian skipped off while I made a mental note to cut David's brakes, you know, when Blake wasn't in the passenger seat. I wouldn't harm a hair on her head. But David? Let's just say I wanted to rip him limb from limb.

"Blake paid us," Lex announced when I walked into the house and set all my school stuff out on the table.

"I did the right thing." I was saying that a lot lately. In my head while showering. Right before bed when I still smelled her on my sheets, regardless of how many times I washed them. Before class, after class. So basically it had become my new mantra. *I did the right thing.*

Exactly seven hours later, I was still repeating that to myself as I lay across the couch and wondered how much pizza one man could consume before he actually ate himself to death.

Would it be less painful than drowning?

Would Lex mourn me? Or simply cash in on the fact that I'd over-dosed on pizza and get Domino's to name a pie after me?

Deep thinking. That's what my life had turned into. Well, that, no showers, overeating, and *Game of Thrones* reruns.

In a moment of complete pizza-drunk weakness, I sent a text to Blake.

```
Ian: I miss you.
```

She texted back right away.

```
Blake: You dumped me for my own good and
    rejected me when I said I loved you.
    Go. To. Hell.
```

She punctuated the text with a smiley face.

A smiley face meant there was still hope. Right?

Oh shit, and the teacher becomes the student. I always tell my clients a smiley face does *not* mean "I want to have sex with you"; sometimes a smiley face just means "I'm happy."

Did that mean she was happy for me to go to hell?

I frowned as yet another main character on *GoT* was slaughtered in front of me.

And I felt nothing.

Shit, life was bad when you felt nothing after the death of one of your favorite characters.

"Get up," Lex barked.

With a very solid double middle-finger salute, I let him know my opinion of that suggestion and continued watching as blood poured out of the dude's chest.

Huh, maybe I should become an actor and get myself killed. Better than death by pizza. I didn't want to smell like pepperoni in my casket.

I reached for the bottle of Jack Daniel's. Not a drop rolling around the bottom. Well, damn.

Lex snatched the remote from the table and turned down the volume. "Seriously, get the hell up and stop moping around. It's scaring the shit out of me. Let's go to a bar."

"No."

"Dude." Lex fell onto the couch. "You're seriously killing me here. The stats for their relationship success don't lie, fine. The fact is, they have a higher success rate. BUT SHE LOVES YOU!"

"*Must* you shout?"

"Please, that empty bottle has been sitting there since ten this morning. You've been drinking water and eating pizza—that's how you deal. Pizza. You disgust me."

"Pagliacci delivers, man. Can't beat that. And no hangover."

"Look." A thick folder landed in my lap.

"What the hell is this?"

"Your background info against hers."

"Lex." I growled his name like a curse. Sure, grab some salt and pour it into the gaping hole that is my heart. Really, I'll just sit here and take it. "I don't want to get more depressed." I shoved the folder away.

Lex sighed loudly. "I love you like a brother. But this folder is ruining your life. I want you to see the stats. The real stats."

"Real stats?" I repeated, sitting up straighter, interest suddenly piqued. "What do you mean *real* stats?"

"Look." Lex held up his hands innocently in front of him. "I may have . . . tweaked the numbers a bit . . ."

"'A bit,' meaning you rounded up instead of down?"

Lex coughed into his hand.

"Lex!" I lunged for him, but all the pizza made me slow and sluggish. "What the hell did you do?"

"What I had to do," Lex shouted. "You are seriously such an idiot."

"Thank you?" I shook my head. "And I repeat, what the hell did you do?"

"I know you."

"I know me too, thanks."

"No, I really know you." Lex ran his hand over his buzzed head. "You slept with a client. A client, Ian. Our business is based off your ability to, first off, not do that, but also to be damn good at what you do. Remember when we first started? What's the oath we both took?"

I swallowed the bitterness in my throat. "Never fall in love."

"Right." Lex nodded. "And on that same drunken night, what did you make me swear to you?"

I didn't answer.

"Ian, damn it! What did you force me to do?"

"I made you promise not to let me."

"And why is that?"

"Because I was tired of losing shit . . . I lost my ability to play, and I moved on, but I didn't like the emotional pain. Hell, who would? So I told you to always have my back."

"So"—Lex opened the folder—"I did."

I glanced down at the sheet and nearly tackled him to the floor. "Holy shit! How is this supposed to make me feel better?"

Lex burst out laughing. "I couldn't do it. I changed the numbers by five points, man. Five whole points. And it was enough to ruin you. Don't you get it? Fifty percent? Fifty-five percent? It doesn't matter. Numbers can lie. The heart—"

"Damn poet. That's how you get so much ass," I said in an irritated tone.

"I rarely have to use my words, Ian. Rarely."

"So she'd still be settling with me."

"Only one way to find out." Lex stood and offered his hand. "I know for a fact where David's partying tonight, and word on the street is he's at it alone while Blake hangs out with Gabs. Care for a drink?"

My eyes narrowed. "What? You think Mr. Goody Two-Shoes Oh Look a Butterfly Let's Rescue It Then Go Hug a Tree is actually as bad as I wish he was? Believe me, I wish that were the case."

Lex shook his head. "No, man, because you look like shit. I highly doubt you could even board an airplane without hitting the weight limit."

I lifted my shirt. "Six-pack, you were saying?"

"Stop flashing me." Lex looked away and covered his eyes. "Where the hell do you put it?"

"You know, a girl asked me that once. I didn't answer, just shoved my giant—"

"Clearly you're feeling better." Lex held out his hand again. "Let's toss you in the shower and get some 'sex me' clothes on. Remember one of the most important stats? Guys typically mess up within the first two weeks of a new relationship. And why is this?"

"God complex sets in," I grumbled. "They finally won the lottery, and they want to buy everyone a drink."

"God complex." Lex nodded. "Translation: I stole a sexy piece of ass away from Ian Hunter, which means I could have any chick I want, so come hither, my little pretties, and let me show you what a real man can do."

I made a face. "Please, like they'd even feel him."

"Hah." Lex nodded. "Alright, my work here is done. Go get your shit together. We leave in fifteen."

CHAPTER THIRTY-SIX

The bar scene had always been my thing. Actually, give me any location with willing girls and alcohol . . . and you'd have my perfect night.

Except tonight.

The girls all seemed too eager and fake.

The lights too dim.

The crowds more irritating than exciting. And to top it off, Lex had already claimed the one chick who looked exactly like Gabi. When I pointed that out, it must have traumatized him, because after that he took three shots of tequila and mumbled, "Not a chance in hell."

We'd taken a cab to the bar, and it looked like I'd be riding back solo. Something that hadn't happened in years.

The alcohol wasn't doing its job properly; I needed it to numb the pain that still stabbed me in the chest every time I thought about Blake.

And David had yet to arrive, even though Lex swore that he would be there. All in all, it was a shitty night, and thanks to all the pizza I'd had, the alcohol wasn't really affecting any part of my brain, not yet.

"Hey there." A tall Asian girl raked me over with interest. She looked like a Victoria's Secret model. "Do I know you?"

"Everyone knows me" had once been my line.

Tonight? "Nope." I offered a polite smile and sidestepped her, making my way back to the bar.

"Jack on the rocks. Make it a triple," I called out to my new best friend, the one who'd help me get drunk and forget the fact that at this very moment David probably had his pathetic hands all over Blake's body.

Damn Lex. Tonight was going to be a dead end.

I was far from drunk. Only one way to rectify that.

I lifted my glass into the air. I was just about to take a sip when, through the bottom of my ice-filled glass, I saw a tall figure make his way through the crowd.

David.

I lowered my glass, eyes zeroed in on whoever he was with. Because it sure as hell wasn't Blake. I didn't want to jump to conclusions. It was too soon. She could be a friend, or even a girlfriend of another team member. Athletes hung out together all the time, so it wouldn't be a stretch.

He laughed loudly, already sounding drunk, then lowered his head to hers . . . and kissed her sloppily on the mouth.

Whoa. Not a friend.

My grin widened as he kissed her harder and then grabbed her short prostitute-looking friend and kissed her as well.

The short chick was wearing a painted-on fuchsia dress that any hooker could buy for five dollars and a line of coke.

"Come here, bitches!" he yelled, slurring a bit, then rocking his sad Jolly Green Giant body toward girl one while girl two smacked him from behind. The crowded dance floor made way for them. Fascinated, I watched. He couldn't dance worth shit, but clearly he was too plastered to care.

"Like I said," Lex said from behind me, seeming to appear out of thin air. "God complex."

"Happens to the best of them," I said, feeling smugger by the minute.

"And the worst." Lex winced and shook his head in disapproval as David started swiveling his hips and thrusting back and forth.

"Hell, he must be shit in bed, if the man can't even move to the beat." Lex shivered. "I actually feel sorry for the drunk girls."

"Right?" I turned around and started making my way back toward the bar. Lex followed.

"Hey." I motioned for the bartender to come over.

"Don't like your drink?"

"Drink's great." I slid him $200 cash. "But I have a job for you."

He looked down, covered the cash with his hand, and said, "What do you need?"

"See Jolly Green Giant over there?" I pointed. "I want to know what he orders, who pays, the story on the chicks. And give him at least four drinks on the house so that you loosen up his lips a bit, got it?"

"Cool." The bartender stuffed the bills in his back pocket.

"I'll be back in an hour or so. Try to keep them here. If they end up partying hard, I'll pay the entire tab, whatever it takes."

"I'll try, man."

"Classic move." Lex sipped his drink. "I think our work is done here. I'll catch you at home. Just make sure she doesn't scream too loud, cool?"

I rolled my eyes, trying to ignore the rapid beating in my chest. If she came home? Hell, if she came home, I was just going to tie her to my bed so she never left again.

I fired off a quick text to Blake, asking her where she was and letting her know that if she didn't get her cute ass downtown, I was going to sing drunken opera outside her window until four in the morning.

And when she still didn't respond, I lied and told her I needed a ride and asked if it was normal to see Pinocchio after doing 'shrooms.

My phone lit up within a minute.

And just like that.

I was back in the game.

~

"You don't look high as a kite." Blake scowled, slamming the car door behind her and pulling down the gray knit dress so it covered her ass. It barely did, by the way, and I offered up a prayer of thanks. I tried to appear inebriated, which was difficult, considering I wanted to kiss her and actually hit her lips, not pretend to miss and make love to the damn telephone pole.

"I'm high." I nodded. "Superhigh. Hey, want a drink?"

"No," she said, seething, and slapped my hand. "I don't want a drink. I'm not your girlfriend anymore, remember? And the only girl you're friends with tried to kill you in your sleep."

"Gabs exaggerates that story every time she tells it. I wasn't asleep, I was faking it."

"So the knife wound was faked too? And the blood?"

I winced, remembering the time Gabi accidently stabbed me in the arm after trying to scare me on Halloween. "We're getting off-topic."

Blake scowled. "Just get in the car so I can drive your drunk, high ass home. I can't believe I actually came. What's wrong with me?" She was doing that cute talking-to-herself thing, and chewing on her thumbnail like it would answer her question.

"Nothing." I checked her out, my eyes homing in on her legs. "Seriously, nothing at all. It's a problem."

"Excuse me?" She thrust out her hips, placing her hands on them. I held my groan in, which was difficult. Just about as difficult as not kissing her, then tossing her over my shoulder.

"Cute. Did Gabs teach you that head-swivel thing?" I laughed.

"Geez, you are drunk. Last time we talked, you nearly killed David and managed to simultaneously break my heart in the process. I hate you right now, but thankfully you won't remember it in the morning."

"Not drunk." I steered her toward the bar while she tried to drag me back to the car. "But I do have a confession to make."

"Oh?" She stopped fighting.

"And I realize this isn't romantic, but"—I shrugged—"I love you."

Blake stilled. "Did you just toss out an 'I love you'? While high?"

"I lied about being high," I offered lamely. "And yeah, I tossed it out, because it's true. Because in a complicated world, where an ex-NFL player decided to change the map of the dating scene, he somehow lost his way and fell ass-over-heels in love with one of his clients."

Blake didn't look convinced.

I wouldn't be either. Shit, here I'd been handing out relationship advice for the last year, and I couldn't even make a convincing speech!

"The stats told me we weren't a match. Lex messed with them, but only by five percent. We still have only like a fifty-five percent chance of working. And you want the truth?"

She nodded. "If you're able to come up with such a thing."

"I desperately"—I tugged her against my body—"want you. Need you. Crave you." I grasped her by the back of the head and jerked her toward me. Our lips met forcefully, my tongue sliding against hers before retreating. "But I was scared."

"Ian Hunter? Scared?" Her lower lip trembled. "I don't believe it." She clung to me now, her hands gripping my shirt.

"David was in the eightieth percentile," I admitted, feeling the need to come clean. "And the numbers don't lie—they never have. I was scared that you'd be settling if you stayed with me when he was the one you've wanted all along." I felt my body tightening with the wrongness of the situation. "There, I said it, my insecure confession is done now. If you'll excuse me, I'm going to go get drunk off my ass and forget I just told you I can experience fear when it comes to relationships."

She caught me by the shirt and tugged me back. "Oh no you don't. You can't just make epic speeches and stomp off."

"Wasn't epic," I said. "And I never stomp. I swagger, but I never stomp. Sometimes I've been known to tiptoe, but only when sneaking out of a girl's bedroom, and I don't think I have to explain the why behind that."

Blake's eyes were still filled with tears. "Prove it."

"You want me to swagger?"

"Prove your love." Her eyebrows arched in challenge. "I want you to prove it to me. You made an epic speech, you told me you loved me back, and I can maybe, sort of, understand the method to your madness. But as far as I know, you just don't want David to have me. How do I know I belong to you?"

I thought about it for a minute. "Honestly?"

She nodded.

"You don't. You never will. Just like the stats failed me"—I sighed, struggling not to frown—"words fail me too. Hell, I think they fail everyone sometimes, especially when you need them the most. It's like, the one time I want to be eloquent, my tongue decides to stay glued to the roof of my mouth."

I paused, nervous about how to convince her about how I felt. "I can get into any woman's pants I want"—Blake snorted—"but yours. I could turn around, march into that bar, and leave with anyone but the one I actually want. Probably because when the words actually mean something, when they hold something powerful behind them, they will always, and I do mean always, fall flat. My actions"—I shrugged and grabbed her hand—"they'd fail too.

"You'll have moments of doubt, especially considering the type of business I'm in. At the end of the day, the only thing that will really be on our side is us, and the fact that we love each other. We aren't promised time. We aren't promised it will be perfect. And I can't promise I'll get it right on the first try. I mean, look at the mess I've already made. But"—I jerked her against my chest—"I do swear this." My lips brushed hers. "It will only ever be you, Blake, who I take home at night, who I want to wake up to every morning. I love you. And if you give me time, I'll prove that. Every minute of every day that you allow me to be with you."

"Whoa." Blake wiped her eyes. "That was—"

"Wah-wah," Lex's voice said from somewhere behind us. "Just kiss him already so you guys can go home. Also, David's plastered, so—"

"David's here?" Blake jumped away from me.

"Oh yes, that." I nodded. "So David's here."

"Got that," she said through clenched teeth. "Not that it matters, since we aren't dating."

"You aren't?" I said.

Lex chuckled darkly.

"You"—I turned and subjected him to a glare—"are a sick bastard. You knew?"

He shrugged, and I turned back to Blake.

"David's an idiot," Blake said. "When I told him I couldn't date him because I was in love with someone else, he said, 'What does love have to do anything? I just wanna screw you, now that you're hot.'"

Lex and I stared at her, dumbfounded.

"Well then." I shrugged. "I guess I don't need to lure you into the bar so you can see for yourself how far our young David has fallen. I'm pretty sure he's with a prostitute, possibly two. If you want to find out, all I need to do is call the police." I held up my phone.

Blake burst out laughing. "Sounds kind of fun. I could use a drink after all that confessing."

"Pussy," Lex coughed.

I rolled my eyes. "Just wait, Lex."

"Hah." He slapped me on the back. "No, thanks. I love my life. There will be no waiting for any girl to sweep me off my feet."

"I should hope not, since you have a dick. That's really not how things work."

"Guys?" Blake cleared her throat. "Who's buying me my first drink?"

"That honor goes to your boyfriend." Lex slapped me on the back. "Think I'll go hang out with Gabs for a while . . . Have fun."

"Wait, what?" I narrowed my eyes. "You hate Gabs."

"Oh, did I say hang out?" Lex laughed. "I meant torture. Heard she's home alone tonight, and she still hates clowns. I just happen to have a clown wig and a horn in the back of my car. What are the odds, right?"

"Don't get shot, man." I fist-bumped him.

"No promises." He waved us off and walked toward a waiting cab.

"For hating someone so much, he really does spend a lot of time . . . annoying her." Blake watched Lex walk away.

I let out a snort. "Been that way for ages, and it will continue to be that way. It's best to just ignore them," I said, nuzzling her neck as we weaved through the crowd.

Sure enough, David was front and center, dancing with a few drunken girls.

"You smell good," I said.

Blake chuckled, then turned abruptly and pressed her mouth against mine while I waved over the bartender.

"Two shots of tequila!" I yelled, upon coming up for a breath. Then I twirled Blake in front of me, stopping her so she could watch the free show David was giving.

I leaned down and murmured in her ear, "Admit it, you so wanna tap that." David was dry-humping the short chick, but since he was so tall and she was so short, it was like he was trying to fit his tiny penis into her armpit. "Maybe I should draw him a diagram or something."

Blake leaned back against me.

I hissed out a breath, and she thrust her ass against me as she met my gaze over her shoulder. "Yeah, because if anyone knows the game plan to score . . . it's you."

"I love it when you compliment my sexual prowess . . . Do it again." I kissed down her neck while her hands reached back for me. She tried to turn around, but I kept her pinned in place, then slowly moved her so that she was facing the bar. "Hands on the wood."

She reached behind her.

"Cute." I tugged her ear with my teeth. "Wrong wood, sweetheart."

Slowly, she inched her hands away from me and placed them on the bar top.

"Bend over."

She froze, then glared back at me. *We're in public,* she mouthed.

"Exactly." My body heated. No, it freakin' began to hum with awareness. "Just a little preview, only for me. Nobody else is watching, not with *The David Show* going on."

She glanced back, and so did I.

Sure enough, every eye was glued to the catastrophe taking place over on the other side of the room. The girl's poor armpit was going to have a penis print on it, along with a zipper scrape. Such a sad, sad morning in store for her.

"Fine." Slowly, Blake leaned over the bar and reached for our shots. The view was beautiful. I saw just the slightest hint of ass cheek, enough to make me want to become an exhibitionist.

"Gorgeous." I squeezed her ass before I slowly turned her around, took a shot glass, and clinked the glass against hers. "To new beginnings?"

"And happy endings."

"And so the virgin turns into the slut. My work here is done."

"Says the whore."

"Who's going home with you," I countered. "Now, shake that ass toward the door. I have some ideas that involve rope and zip ties."

Blake's eyes widened. "Ian!"

"What?" I said with a shrug. "I was talking about home improvement, you dirty, dirty girl."

A blush stained her cheeks.

"Now, let's get out of here before I maul you in the closest bathroom. Gotta keep things classy where you're concerned."

"I don't know . . ." Blake stopped walking. "I could go for the bathroom."

"Hmm." I continued leading her out. "Maybe next time . . . But tonight? I want you in a bed . . . I'm not going to confess love, then take you in a bathroom stall, no matter how sexy you look in the dress that I really can't remember buying for you."

"It's Gabi's."

"Sometimes I love her."

"And sometimes, on very rare occasions, she loves you."

Laughing, I kissed Blake on the head and whispered, "Let's go home."

CHAPTER THIRTY-SEVEN

Never in my life had a car ride taken so long. It didn't help that a few streets downtown suddenly decided they needed construction on the way to my house, so the drive that should have taken a few minutes took close to twenty.

"You alright?"

"Nope." My entire body was tight, aching.

"Ian?"

"Hmm?" I turned to look at Blake. Her hands were folded in her lap, her knit dress was almost indecent as it inched up her thighs. I reached out to grab her hand, but she pulled away. "What's wrong?"

"I *did* kiss him back."

"Shit." There went our fun night. "Blake, I really, really don't want to talk about him. It's done. A moment of weakness—"

"Moment of weakness?" She burst out laughing. "No, more like, I kissed him back to make sure."

"Make sure?" The construction worker flagged me forward. We were moving at a turtle's speed over a bridge. I couldn't look at Blake anymore, but I could sense her apprehension as if it were my own. "Make sure of what?"

"My feelings."

We were almost at my house. I stole a sidelong glance at her. "Your feelings for David?"

"No." She swallowed. "My feelings for you."

"Blake, no offense, and I mean this in the nicest way possible, but what the hell were you thinking?"

"I wasn't!" She threw her hands into the air. "I just . . . I wanted to make sure. You were my first . . . everything, and I just didn't know, and I was falling too fast.

"And then he leaned in, and I thought, well, at least I'll know for sure that I love Ian." She gulped in a huge breath, then finished softly, "Because I do . . . I love you."

"And yet"—I turned into my driveway and shut off the car—"he kissed you."

Blake sighed heavily. "I let him kiss me. I didn't push him away at first because I was so shocked by how horrible it felt, how wrong everything felt. The way he kissed was—"

"Please." I held up my hand while my stomach tied itself into knots. "Spare me the details."

"He tasted funny."

"Did you not hear me when I said spare me the details?" I pulled the keys out of the ignition. "I guess . . . I can maybe understand why you let it happen, but, Blake, that kiss was at least seven seconds. Believe me, I counted."

"Of absolute torture," she pointed out. "And when we were finished, he wiped his mouth."

"Well, shit." I chuckled. "Lots of spit?"

"Maybe he was a merman in another life, and the only way he can survive on dry land is to keep as much liquid inside his mouth as possible."

"Believe it or not, this conversation isn't turning me on, sweet cheeks."

"Think of me!" Blake threw her hands into the air. "I have to live with that memory."

"I think," I began, leaning across the console, "I have a few ideas on how we can . . . expunge it."

"Oh yeah?" She smiled, grabbing me by the back of the head and forcing our mouths together. "You always taste good."

I pulled back. "I'm Ian Hunter. Of course I do."

"Cocky."

"For you?" I kissed her harder. "Every damn second of the day."

We made it inside the house with clothes intact, but the minute the door slammed behind Blake, her shoes went flying by my head, and her arms were already halfway out of her dress as it pooled around her waist. It was near impossible to take my eyes off of her round breasts, which were for once not covered in a pink sports bra but perkily sitting under a black sheer piece of lace that I knew I'd be pulling off with my teeth later. She slowly slid the dress from her waist, her eyes watching mine as it slid across her bare thighs and then kissed her ankles. I licked my lips in anticipation.

"Eager?" I grinned, enjoying the private show more than she would ever realize.

"Hmm?" She turned around, her dress still at her ankles. "Nope, just don't like wasting time." She kicked the dress to the side and pulled off her bra, then very quickly stepped out of her sexy little boy-short panties.

Moonlight flickered in from the living room, casting a sensual white glow across her body. Wavy hair fell in cascades around her shoulders, giving her a dreamlike, ethereal look.

"Tell you what." I stalked toward her. "I'll love you no matter what you wear—basketball shorts, scrunchies, Adidas flip-flops. Just swear you'll always come to my bed naked."

She licked her lips. A blush tinted her cheeks. "But what if I have some really sexy lingerie?"

"Well, I guess I can make exceptions." I tugged a piece of her hair, causing it to caress her breasts the way I wanted to. "But only on special occasions."

"What would those occasions be?" Her eyebrows rose as she dangled her arms around my neck.

"Christmas." I nodded, kissing the corner of her mouth. "New Year's."

"Hmm, I can deal with that."

"Not done yet." I pressed a finger to her lips and kept talking. "Valentine's Day, Presidents' Day, Groundhog Day." She laughed against my hand. "Flag Day's a given—I mean, c'mon."

"Of course," she whispered against my mouth.

"Fourth of July." I squinted. "Because of the fireworks."

"Any other days?"

"Wednesdays." I added. "Mondays too."

"So, every day?"

"Almost. Tell you what, I'll make a calendar, and on the days that say 'naked,' you have to be naked. The other days I'll give you a pass on—you can be as creative as you want."

"Sounds to me like you're scheduling sex?"

"Does it? Because to me it sounds like I'm scheduling playtime, but I can see how your innocent mind would be confused. And of course"—I pressed a kiss to her lips, drawing it out—"birthdays are always special."

"Naturally."

"I'll send you instructions on the striptease and what flavor of cake I want you to jump out of."

"You're extremely bossy."

"I like nice things." I lowered my hands to her hips and tugged her against me. "Is that so bad?"

"No." Her head fell back. "It's very, very good."

"Why, thank you." I chuckled darkly as I kissed her on the mouth again, the heat of the kiss nearly setting my clothes on fire as I cupped her breasts, then leaned down and flicked her nipple with my tongue.

"Enough." Blake pulled at my shirt. I threw it off over my head. My jeans followed, getting hung up on my shoes as I stumbled with her toward the couch and pulled her on top of me. "No boxers?" she said.

"No need," I said, smirking. "Takes too much time to take them off."

Her alluring blue eyes raked over me, stopping at my waist. She lifted a hand and pressed it against my hip, then inched lower.

"Exploring?" I teased.

She nodded, then gripped me with one hand.

My knees weakened briefly before a strangled growl escaped between my lips. Her touch was electric, as if her fingers pulsed straight waves of energy through my skin. Her swollen lips pressed together in concentration.

"Enough of that"—my nerve endings leapt in response to her rapt fascination with my body—"or I'm going to embarrass myself, and nobody wants that."

Blake's eyes snapped toward mine. "I can think of something *I* want."

"Oh yeah?" I relaxed my grip on her hips and brought my hands behind my head in a relaxed motion. "What's that? Cake?"

"Yeah, Ian." She lowered herself over me, her searing skin almost painful as her body made contact with mine. "I want cake."

"Fresh out." My eyes felt lazy, drugged by the hypnotic way she moved above me. "But I have a few other ideas."

"Good." She grinned.

She visibly relaxed.

Bad move.

Within seconds, I'd flipped us both onto the floor, the soft thick rug catching our bodies as we rolled for a few seconds and then stopped with me on top, her on bottom. "Better than cake . . . Let me taste you," I said before lowering my head to one of her breasts, taking her nipple captive, and rolling my tongue around it.

"Ian!" Blake laughed and then bucked beneath me as she wrapped her ankles around my back.

"Shh, I'm having a moment here."

"With my boobs?"

"We've never really had one-on-one time, you know? And it's important not to show favoritism in the bedroom—that's another rule." I blew against the skin where my lips had just been. "In case you were wondering."

"What are you doing to me?" she groaned.

"Everything I can possibly do without dying of dehydration or getting us arrested. Is that okay with you?" I moved to the other nipple. "Because I'd like to continue this conversation over here." I licked down the valley of her breasts. "If you're done talking?"

She shut up.

Except for the moans that came out of that bee-stung mouth of hers.

Touching Blake was like jumping right into a fire only to realize that rather than burn you, the flames infused you with a need that couldn't be met, no matter how hard you tried. Every kiss had to be followed by another, every taste of her skin—a mixture of salt and honey—just made me ravenous for more. I'd never experienced that kind of need before, which made me more frantic in my attempt to cover every inch of her body with my mouth.

Blake reached for me, but I slapped her hands away, then pinned her arms high above her head. "I'm not done."

"I am!" She squirmed beneath me.

"You're close."

"So close."

"Then let go." I kept her wrists pinned with one hand while I slid my free hand down her hip, my fingers hovering exactly where I knew she wanted them.

"Ian!"

Smirking, I moved onto my knees, then flipped her onto her back and brought her slowly into my lap.

"Whoa," Blake said. "What's—?"

Our bodies joined.

Her head fell back against my shoulder, and my lips moved against her neck in the same cadence as our bodies slammed together, each thrust met with another kiss.

Blake's hands gripped my wrists as she pushed her body back against mine. Her eyelids fluttered closed as I brought us both close to the edge, only to stop.

Her eyes jerked open. "Ian, I'm not into begging."

"And I'm not into the girl I love closing her eyes while I watch her come apart in my arms."

Her eyes stayed open as I thrust into her wildly, groaning as her body clenched tight around me. She fell against me, boneless, while I slid my hands down her silhouette, taking in the feel of her, the velvet skin almost too soft to be real.

"You love me," she whispered.

"I do."

"Tell me"—her voice was hoarse—"was it the Caboodle or the sandals?"

"Both." I laughed. "Definitely both."

CHAPTER THIRTY-EIGHT

We made it to the bed after briefly stopping in the kitchen and grabbing as many snacks as we could.

My room was blanketed in grays and blacks, masculine but not so masculine that a girl would feel like she wasn't welcome, which was weird since I'd never welcomed anyone except Blake into my bed.

ESPN blared in all its glory on the large flat-screen TV across from the bed. Colors from the screen played a kaleidoscopic light show across the white down comforter. Blake made a beeline for the bed and flopped into the center. As the colors flickered across her face, making Blake part of the show, my throat went dry and I had an honest-to-God "moment." She was really here, really with me. The fantasy had become the reality.

Was I up to it?

"You have throw pillows," Blake stated as she pulled out a box of Ritz Crackers.

Hell yeah, I was up to it. A smile pulled at my lips.

"And you're just now noticing?" I grabbed the pillows and chucked them off the bed. Four of them landed in my black leather armchair while the other nearly took out the dresser.

"I noticed it before." Blake crunched down on a cracker. "But I'm only now mentioning it. Is that you or Gabs?"

"All me, sweet cheeks." I winked and stole the cracker out of her hand. "Don't I look like I can decorate?"

She eyed me up and down and frowned. "I guess so, but why have them if you've never brought girls back here? I mean, throw pillows make the bed look inviting."

"Wow, it's like you've jumped into my head," I grumbled. "They look nonthreatening, if that's what you mean."

"Exactly!" Blake pounded the spot between us. "Almost like, 'Oh, hey, this isn't a one-night stand. I have throw pillows.' Do one-night stands have throw pillows?"

"Hell no." I shook my head. "It's scary that you're picking up on things like that. Hey, want a job?"

"Riding you isn't a job, sorry."

"Damn it!" I stole another cracker from her hand while she glared daggers in my direction and then shoved the box into my face.

"Stop stealing them from my fingers. Grab them from the box like a normal human being or I'm not letting you touch my boobs anymore."

"Tits—they're tits. 'Boobs' is what a middle schooler calls them, all the while getting embarrassed that the mere mention of the word is giving him an erection in front of the class while he's giving a speech on his favorite grandma."

Blake's horrified expression said it all. "Please tell me you made that up."

"Ask Lex if I made it up. Just do it when I'm not in the room. I'd hate to get punched again."

Blake burst out laughing and handed me the cracker she was munching on. "For that, you don't have to work for the cracker."

"That's my girl." I chomped down on it and reached for the bottle of wine we'd brought into the room. "But seriously, want a job?"

"Ian . . ."

"Don't Ian me. Damn, it's like Gabi told you how to draw out my name as long as possible, in turn making me feel guilty as hell before I even ask for a favor!"

"So it's a favor?"

"Not really." I frowned. "More like a joint venture. Care to listen?" I held up the bottle. "I'll pour you a double."

Blake hesitated, then held out her hand for the cup. "Double me."

"If the lady would like a double, the lady gets a double." I poured the wine nearly to the rim and handed it over. "So I've been thinking."

"That's fascinating, Ian, do continue. What are the big thoughts taking place down here?" She pointed to my dick.

"Hilarious." I rolled my eyes. "It's like now that you've made his acquaintance you don't care about public shaming anymore. Good to know. Storing that information for later." I poured myself a glass of wine and leaned back against the headboard. "I can't really continue working the way I am. Now that I have a girlfriend and I'm in a com- mitted relationship, if it gets around that I'm seeing you, Wingmen Inc. won't work, so I need to come up with a different plan."

"Hmm." Blake sipped her wine quietly, her expression unreadable. After her second sip, she said, "Well, you can still offer advice and take girls through the steps. In most situations, that should be enough. Almost like a life coach. I *did* used to call you the love coach, so there you have it."

"Yeah." I frowned. "And Lex could probably do more of the grunt work, since he's completely single and will probably die alone."

"I'm sure he appreciates your optimism about his future."

"Last time he agreed. Trust me, he embraces it with a scary joy that I'm sure is only matched by pubescent boys when they watch *Baywatch* reruns."

"I'm sure he won't mind, then." Blake stared at ESPN and frowned, then leaned forward and frowned harder. "Um, Ian? Do they still run stories on you?"

"What? Why?" I glanced at the TV. They were showing reruns of last year's most promising drafts.

I'd seen the footage a thousand times.

And each time it stung.

But it didn't now.

I used to turn it off, walk away, work out, get drunk, or just try to focus on something else, but with Blake in my bed, eating crackers, it was less painful. The sting was gone, and in place of the hole that had once been there . . . I had her.

Reaching for her hand, I squeezed it and then turned up the TV.

"Wow"—Blake watched with rapt fascination—"you're amazing!"

"I was a safety. Hardly the quarterback," I said, though my chest puffed out a bit more when her eyes widened at the next play.

The ESPN announcer's voice popped on and explained which guys had been drafted and what their numbers were, and then my name popped up again.

"Ian Hunter, Heisman nominee." Blake clenched my hand tighter. "The most promising draft pick played only two games before a freak accident ended his career, but I'm sure that ten-million-dollar signing bonus helped ease the sting a bit." The announcers chuckled while Blake's mouth dropped open in absolute shock.

"You bastard!" She launched herself and her wine toward me. "You're worth ten million dollars, and you charge over two hundred dollars a day!"

"In my defense," I said, laughing, "if I charge too little, it seems like I value my expertise too little. And we didn't cash any of *your* checks. But if you're this pissed, maybe we should reconsider what Wingmen Inc. charges?"

"You think?" She threw her hands into the air. "I mean, you don't want it to be charity, but clearly you don't need the money."

"Even without the NFL, I wouldn't have needed the money," I said slowly, warily, concerned that we might be entering deal-breaker territory.

"Oh, right, your parents?"

"Left me this house—and a few others." I shrugged, not fully ready to let her know my net worth. Because what was the point? It was money. And it had always made me feel empty.

Football had given me something.

But Blake had given me so much more.

A wry smile teased her lips upward. "Sorry for freaking out."

Hard to say exactly what emotion washed over me at her words, but I think it was relief. I could never let Lex know I was beginning to analyze my feelings like a girl.

She winced and pointed to a red wine stain on the white comforter. "And sorry that I ruined your comforter."

"I'll make you work it off." Confidence returning, I nodded and sent her a smug grin. "Hard labor. Bedroom-style. You interested?"

"For how long?" Her eyes narrowed.

"Forever."

"Hmm, I better get started now, then."

"Great." I set my wine down and then whispered, "On your knees, sweet cheeks."

EPILOGUE

I watched them.

But they didn't know it.

I wasn't sure if that made it more or less inappropriate. Not that I gave a shit. At least when sober I didn't give a damn.

But I was shit-faced.

And there they were.

Kissing, hugging. Holding hands. I seriously wanted nothing more than to slam my beer bottle over Ian's head, give him a good shake, then yell, "What the hell are you doing screwing with the perfect life?"

He'd had it all.

Even after his accident he'd still had it all—women, sex, more women. Did I mention sex? Because he'd had a lot of it.

And now? He was giving that all up. For what? A piece of ass? Like he didn't have prime pick on campus?

"What a loser," I huffed, though part of me felt like I was somehow losing, even though I was clearly at the top of my game.

As the bartender slid me another beer, she leaned over, her perky tits damn near falling out of her low top. "Rough night, Lex?"

"Does it matter"—I said with a grin—"when you know you're going to be making it even rougher?"

She smirked. "What makes you so cocky?"

"Look at you," I said. "Two minutes in, and you're already talking about my favorite subject."

Her eyebrows arched. "Even drunk you're good."

"Baby . . ." I stood, placing my hands firmly on the bar and leaning in so that I could brush my lips against her ear. "I'm the best."

"Hmm." She nodded. "My break's in five minutes."

"Of course it is." Their breaks were always in five minutes, just like they *never* did this. I was more used to girls screaming that during sex than my actual name. But whatever made them feel better about getting screwed in the hallway of some cheap bar.

I felt a slap on my back as Ian fell onto the barstool next to me, followed by Blake.

"So . . ." Ian said, his eyes darting between me and Blake. "I have this idea."

"I'm drunk. Let's have you and your ideas tomorrow." I eyed the hot bartender over the mouth of my beer. "Besides, in five minutes I'm getting laid."

"You're always getting laid in five minutes, sometimes ten. Learn to last longer, dude." Ian smacked my cheek twice. "In any case, not the point. Focus."

My eyes blurred as I stared into his face. "You have three minutes. She's giving me sex eyes, and I'm bored."

"When are you not bored?"

"When I'm having sex."

Blake cleared her throat. "I'm sorry he asked."

"Jealous?" I winked at her.

Ian punched me in the arm. "Sorry," I wheezed. "Drunk, remember?"

"Gabs is in," Blake blurted.

"Smooth." Ian nodded, then looked heavenward. "You couldn't at least lead with 'This really hot chick that we both know, who needs to pay for college, needs a job. Oh, hey, look we have an opening!'"

"Gabs." I could taste her name on my tongue, like she was a red Sour Patch Kid that I'd just accidently ingested. "Hell. No."

I moved to stand.

"Wait." Ian grabbed my arm, pulling me back into the barstool. "She has to pay out five grand in tuition before the end of the semester. It's an easy way for her to make money, and you did say you wanted to branch out and start accepting guy clients. So why not? What's the harm?"

"Oh, I don't know." I chugged my beer, then pounded my chest a few times to alleviate the air. "She might kill me? Run me over with her car? Poison my Lucky Charms? Oh." I snapped my fingers. "Also, she hates me. And I hate her. It's a very mutual hate that works really well for both of us, so"—I stood—"sorry, but not sorry."

Ian shifted in his seat, his eyes meeting Blake's, hers looking down at her clenched hands.

"Aw, shit, what did you do?"

"I kind of"—Ian waved his hand into the air—"already told her it would be cool."

Beer rolled around in my stomach, then did some flip-flops, a couple more tumbles, and a jumping jack, then threatened to come right back up.

"No chance in hell I'm training her," I spat. "No. Freaking. Chance. I will literally strangle her to death."

"Great," a light feminine voice said from behind me. "Then the feeling's mutual."

I turned, slowly, and came face-to-face with my nemesis, the one girl I seriously couldn't conjure up anything but hate and distaste for, no matter how sexy her ass was. "Oh baby." I leaned down and bit the outside of her ear just to piss her off. "You know I'd dig the strangling part if I could have my dick inside you at the same time. I heard you're into that."

It happened all at once.

The beer bottle flying across my head.

The knee to the groin.

And then the searing pain as I fell to the floor, with the devil standing over me, her hot-as-hell heel pressed hard against my chest.

"Yeah." Ian nodded. "I think this new partnership is going to work just great. Don't you?"

"Just great," Gabi said.

"Yeah," I grunted as all the beer I'd consumed threatened to come back up and make an appearance across her shiny red heels. "Freaking. Great."

ACKNOWLEDGMENTS

I release a lot of books . . . meaning I do a *ton* of acknowledgments, and I *still* always manage to forget people that made the book possible . . . like the checker at Albertsons who didn't judge me when I bought two bottles of wine and announced that I had a date with my computer and a scene I really didn't want to write. Okay, I didn't drink two bottles, more like one, over the course of a few hours. But seriously, people, it takes a village, and I'm so thankful that I have such an amazing team around me.

Skyscape, you guys work your butts off to make sure that every book you release is pristine. Thank you for constantly challenging me to be better, which of course plays into Melody, my editor . . . you are *hard*. I'm not just saying that. You're the type of editor who makes me want to cry into an empty cereal box while trying to justify whiskey in my morning coffee, and I *love* every minute of it. You make me a better writer, and for that I'm eternally grateful!

To my beta and editing team on the front end—Katherine Tate, Kathleen Payne, Jill Sava, and Liza Tice—thank you for making sure that each and every book has its own special flavor!

My amazing agent, Erica Silverman, is as usual the total voice of reason in *all* situations. Thanks for being such a dear friend. I feel like we are family. ;)

To my publicist, Danielle Sanchez at InkSlinger PR, thanks for all your hard work with each and every release. Blood, sweat, tears!

Bloggers and reviewers, you are incredible! It never ceases to amaze me that you are willing to take a chance on each and every release; you guys do *so much* for me, and I'm so thankful!

And readers . . . I really don't even know what to say. I'm so blessed to have you guys. Let's make a deal: I'll keep writing, and you keep reading. Yes?

And finally, I *need* to thank God. He's first, always first, in my life. Without him, I am nothing.

Nate and Thor, you are both *real* live superheroes. I am blessed by you guys in so many ways!

As always, thank you for reading! Stay tuned for the next Wingmen Inc. book. You won't want to miss Lex's story. After all, there's a very fine line between love and hate, don't you think?

See you guys on the flip side! You can follow me on Instagram @RachVD or text MAFIA to 66866 to keep up to date on releases!

Hugs,
RVD

About the Author

Photo © 2014 Lauren Watson Perry, Perrywinkle Photography

A master of lighthearted love stories, author Rachel Van Dyken has seen her books appear on national bestseller lists including the *New York Times*, the *Wall Street Journal*, and *USA Today*. A devoted lover of Starbucks, Swedish Fish, and *The Bachelor*, Rachel lives in Idaho with her husband, son, and two boxers. Follow her writing journey at www.rachelvandykenauthor.com.